ADDITIONAL
THE BARKERY & B

Bite the Biscuit
"Recipes for both dogs and people add enjoyment in this clever cozy that will taste just right to fans of both foodie and pet mysteries."
— *Booklist*

"Kicking off a cozy new series, prolific Johnston blends mystery and romantic intrigue."
— *Kirkus Reviews*

"An enjoyable mystery."
— *RT Book Reviews*

To Catch a Treat
"A mystery to delight dog lovers."
— *Booklist*

"A tale filled with fun, mystery and excitement."
— *Suspense Magazine*

"This sophomore outing is as delightful as its predecessor."
— *Library Journal*

Bad to the Bone
"Veteran Johnston has her formula down."
— *Kirkus Reviews*

"This cozy will appeal to fans of Susan Conant's Dog Lovers' series and is also reminiscent of Joanne Fluke's Hannah Swensen novels."
— *Booklist*

"Dog lovers (not to mention lovers of great mysteries) will be thrilled to see this third book in the fantastic series … A whole lot of fun and the animals who are all about spreading warmth and friendship come alive on every page."
— *Suspense Magazine*

OTHER BOOKS BY LINDA O. JOHNSTON

PET RESCUE MYSTERIES, BERKLEY PRIME CRIME

Beaglemania

The More the Terrier

Hounds Abound

Oodles of Poodles

Teacup Turbulence

KENDRA BALLANTYNE, PET-SITTER MYSTERIES,
BERKLEY PRIME CRIME

Sit, Stay, Slay

Nothing to Fear but Ferrets

Fine-Feathered Death

Meow is for Murder

The Fright of the Iguana

Double Dog Dare

Never Say Sty

Howl Deadly

Feline Fatale

HARLEQUIN NOCTURNE

Back to Life

The *Alpha Force* miniseries

HARLEQUIN ROMANTIC SUSPENSE

Undercover Soldier

Covert Attraction and *Covert Alliance*

Second Chance Soldier (K-9 Ranch Rescue series)

SUPERSTITION MYSTERIES, MIDNIGHT INK

Lost Under a Ladder

Knock on Wood

Unlucky Charms

BARKERY & BISCUITS MYSTERIES, MIDNIGHT INK

Bite the Biscuit

To Catch a Treat

Bad to the Bone

— A BARKERY & BISCUITS MYSTERY —

PICK AND CHEWS

LINDA O. JOHNSTON

MIDNIGHT INK
WOODBURY, MINNESOTA

FIRST EDITION
First Printing, 2018

Book format by Bob Gaul
Cover design by Ellen Lawson
Cover illustration by Christina Hess

Midnight Ink, an imprint of Llewellyn Worldwide Ltd.

This is a work of fiction. Names, characters, places, and incidents are either the product of the author's imagination or are used fictitiously, and any resemblance to actual persons living or dead, business establishments, events, or locales is entirely coincidental.

Library of Congress Cataloging-in-Publication Data
Names: Johnston, Linda O., author.
Title: Pick and chews / Linda O. Johnston.
Description: Woodbury, Minnesota: Midnight Ink, [2018] | Series: A Barkery & Biscuits mystery; 4 |
Identifiers: LCCN 2017054913 (print) | LCCN 2017057363 (ebook) | ISBN 9780738755953 () | ISBN 9780738752457 (softcover: acid-free paper)
Subjects: LCSH: Dog owners—Fiction. | Murder—Investigation—Fiction. | GSAFD: Mystery fiction.
Classification: LCC PS3610.O387 (ebook) | LCC PS3610.O387 P53 2018 (print) | DDC 813/.6—dc23
LC record available at https://lccn.loc.gov/2017054913

Midnight Ink
Llewellyn Worldwide Ltd.
2143 Wooddale Drive
Woodbury, MN 55125-2989
www.midnightinkbooks.com

Printed in the United States of America

Pick and Chews is dedicated to people who love their pets, as are the other books in this series and all of what I write.

I want especially to thank and hug those people who were affected by so many difficult situations last year while I was writing this book, such as Hurricanes Harvey, Irma, and Maria, the horrible wildfires in Los Angeles and other parts of the country, and the flooding and mudslides. People often had to evacuate their homes, yet brought their pets, their furry family members, with them. They might not have had much choice in what they and their pets ate—healthy and tasty or not—but at least most of them survived, and hopefully have regained normalcy in their lives.

Pick and Chews is also dedicated to mystery readers who enjoy stories involving pets and food—especially those who have read the Barkery & Biscuits Mysteries.

And, as always, I dedicate *Pick and Chews* to my dear husband, Fred, who acted as my servant and fed our dogs—and me—as I healed last year from a broken knee!

ONE

As always, I loved being here at the Knobcone Veterinary Clinic, even in the chill of March in the San Bernardino Mountains. A few minutes earlier, I'd dropped off my wonderful dog, Biscuit, a golden toy poodle/terrier mix, at the doggy daycare facility at the back of the clinic. After leaving my jacket in the locker room, I donned my light blue scrubs and hurried toward the vet tech room to check in for my shift. But as I passed the offices along the inside hall, a door opened.

Dr. Arvus Kline, wearing his traditional white medical jacket, stepped out of his office holding a clipboard. Arvie was the head veterinarian, one of the clinic's founders, my boss, and one of the most wonderful people I'd ever met. Although only in his sixties, he looked older, with wispy, silvery hair and a deeply wrinkled face. But his attitude was young, particularly toward his staff, the animals he helped to save … and me.

"Good afternoon, Arvie." I smiled.

"Good afternoon, Carrie." Arvie stepped farther into the wide hallway that just beyond us was lined with doors into examination and treatment rooms. A man followed him out. "Carrie, this is Dr. Oliver Browning. He's one of the vets Reed recommended from the San Diego Pet Care Center."

"Hi, Dr. Browning," I said.

The short, slender man wearing a brown suit and a huge grin on his narrow face reached out his hand, and I shook it. What was left of his hair was dark. "Hi, Carrie. Call me Oliver. Very nice to meet you."

"Oliver, Carrie's a part-time vet tech here. She also owns a couple of bakeries nearby. Her Barkery and Biscuits shop sells homemade and healthy doggy treats, and she developed some of the recipes when she was working here full time. Her other bakery, next door, is Icing on the Cake, and—"

"And I'll bet she sells homemade and healthy people treats there," Oliver interrupted, "though I doubt she developed the recipes while working here."

We all laughed, and I said, "I'm not so sure how healthy those recipes are either, but fortunately people seem to enjoy them."

"Well, I'll definitely have to stop over and visit your shops while I'm in town," Oliver said. "And hopefully I'll move here soon and be able to patronize them a lot."

He leveled a gaze straight at Arvie, who only smiled a bit. I knew why. One of the other vets who founded the clinic was retiring, and Arvie was searching for a really good replacement. Dr. Reed Storme, one of the less-senior vets and a very good friend—well, more than a friend—of mine had given him a couple of referrals from the animal hospital where he'd worked before coming to Knobcone Heights, and this Dr. Browning had to be one of them. I'd heard Arvie would be interviewing soon but hadn't known when. Was the other applicant around, too?

"I'm giving Oliver a brief tour now," Arvie said. "We won't hold you up any longer." In other words, I was to check in and start my vet tech duties for the day. Fine with me.

"Great meeting you, Carrie," Oliver said. "Hope we get an opportunity to work together soon."

I thought he was laying it on a bit thick, but maybe he really wanted the job here. I could understand that. This clinic was a great place to work—thanks to Arvie and Reed and the others on the staff, even including me. Plus, Knobcone Heights was a wonderful location to work—and play.

I didn't know what Arvie's criteria were for choosing the successor to Dr. Angela Regles, but I knew whoever won the position would have to be smart enough to diagnose and treat all kinds of pet ailments, and caring enough to treat every animal—and their owners—with compassion. That was true of the vet techs, too, although we did more treatment than diagnosis, and anything we diagnosed had to be confirmed by a licensed vet. But caring? Oh, yes.

"See ya," I said with a wave to Oliver, intending to be totally neutral. It was Arvie's call whether this guy and I ever worked together.

My boss apparently appreciated my attitude, since he raised his brows and smiled at me as he led his interviewee down the hall. I figured I'd learn more later.

I hurried into the room where veterinary technicians like me signed in, then said hi to Yolanda, one of the other techs, who happened to be in there on the computer. Attractive, dark-complected, and highly competent, she grumbled a hello, which was normal for her these days.

"Anything exciting going on?" I asked.

"Not really. But if you want, you can go into the reception room and grab the dog in there who's here to get neutered. I don't think

3

Reed is ready yet, but that's next on the agenda." She pointed to the computer screen at the combined schedule for the whole place.

"Sounds good." I turned away and hurried to the reception room. It was a good-sized area, with an abundance of chairs and a tile floor in case of doggy or kitty accidents. Along one side was the reception desk, which today was staffed by Kayle, another of our vet techs. Like me, the young guy was in blue scrubs, and his light brown hair matched the hint of beard on his cute face.

A guy stood beside Kayle, looking down at him. He wore a suit, like Oliver. Was this the other interviewee?

"How long have you worked here?" he asked Kayle—almost as if he were conducting an interview.

"Almost a year." I knew Kayle was interested in applying for veterinary school but wasn't aware whether he had yet.

"Do you like it?" the guy persisted.

"Very much. Oh, hey, Carrie," Kayle said, apparently noticing me for the first time. I thought I heard relief in his tone. "Could you take Fizzler back to Dr. Reed's examination room? He's here to be neutered."

There was only one dog in the reception area, plus several portable crates on the floor, or on laps, that I assumed held cats. Each was accompanied by a person, and at Fizzler's name his owner, a woman who appeared about my age, approached with him on a leash. Fizzler was mid-size, gray, and appeared to be a miniature poodle mix.

"Of course," I said. Then, looking at the guy who'd been interrogating Kayle, I added, "I hope you enjoy it here in Knobcone Heights and at this clinic."

"You know I'm a new arrival?" He was a bit better-looking than the man I assumed was his rival for the job: maybe six feet tall, slender, with a full head of medium brown hair and darker brown eyes that seemed to study me.

"I guessed. And before you ask, I've worked here for over five years, though I'm part-time now. This animal hospital is a wonderful place to work, and you can't go wrong if you're the one who happens to land the job here."

"That's what I'm hoping for." He pulled a smartphone out of his pocket, poked at it, and said, "My interview's in about five minutes, with Dr. Arvus Kline. Can I tell him you're rooting for me? I'm Dr. Jon Arden." He aimed a toothy grin at me.

"Only if you qualify that by saying I'm rooting for you if you happen to be the best." My turn to grin.

"Of course I am."

This discussion had gone on long enough. "Well, if so, good luck." I picked up Fizzler's paperwork from the desk and learned the dog's last name was Vink. I turned to Fizzler and his owner. "Are you ready to see Dr. Storme?"

"I am," Ms. Vink said, "but I suspect poor Fizzler would rather be anywhere than here, if he happens to understand what's going on."

I laughed. "I'd imagine so. Please come this way." I began walking toward the door to the inside of the clinic, and glanced back to make sure that leashed Fizzler and his owner were following.

The examination room Reed was scheduled to use that afternoon was a few doors down the hall. The smile I'd had on my face before grew larger. It would be the first time I'd seen Reed that day, though we had talked on the phone earlier. We hadn't been able to get together for dinner the past several evenings and had made plans for that night, once he was off duty at the clinic and I'd closed my shops. Dinner was our standard get-together time, and we did it as often as we could.

We wouldn't discuss dinner now, though, but we'd probably share some glances to suggest we both were thinking about it.

But when the patients and I reached the door to that room, I heard voices raised inside—and no one was scheduled to be in there. Once I had Fizzler and his owner situated, I was supposed to go get Reed. And one of those voices sounded like his. I didn't recognize the other but it was female.

What was going on?

"Excuse me just a second," I said to Ms. Vink. "I need to check to see if we should go to a different room."

A displeased look passed over her face but I didn't wait to explain. I opened the door, stepped inside, and closed it behind me.

Reed was there, as I'd figured. So was a woman I didn't know. She stood close to Reed, looking up at him and scowling. She'd raised one finger as if she wanted to poke him in the eye with it. She wore a tailored blouse and skirt that appeared nearly as businesslike as the outfits of the men who'd come in to interview. But Reed had only mentioned two former colleagues, both men.

Reed looked at me, though the woman didn't. His intense dark eyes flashed, and a scowl marred his usually great-looking appearance. Like Arvie, he was dressed in a white medical jacket. "We'll be out of here in a minute, Carrie." His gruff voice suggested he wanted me to leave.

"I've got your patient and his owner in the hallway," I said. "Are you going to be able to handle his neutering?"

The woman gave a burst of nasty laughter. "Oh, he's good at neutering, literally and figuratively."

I didn't want to think about what she meant by that. Did she have a relationship with Reed? Had he somehow hurt—neutered—her?

I'd learned a bit about Reed's background before he started working at the Knobcone Vet Clinic a year ago: former military, a K-9 handler, and then veterinary school, followed by a first, short-term practice in San Diego. He'd never mentioned any former relationships, but then, neither had I.

"Oh, can it already, Raela," Reed snapped at the woman. "The last thing I want is for us to work together again. That's why I invited Oliver and Jon here to interview but not you. Don't you have any kind of a conscience? No, don't answer that. I already know. For one thing, if you did, you wouldn't have taken time off at the San Diego clinic when you knew two other vets were going to be gone."

"If I didn't do it now, I knew there'd be no possibility of getting the job here. And from the way you've described it, it's veterinary heaven."

So her name was Raela? I definitely wanted to know more, but this wasn't the time. "Excuse me, Raela," I said. "I don't know about the interviews or how they're being scheduled, but I do know about the scheduling of our patients, and one is waiting right now for Reed. I'd appreciate it if you'd step out of here for now. You can continue this later, if you want to." More important, if Reed wanted to.

"So who are you?" she sneered. She looked me up and down, and at the same time I had an opportunity to look her in the face. She definitely had pretty features: high cheekbones, smooth skin, full lips, and gorgeous long medium-blonde hair framing it all. "A technician or other minion, I assume. I'm a veterinarian—*Doctor* Raela Fellner."

No wonder Reed hadn't wanted her to interview at the clinic, not with that attitude. I certainly wouldn't want her to start working here and be one of my bosses.

I wondered if she was a reason Reed had left his former job. Well, I'd find out later.

For now—

"Get the hell out of here," Reed said through gritted teeth, stating what I'd hoped to say more tactfully, but this was better. Reed moved away from her even as he clenched his fists.

As much as I'd have liked to punch her, too, I didn't think that was a good idea. I pulled my phone from my pocket.

"I'm not going anywhere," she countered angrily.

I glared at her. "Once I call the cops," I said, "I suspect you'll have … oh, maybe five minutes at the most to leave without getting arrested. We know them around here, and you don't." Of course I was bluffing. Yes, I knew some of them. But get them to do something I requested, even if there was some kind of law being broken, or danger involved? Though in this case any danger might be *to* the miserable cause of the problem, not *from* her. Well, I doubted we'd see them that quickly anyway. If at all.

"Oh, I'll get out of this room right away so you can go ahead and get your *neutering* started." She stressed the word as if she wanted to perform that kind of surgery on Reed. "And you know what? I rather like what I've seen of this town. I think I'll hang around, interview or not. Or maybe I'll just go over your head to get that interview after all. I'll be the one to decide."

She again leveled a nasty grin at Reed, then at me, and glided out of the room.

TWO

FIRST THING AFTER RAELA left, I took Fizzler from her owner to see Reed. Ms. Vink, back in the reception area, was clearly not a happy patient parent after being forced to wait as she had. I understood that. And though I was Reed's assistant during the neutering, we certainly had no chance to talk then about what had just occurred.

Judging by the grim look on Reed's face, that was the way he wanted it. But he fortunately was one excellent vet, and I could tell, thanks to all my experience during such procedures, that he didn't allow any emotions to interfere with what he did.

When we'd finished, and with Reed's okay, I went out to the waiting room to assure Ms. Vink that all had gone well and that she could pick Fizzler up in a few hours after our staff watched him for a while to make sure all remained okay and he woke up soon.

"Thank you," she said with a soft smile, apparently over her justifiable earlier irritation with us.

"You're welcome."

Though there were still some people with cat carriers in the waiting room, Dr. Jon Arden wasn't there any longer, so I figured Arvie must be interviewing him. I was curious how that was going. But as I stepped back into the hallway, I noticed Reed and Arvie talking outside the restrooms several doors away from Arvie's office.

Talk about curious ... I had to find out what they were talking about, so I hurried in their direction.

"I don't want to hold you up from talking to Jon," Reed said. "I think you'll like him."

"He's waiting there"—Arvie nodded down the hall toward his office—"so I'm about to find out."

I wondered how things had turned out with his interview of Oliver but didn't ask ... yet. Particularly because Reed leveled a look at me that suggested he wanted me to stay quiet. I had no problem with that. I had an idea of what he was about to say, and I was right.

"By the way, there's someone else visiting here from my old haunt," he told our boss. "She might contact you for an interview, but I don't think you'd like her. She showed up without an invitation because she knew Oliver and Jon were coming. I've told her to go back to San Diego, and if you hear from her I'd suggest you do the same. She wouldn't be a good asset here."

Arvie clearly hadn't met Raela, since, frowning, he asked, "Who's that?"

"It's me, damn you!" The ladies' room door burst open and the woman being discussed stomped out. "And you, Reed Storme, are a fool—and a damned sorry excuse for a vet. That's why you left San Diego. We all knew it."

"No," Reed growled. "Everyone but you realized that one major reason I left is that you were there. Even our bosses couldn't get rid of you, though they were working on it."

10

"No way!" she shouted, and I looked around. Fortunately no one else was in the hall, though undoubtedly a lot of people had heard it. Certainly their dogs did, with their superior hearing, and a couple started barking. "I'm a much better vet than you'll ever be," Raela continued. "I was nice to you then because you seemed so lost, and because ... well, you seemed interested in me, not that I saw you like that."

"Get over yourself." Reed looked anything but interested. Now, at least. But I couldn't help wondering about then.

"Oh, I'm way over you. And now, now—well, it's time for me to make sure you don't hurt any animals. I've never been to Knobcone Heights before but it seems nice. I just might open my own veterinary hospital here. I've been thinking about breaking out on my own anyway, and a couple of well-qualified vet friends will undoubtedly be delighted to join me."

I glanced toward Arvie. He didn't look pleased. Because of the potential competition? Maybe, but I figured it was also because of his affinity for Knobcone Heights and the distressing idea that such a terror of a female vet might wind up living here.

"Forget it." Reed's voice was a snarl. "You in charge? Talk about the possibility of animals being hurt or worse ... that would do it. The only thing you might be able to manage, with effort, is a dog-walking business, with yourself as the only employee, not a successful veterinary clinic that does the best job for its patients."

"Just wait," Raela said. "You'll hear from me again."

This time, she stomped down the hall, through the reception area, and out the front door. I knew because I followed at a careful distance.

When I turned again Reed wasn't there, though Arvie was. "Any idea what that was all about?" he asked as he joined me.

"I was going to ask you the same thing." The looks we traded were bewildered yet compassionate, or so I believed.

"Do you think she was the main reason Reed came here?" Arvie asked.

"I wouldn't be surprised," I said. Or would I?

I hoped Reed and I still would get together for dinner that night. I'd try to get more answers then.

Arvie left the reception area, probably heading to his office for his next interview. In the meantime, Kayle asked me to prepare an exam room for Princess, the next patient: a young kitten here for her first checkup. Dr. Paul Jensin, another vet who'd helped start the clinic, would be in charge. Helping him was fine with me. Staying out of Reed's presence might be best for now.

Once the room was ready I headed into the reception area to get Princess and her owner, greeting some of our other arrivals but hurrying to bring our new patient to Paul, whom I saw in the hallway. He was a tall guy, thin and gaunt-looking, and judging by the way he talked to people versus pets, he greatly preferred the latter—which I could understand.

In the exam room, Paul gave some extra cuddles to the cute Persian kitty, and so did I, and fortunately the little girl checked out just fine, pending the results of the blood test we took.

It was nearing the end of my shift, which was short that day, but I accompanied Princess and her mom back to the reception area. Kayle still presided there, and the only patients in the room had been present earlier, too—Shea Alderson and his two dogs: Earl, a pit bull mix, and Buffer, a yellow Lab mix. Both had been in a few weeks earlier for a checkup, but, as I recalled, they were due now for shots.

"Hey Carrie, how's it going?" Shea asked.

"Fine, thanks," I replied. Shea also knew me from my shops, or at least the Barkery, since he brought Earl and Buffer in there every week or so. Plus he was a nice guy who volunteered at Mountaintop Rescue. I'd run into him there several times.

"How are your guys?" I bent to give both dogs a hug.

"Not so thrilled about the idea of shots, but hungry for some special Barkery treats." Shea grinned. "I don't suppose you have any here?"

I had brought in a couple bags of items that were starting to age a bit—not bad yet, but in danger of not being edible soon. I'd planned to leave one bag at the clinic when I left and, assuming I had enough time, I'd take the other bag to Mountaintop Rescue, which was not far from the clinic.

But how could I resist a request like Shea's?

"I might be able to scrounge up a few." I glanced toward Kayle, who rolled his eyes toward the ceiling. "As long as that's legal."

"I can provide a legal opinion," Shea offered with a smile.

I'd learned during one of his visits to the Barkery that Shea was a lawyer, and also relatively new to the area. He had his own firm in a different downtown location than Ted Culbert, another attorney in Knobcone Heights, whom I'd hired in some difficult circumstances and now referred others to as well. Ted was a criminal attorney, but I gathered that Shea had more of a general practice.

Shea put his index finger on his chin and furrowed his brow. "Okay, here it is. Barkery treats can always be scrounged up and fed to my dogs as long as they're made from healthy ingredients and taste good."

"Then we've got a deal. Wait here for just a minute." I hurried to the vet tech room, which now was empty, and grabbed my bag of Barkery treats. When I returned to the reception area, Kayle wasn't present. In fact, Shea was the only human there.

I pulled out a couple of my special carob biscuits and handed them to the two dogs.

"So tell me," Shea said as the pups started begging for more. "What was going on earlier? I saw a lady storm through here as if she'd literally been kicked in the butt. Does she have a sick pet at the clinic?"

"No, she was involved in a little disagreement," was all I said. Raela was the one who seemed sick—in the head. But I wasn't about to tell Shea that. "Anyway, come on back and let's get these beautiful boys taken care of. Oh, and to encourage them…" I broke another treat in half and gave one piece to each dog.

Arvie was the vet who came into the exam room to take care of Shea's dogs, so I figured his interview with Dr. Jon Arden was over. I wondered how it had gone—and what Jon was like. Clearly, he'd be better than Raela. Anyone would be better than her.

Oh, well. At least she wasn't at the clinic any longer, though she'd indicated she was staying in town, at least for now.

It turned out I was wrong about where she was.

I soon clocked out, changed out of my tech scrubs, and hurried to the doggy daycare facility at the back of the clinic to get my Biscuit. The place consisted of a large room with a shiny beige linoleum floor that could easily be cleaned in case of accidents. For those pets who didn't deal well with others, crates of different sizes sat along the walls.

My little Biscuit got along well with everyone. She was loose in the middle of the room with other dogs, ranging from a golden retriever to a little Yorkie mix, with four others also in the game. And standing at the reception desk talking to Faye, manager of the daycare, and her assistants Al and Charlie, was my good buddy —not—Raela.

As soon as I came in, Raela turned her head to look at me, and the grin she leveled on me appeared evil. "Oh, hello," she said. "I understand one of those dogs is yours."

I assumed Faye had told her this—but what had Raela asked? I'd figured Raela knew nothing about me except that I worked at the clinic as a vet tech.

"That's right," I said. I wished I didn't have to indicate which dog it was, but Biscuit and I needed to leave. "Do you have a dog here, too? You know, this is a place where pets are dropped off, and only the people who work here hang around." I hoped this was a round-about hint that if she didn't have a pet present, as I assumed, she didn't belong here.

"I just wanted to check it out." Raela's voice was calm, her expression much too angelic. "For when I open my own veterinary clinic in the area. In case I decide to do something similar."

Faye's brown eyes opened wide and she looked toward me as if totally puzzled. I figured that whatever Raela had told her, she hadn't indicated that she was looking into doing something competitive.

Faye was in her forties, thin and energetic and dedicated to making sure her charges were all cared for well. Al and Charlie, who both wore standard red shirts that said *Knobcone Vets Rock* over their jeans, were twenty-something guys considering veterinary school. I wondered if Raela would attempt to advise them at all. I certainly hoped not.

"Er … excuse me," Faye said, "but I thought you wanted to know how we handle things around here so you could feel comfortable bringing the little French bulldog you described for a visit soon." Her voice was a little higher than usual, and she kept glancing from Raela to me and back again.

15

"Oh, I just like French bulls," Raela said. "Other dogs, too, of course. And cats. And other animals. I'm a damned good vet, a whole lot better than your staff. Anyway, I'm out of here now, but see you again soon."

Then she left the daycare, too—swaying in her businesslike blouse and skirt this time instead of stomping. She seemed to be gaining confidence somehow. About what? She knew she wasn't getting hired at our clinic.

But she had threatened to open a competing clinic. Was she serious about that?

Well, any new clinic she launched wouldn't be successful. All of us would be sure to tell the world how nutty the woman was. Right? But judging by Al's and Charlie's looks, they found her attractive. Faye, at least, seemed to recognize that there was something wrong here.

I was looking forward to my dinner that night with Reed, for multiple reasons. Raela had definitely made a bad impression on me, and I didn't want to get to know her any better. But I did want to learn what was really going on with her, and I felt fairly certain that the only person who could explain anything about her was Reed.

I shuddered inside about what I might learn from him regarding who she was—and what his relationship with her had been.

For now, I called my Biscuit. She ran from where she'd been playing and all but leaped into my arms as I knelt. "Hi, sweetheart." I snuggled my face against her soft, warm fur.

"Carrie, if that Raela woman comes back, should I tell her to get lost?" Faye asked, standing beside me on the linoleum floor.

I rose. "That's up to you. I'm not sure why she was back here in the daycare area, but then I'm not sure why she visited the clinic at all—except possibly to give Reed a hard time."

"Really?" This time Faye's eyes were narrow, and she appeared highly curious. Of course, she knew Reed and I were seeing each other, so I suspected she wanted to know what I was thinking.

I wanted to know what I was thinking, too, but I wasn't going to focus on anything till I had a chance to discuss this odd situation with Reed.

"Yeah, probably," I replied. "Anyway, I've got to leave. If I learn anything interesting, I'll let you know." That sounded good, but it would depend a lot on what, if anything, I found out. "See you at my next shift."

I'd already grabbed my jacket from my locker, since the spring day remained chilly. At least we didn't currently have snow in the San Bernardino Mountains, which was a good thing—especially since I intended to take a few minutes to drop in at Mountaintop Rescue to leave my other bag of doggy goodies.

I'd driven my aging white Toyota sedan to the clinic today, though I often walked. But I'd wanted to run some errands after my shift, plus this way I could leave that extra goodie bag in the trunk.

The rescue shelter was only a couple of blocks from the vet clinic, but the streets were a bit crowded, so it took me a little longer than usual to drive there. Plus, I stopped to get gas. But I soon parked at the rear of the attractive, gold-colored administration building and heard dogs barking from the enclosed kennels inside the fence. Before I went in, I gave Biscuit a brief walk in case she needed to relieve herself, but she mostly just sniffed the air and moved her long, fluffy ears as if listening. I tugged gently on her leash to get her attention, and then we walked to the front of the shelter and entered.

One of my favorite receptionists, Mimi, was at the large, chest-high wooden desk that helped to keep visitors contained until they were welcomed inside. As always, she wore a shirt with either a dog or cat on it—this time, a cartoon hound with a huge tongue. Mimi's youthful face lighted up with a big smile, as usual. "Hi, Carrie and Biscuit. I assume you want to see Billi, right?"

Billi was also known as City Councilwoman Wilhelmina Matlock. In addition to running the shelter and serving as an elected official, she owned Robust Retreat, a day spa. She and I had become good friends.

"Yes," I told Mimi. "Is she here?"

"She is, but she's got someone with her. I'll let her know you're here, though."

"Oh, that's okay, if she's busy. I can just leave my treats with you." I held up the bag and handed it over the desk to Mimi, who seemed to welcome it.

"Thanks. But Billi won't be happy if I don't at least tell her you're visiting." She picked up a cell phone and pushed a button, but before Billi could have heard it, she appeared at the top of the steps behind Mimi, off to my right.

"Hi, Carrie," she called.

As I waved and started to respond, I noticed she wasn't alone. Raela was with her.

What—here, too?

Plus, Shea suddenly appeared from the doorway that led into the shelter area.

I felt rather stunned. Were Reed and Arvie and Faye going to show up here as well? I'd just seen them recently too, after all.

Raela and Billi reached the bottom of the steps, and Raela faced me over the tall desk. "Are you following me, Carrie?" she demanded—though her snide expression suggested she wasn't as taken aback as I was.

"Nope," I said. "How about vice versa?"

"I was here first," she retorted.

Then Shea, who'd walked over to us, chimed in. "Or maybe you're following me, Carrie. It's legal to follow a lawyer, you know, as long as I don't feel threatened." But he was smiling and I knew he was joking.

"I thought I'd heard you're a lawyer." Raela's tone sounded excited and she bounced between Shea and me, facing him. "I might need to hire a lawyer for what I want to accomplish here in Knobcone Heights, like opening my own veterinary clinic. I'm a better vet than anyone in town, you know."

Shea's glance at her appeared as dubious as it should. "I doubt that." He moved away and nodded toward me. "There's already a very good veterinary clinic in town."

"Then you won't represent me?" Raela seemed to pout.

"I didn't say that. But you'll have to set up an appointment with me one of these days to talk."

"Yeah. Sure. I will. Someday."

Her tone indicated to me she'd never meet with him now.

"Care to see any of the pups I've been volunteering with here today?" Shea asked me. "And in case you're wondering, my own dogs are back at home."

I had wondered about that for an instant when I first saw him. As my gaze met Billi's, though, I spoke only to her. "I was here dropping off some treats, and Biscuit and I have to run back to the shops now."

"Thanks." Billi looked as puzzled as I felt. "Let's talk later."

"Great." I left, feeling all those sets of eyes on me.

Puzzled? I was stymied—as if I'd leaped into some kind of odd sci-fi adventure. Why had Raela come to the shelter? And why right now?

19

On the other hand, I mused as I harnessed Biscuit into the backseat of my car, as a vet who'd just arrived in town, Raela would naturally have some interest in the local shelter. And I already knew that Shea volunteered there. There really was nothing particularly *woo-woo* in either one showing up there.

But when I arrived at the rear of my two shops a short while later and started getting Biscuit out of the backseat, I again had a sense of *woo-woo*-ness. My phone rang, and when I answered, it was Reed.

"Sorry, Carrie, but I have to call off our dinner tonight. Gotta run now, but let's reschedule for tomorrow, okay?"

I had nothing in particular going on the next night, so I said yes.

And then I wondered what the heck was wrong with my life, and its karma, that day.

THREE

AT LEAST NOTHING APPEARED to be going wrong at either of my shops: Barkery and Biscuits, my healthy doggy-treat shop, or Icing on the Cake, with its fun people treats. After parking in back, I walked around to the street at the front of the building since Biscuit was leashed beside me. The two shops shared a kitchen, which opened into the parking lot, and dogs weren't permitted by the health laws to walk through it. But Biscuit could hang out in the shop part of the Barkery all the time, if she and I wished—and she did manage to spend a lot of time there, nearly as much as I spent at my dual venture.

First stop: the Barkery. It looked delightfully busy as I opened the front door. Of course, the bell rang. I'd installed a bell over the doors to each of my stores. If my assistants and I were all in one store, or the kitchen, we'd know when someone entered.

My full-time assistant Dinah Greeley, in a beige *Barkery and Biscuits* T-shirt, was behind the counter portioning out some of my healthy dog treats and talking to an older woman accompanied by what appeared to be a Shih Tzu puppy. Six other customers—some with dogs, including a golden retriever mix and a French bull—stood in line or peered through the glass into the refrigerated display case. Dinah didn't appear rattled at all about the busyness of the place, though she shot me a welcoming grin as I came through the door.

I'd inherited Dinah when I bought the original Icing on the Cake shop from my friend Brenda Anesco, who'd had to move away from Knobcone Heights to take care of her ailing mother. She had wholeheartedly approved of my turning it into the two shops. I always got a kick out of hard-working, dedicated Dinah, whose pudgy appearance always suggested that she got a kick out of working in a bakery and sampling its products. But Dinah was hard-working in other ways, too. She was a writer in her spare time and was always asking questions. So far she'd had some articles published, and she was also writing fiction.

I wondered what she would think of Dr. Raela Fellner—and feared I'd have the opportunity to find out if the vet really did decide to settle in the area.

Ugh. I didn't need to think about that now. Instead, I maneuvered Biscuit and myself around the few tables. The blue tile floor of the Barkery was decorated in the center with a beige representation of a bone. I glanced through the door that led into my other shop. Three customers were present in Icing, and Vicky Valdez, one of my part-timers, seemed to have things under control. I got Biscuit situated in her open-topped pen in the corner of the Barkery and turned to face the crowd myself, smiling as I made my way behind the counter and through the door into the kitchen.

I scrubbed my hands in the large sink located against the wall near the door. Since Dinah appeared to need more help than Vicky, that was where I headed. Of course, I also felt more of an affinity for the Barkery, since all the treats we sold there were either my own creations or had been developed on my behalf by a chef friend. Plus, I loved being around and thinking about animals, especially dogs.

But like a lot of my customers, I enjoyed Icing and its products, too, so I seldom admitted my preference—although I assumed my closest friends could figure it out. My brother Neal, who lived in my home with me, certainly knew it.

"Okay," I called out as I got behind the counter beside Dinah. "Who's next?"

For the next half hour, we chatted with customers and filled their orders. We got a lot of positive feedback—and it didn't hurt that I also gave out a few sample dog munchies to the canines who were present.

A few of our visitors were repeat customers. Others were probably newcomers, maybe visitors to Knobcone Heights. All, of course, were welcome in my shop, and so were their dogs.

When the line shortened to only two, I let Dinah know I was headed next door. "Glad you were here," she said, a grin lighting her face.

"Me too."

It was nearing closing time, and when I entered Icing there was only one customer present, a young woman with a child who seemed smitten by the different kinds of cookies. Icing was like a mirror image of the Barkery, although of course there was no dog enclosure. But it had a refrigerated display case, tables, and a floor composed of pale gold and brown tile meant to resemble the most luscious baked goods created for people.

As I'd done in the Barkery, I gave the child a sample treat—a sugar cookie—with his mom's okay. They then ordered a couple dozen cookies to take home.

When they were gone, I looked at Vicky and heaved a sigh. Of relief? Of frustration at the way my day had gone earlier?

Probably both.

"You okay, Carrie?" Vicky's black brows arched as she stared through her glasses at me. Was my unease obvious? She was wearing our promotional T-shirt, too—hers light green with an *Icing on the Cake* logo on it.

"Pretty much. Just had some stress at the clinic, but I'm fine now." I didn't need to explain it all. Instead, I changed the subject. "So who's on our schedule for tomorrow?" I'd found that of all my assistants, Vicky was the best at determining our part-timers' schedules.

"I've already contacted Janelle and Frida. Of course Dinah will be here all day, but the rest of us decided to each take a few hours, shifting between the shops like we've done before."

"Sounds good," I said. "Thanks for putting it together."

"It's always my pleasure." Vicky grinned, and I knew she meant it. I certainly was okay at scheduling, but she excelled at it—and at keeping me informed so I could pay my staff appropriately.

I pulled my phone from my pocket. It was nearly six p.m. "Okay," I said. "Let's begin closing up for today."

With her help and Dinah's, I locked the doors, including the one at the back of the kitchen that led to the parking lot. I rearranged the leftovers that would be fresh enough to sell the next day. Then I packed up some treats from the Barkery to give away, either to the clinic or Mountaintop Rescue, and some from Icing for a charity down the mountain who would send someone to get it soon. I let my employees go for the day, but before I left I checked to make sure all the computer and accounting information for both stores was locked in my office off the kitchen.

Then I picked up my purse from its drawer and returned to the Barkery to get Biscuit. She'd been a good girl, of course, greeting doggy customers with nose sniffs if they came up to her enclosure, and sleeping part of the time. Now she was clearly ready to go home.

So was I.

I made sure the lights were mostly off except for a dim one kept lit for security, locked the front door behind me, and walked Biscuit slowly around the building to my car. I settled her into her harness in the back seat and myself into the driver's seat—and just sat there for a minute.

I wondered again why Reed had cancelled our dinner plans without saying why. Was it just his terrible mood after the encounter with Raela?

Or was he having dinner with her?

Now, where had that thought come from? Probably my inner insecurity and curiosity about what their relationship might have been in the past.

I knew that my brother, Neal, was spending the evening with his girlfriend, Janelle, and I didn't want to bother him—or her, for that matter. She was not only his girlfriend and one of my assistants at the shops, but also an excellent professional photographer. And a friend of mine, too.

But I also didn't particularly want to be alone that night—not even with my adorable Biscuit. I decided to call Billi to see if she wanted to meet for dinner.

And was delighted that she did.

This would be a good thing for more than one reason. I would have company that evening—and I might learn why Raela had visited Billi, and Mountaintop Rescue, earlier that day.

We chose to eat at Billi's house that night. She said she would stop on her way home and pick up pizza, and that was fine with me.

As a Matlock, Billi was a member of one of Knobcone Heights' most elite families, so she lived in an amazing part of town. Her place was a gorgeous stone mansion near the top of Pine Lane. Gorgeous? Heck, it seemed majestic. As I often thought after pulling up in front of it, all Billi's place needed was a moat to look like a genuine European castle. The large front door was made of ornately carved wood, and round towers of stone decorated each side.

After parking, I got Biscuit out of my aging car that didn't fit this mansion-filled area and headed to the door. I rang the bell and could hear it toll inside. Billi answered nearly immediately.

"Hi, Carrie." We shared a hug as I entered.

Unsurprisingly, her dogs had barked at the noise and now greeted Biscuit and me. She had two dogs: Fanny, a Beagle mix, and Flip, a black Lab—both rescues she'd adopted from her own shelter.

Despite its vintage outer appearance, the inside of Billi's house looked contemporary and well-maintained. As usual, we headed for the huge dining room, where Billi had set two places at the antique table.

I was still wearing the clothes I'd had on at my shops, including one of my T-shirts beneath my jacket, this one promoting Icing. Billi was dressed more casually than she'd been earlier—in a T-shirt, too, unsurprisingly with *Mountaintop Rescue* on it and a depiction of several dogs and cats.

First off, we got the dogs settled down around us, mostly with gentle commands but also thanks to some treats I'd brought from the Barkery. After Billi poured shiraz wine into fine glasses for us, she and I helped ourselves to the meal she'd laid out on the table, including salads.

Then we began talking.

"So tell me what's going on." She looked at me with her inquisitive deep brown eyes, her head cocked. Billi was one lovely lady in addition to being a City Council member, a spa owner, and an animal lover. She was slender, with long, highlighted dark hair and a beautiful face with high cheekbones and full lips.

"I just had a really weird day," I replied, but before describing it to her I needed to know more. "When I got to Mountaintop Rescue, I saw you with Dr. Raela Fellner. Did you know her?" I assumed they'd just met, but I preferred that Billi explain the circumstances.

"Not really. She came to the shelter a little while before you got there and asked if she could talk with me. She indicated that she'd just come to town to look into the possibility of starting a veterinary practice and wanted to learn all she could about Mountaintop Rescue and whatever other facilities there were in our area for animals. And did I know if there were any legitimate dog or cat breeders, whatever. Why do you ask?"

I described what had happened at the vet clinic, without getting into my concerns about Reed and what he thought of this potential intruder into the area's veterinary community.

But Billi was nothing if not shrewd. "I wondered where Reed was tonight and why you wanted to get together with me. I also wondered earlier why this woman was considering opening another veterinary hospital in this small town when we have a fine one here already. Now I can guess."

"Yeah, me too." I sighed. "As you know, our clinic has a well-deserved great reputation around here. The only way I figure some competitor could succeed would be to spread lies, on social media

27

or otherwise, claiming our patients don't do well. Or maybe she'd cut her prices enough to make it impossible for Knobcone Vet Clinic to remain competitive."

"Or both. And it would be a shame."

"Yeah," I said. "It would." I took a bite of salad and chewed it slowly as I pondered how either threat could be countered appropriately.

"After you and Raela left," Billi said, "Shea and I talked about what he'd seen at the clinic earlier. He mentioned that Raela had seemed completely out of control and angry, and he wasn't sure what was going on."

"I wonder what his legal mind thought of it all."

"Me too. I could just see him cogitating about who could sue whom." Billi laughed, then looked at her slice of pepperoni pizza before taking a bite. "He's been spending quite a bit of time at the shelter. He might be a lawyer, but he's also an animal lover—and that's a good thing."

"Yes," I said, "it is." The expression on Billi's face suggested she was impressed by Shea in more than one way... including romantically?

Maybe. She hadn't mentioned Jack Loroco much lately. Jack was a senior product manager at VimPets, the large and successful pet food manufacturer that had finally succeeded in buying a recipe from me. Billi and Jack had had a budding relationship last fall, or so it had seemed. But although he'd rented a home in the area, he hadn't spent a lot of time in Knobcone Heights recently. Or if he had, I wasn't aware of it.

Maybe that was because he'd been a suspect in a local murder... as had Billi.

I took a sip of shiraz. I could ask Billi who was currently in her headlights, but I figured we were close enough that she would tell me, when she was ready, if there was any change. Otherwise, I could assume that Jack and she remained an item. A long-distance item.

"So are we still on for the adoption event scheduled at the Barkery on Saturday?" Billi asked.

"Absolutely, as far as I'm concerned." Today was Wednesday, so we still had a few days to get everything into place. We'd already held several similar events over the past few months, when Billi and her crew and volunteers from Mountaintop Rescue would bring some of their most adoptable pets to the Barkery and introduce them to my customers and other visitors. Both the shelter and I did as much publicity as we could to lure people in, so that they could at least meet some of the adoptable animals.

So far, we'd found homes for maybe eighty percent of the pets brought to the adoption events. It was a wonderful record. I hoped it remained that good on Saturday.

The rest of our meal went well. We talked a lot about animals—no big surprise. Nothing further about the vet clinic or any potential competition to it, though.

And nothing at all about our respective romantic relationships. I kind of wanted to tell Billi how upset I was with Reed, although I realized I could just be imagining my suspicions.

But he *had* called off dinner with me. And whenever that little fact poked its way back into my consciousness—which was a lot—it hurt.

Eventually, we were finished eating. I insisted on helping Billi bus and clean our dinner dishes. Later, we took our dogs out for a walk.

Then it was time to leave. Time for my mind to go back to—what else? Reed. And tonight. And wondering...

A short while later, I pulled my car up to my house, located in what was probably the nicest middle-class area of Knobcone Heights—pleasant and appealing—but nothing like the mansionized area where Billi lived. A good thing, really. I wasn't sure how well I'd do living in a neighborhood like that.

I drove down the narrow driveway to my charming one-story home, Biscuit now a bit restless in the backseat. She knew where we were. But before I reached for the button to open the garage door, my phone hummed its song. I glanced at it. Reed.

I reached for my Bluetooth button, stopped the car, and girded myself for whatever conversation was to come.

It was in some ways the best I could have anticipated.

"Hi, Carrie," Reed said. "Are you at home?"

"Just arriving. I had a nice evening with Billi." Out of nastiness my mind reached for the name of some guy I could claim to have spent the evening with, but heck. Just because Reed was being difficult didn't mean I needed to be, too.

He might feel guiltier this way, after all.

And he did, in fact, apologize. "I wanted to tell you I'm sorry about how I acted before. It's just that—well, this isn't the time to get into it, although I bet you can guess at least some of it. I'm just getting home, too. I had dinner tonight with the men I used to work with, Oliver and Jon. It was nice to see them again."

"Did they—or you—have any idea which one Arvie preferred? Is he going to make either of them a job offer?"

"I don't know yet, and they didn't either. But they both liked Arvie and the others they met at the clinic, including you. If Arvie does choose one of them, I'll bet whoever it is will accept the job."

"That would be nice." I hoped. Reed knew them, but I didn't.

Either would, of course, be preferable to their female coworker who'd shown up in town ...

I found myself glaring toward my garage door and nearly laughed at myself.

"Anyway," Reed said, "I hope you're still available for dinner tomorrow night. I know you don't have a shift at the clinic, and even if you did, we couldn't really talk there. So will you join me after work at the Arrowhead Diner?"

That was one of our favorite restaurants, out-of-town and cute, with good food.

And a fair atmosphere for conversing.

I nearly played coy, hoping to get him to convince me. But that wasn't really me. Nor was it in keeping with the relationship I thought we were developing.

Even so, I had to ask. "You're sure you'll be able to make it?"

I heard him laugh. "I figured you'd say something like that. And I hope you know I'll get down on my figurative knees and beg you to join me."

"That works for me." I laughed, too. Reed promised to pick me up around six thirty at my house—with our dogs joining us.

We said good night and hung up. And as I finally drove into my garage, I told myself I should be delighted that things appeared to be getting back to normal.

But that would depend on what Reed said in the conversation we were soon to have.

FOUR

I WASN'T SURPRISED THAT Neal was home when Biscuit and I entered. Nor that he was sitting in the living room on the fluffy and aging beige couch, watching a reality show on the TV mounted on the wall—a show that took contestants around the world vying for lots of money and the potential continuation of their fame. It was one of his favorites.

What was surprising was that after Biscuit and I came in and Neal greeted his favorite dog—or "Bug," as he calls her—he looked at me with worry on his face.

A face that greatly resembles my own. Neal was twenty-nine years old, four years younger than me, but taller. We share the Kennersly longish nose and blunt chin, as well as fairly sharp cheekbones. On the whole, we don't look too bad—or at least that's my opinion.

And we are close. Our parents divorced and both remarried, favoring their new families over us. I was now helping my little brother, who made less money than I did, by letting him live in my house and pay me minimal rent. But his emotional support was priceless.

"So how was dinner with Janelle?" I asked. Neal and Janelle did spend some nights together, but I'd gathered earlier that this was unlikely to be one of them.

"Fine. Great, in fact. But . . . "

His expression appeared so full of sympathy that I had to ask, "But what?"

"Janelle heard some stuff about the vet clinic today and told me. I didn't follow it all, but . . . well, has Reed's former girlfriend moved here?"

I closed my eyes and shook my head—not in denial, but because word was apparently getting around about Raela and how she'd happened to choose Knobcone Heights to visit. And the gossip included stuff about Reed, supposedly a prior relationship between them.

Which only made me worry all the more about what Reed and I would really talk about tomorrow night at dinner.

"Several former coworkers of his from his previous employer, a veterinary hospital in San Diego, are interviewing at the clinic," I said. "Two of them are vets Reed recommended. They had their interviews with Arvie today. But there's also a third, and—"

"And I gather she's a she. And that she's planning on staying here even if she doesn't get the position."

"Janelle knew that?" I wondered how she'd heard it. She hadn't been working at my shops today. Even if she had been, all I'd mentioned was that my shift at the vet clinic was stressful. Had either Vicky or Dinah been concerned enough to follow through somehow, learning the situation from someone—who?—and also letting Janelle know?

"Yes, she did. And if you're going to ask how, I haven't the foggiest idea. I can ask her, if you'd like."

"Yes, I would like."

Neal immediately pulled his phone from his jeans pocket and pushed a few buttons. He talked briefly to Janelle, then said to me, "Dinah apparently told her."

Dinah. But how would she know?

"I don't suppose Janelle knows how Dinah found out, does she?"

More conversation over the phone, and then Neal said what I anticipated. "No, she doesn't."

"That's okay," I lied. "I'll check with Dinah tomorrow. But for now … well, I'm tired. Biscuit and I are heading for bed."

Which I knew was a bad idea. How would I sleep with all this on my mind?

On the other hand, it had apparently exhausted me. I fell asleep fairly quickly and didn't awaken till morning.

———

The next day at the shops was fairly uneventful—except that I managed to take Dinah aside and ask how she'd learned what went on at the vet clinic, as well as why she'd passed along that info to Janelle.

We were alone in the kitchen at the time—with me working on Barkery treats and Dinah baking some Icing delights—and I could only call the expression on her face pleased and smug. "You know I like to do research," she said.

"Yes, but—"

"I'm always making contacts at various places and functions, in case something comes up. I'm not about to tell you who told me, 'cause you may get mad and confront the person, but I'm now buddies with someone at your clinic who told me about the strange things the lady vet who showed up there did. I knew you must not like it, and that your brother should probably know about it, so I told Janelle. It was as simple as that."

It probably was simple to Dinah, who really liked doing such things. But… "I assume you've made notes and might use the idea in something you're writing," I told her.

"Of course, but the names will be changed to protect the innocent." Her smile widened, and she looked back down at the Icing counter where she'd assembled the ingredients for our red velvet cupcakes.

I knew that Dinah had a tendency to talk to people randomly, especially if she thought they were involved with something that could lead to a new plot for her novels. For example, I'd seen her having a drink with Jack Loroco when the VimPets executive was considered a murder suspect.

But who was her undercover contact at my vet clinic? And why had that person told her about the Raela situation?

I'd have to find this out… somehow. Dinah clearly wasn't going to tell me at the moment. I'd have to ponder how to get her to reveal all— and then how to handle the situation with whoever it was at the clinic. Raela's arrival wasn't exactly classified information, but even so, gossiping about problems where we worked wasn't the wisest thing.

Especially when it involved people I cared about, like Reed and Arvie and possibly others, too.

And speaking of Reed… as planned, I had a dinner date with him that night. With his Belgian Malinois, Hugo, in his car, he picked Biscuit and me up at our house a short while after I returned home after closing the shops.

I'm always glad to have the dogs along, but that evening I was especially pleased. Since it was a chilly evening, there weren't a lot of people willing to sit outside on the Arrowhead Diner's patio, notwithstanding the heaters on poles that kept the table area relatively warm. That meant we had some privacy, despite the place being nearly as crowded as it usually was. I felt fairly certain we would be able to remove our heavy jackets as we sat there for our meal. Of the few other diners seated at tables not far from ours beneath the heaters, some were dressed warmly while others weren't.

The diner was a popular, family-style restaurant that had long ago been built to resemble a train's dining car. It was outside of Knobcone Heights, off a major road on the way to the town of Lake Arrowhead. It was one of my favorite places to eat, partially because I nearly always went there with Reed.

Since the menu was family style, I got to choose my dinner— from healthy salads to not-so-healthy but definitely delicious regular American entrees. I often did the right thing and stuck with salads, and they were quite tasty here with their variety of veggies and dressings. But tonight I wasn't thinking health … except mental health. I needed something to calm my nervousness over the pending conversation—and what I might learn. So I chose a double-decker burger, though I did ask for a salad on the side. I easily justified the second burger: it was for the dogs.

Reed's order was similar, and we both ordered glasses of beer on tap.

Then, with the dogs lying on the patio beside us, each with a small bowl of water, I finally had an opportunity to look into Reed's very good-looking face.

No scowls tonight. In fact, I once again saw what I believed to be regret for how he'd behaved at the clinic when I'd first met Raela. Or not. I decided to ask—more tactfully than that.

"So how were things at the clinic today?" I asked. In other words, though I didn't say it, was Raela there? If so, did she cause havoc with her threats about opening her own clinic? Or—

"Things were fine. Both Oliver and Jon stopped in, for one thing. I talked to Arvie again about both of them, and though he remained fairly tactful I think he's leaning toward making an offer to Oliver to join us."

"And you'd be happy with that?"

"I'd be happy with either of them. And I'd enjoy having one of them around. We were all good friends back in San Diego."

Ah, my opportunity. I was about to edge my way into the topic of Raela ... but Reed beat me to it.

"In case you're wondering, yes, there were a few other vets at that clinic who were buddies with us, too. But I didn't recommend them as possible candidates for the opening here because I knew they had roots in San Diego—mostly family. A couple of them also helped build the clinic there into something outstanding and I doubted they'd want to leave it. Both Oliver and Jon have been happy there, but I always had a sense of their ambition and interest in trying out other possibilities, so I figured either might be a good fit here. And then there was dear Raela."

Dear? His tone had sounded sarcastic, but what if it wasn't? Not a good time ... but our server happened to show up then with our beers. Maybe it was a good time. After he left, saying our meals would be out soon, I was happy to take a swig.

"So what about dear Raela?" I prompted in a similarly sarcastic tone—I hoped—once I'd swallowed. "Was she a good vet? Did she love the place or have ambition to leave, or—"

That awful scowl I'd seen on Reed's face when he'd talked about Raela before reappeared as he interrupted me. "She was mostly an okay vet, though I didn't like her attitude a lot of the time, with both our patients and their owners. She acted as if she liked our clinic, at least to our supervisors, but every once in a while, when we went out for a drink after the clinic closed for the night, she indicated her dissatisfaction with how things were managed there, and hinted she could do it all a lot better."

So they had gone out for drinks. And more?

"Did the more senior vets like her?" I tried to sound casual. I didn't really care what the senior vets thought of her—but I did care what Reed had though of her.

"I never really asked, but I thought she received fewer, or easier, assignments than the rest of us."

"That suggests they didn't like or trust her work."

"Maybe not, but they didn't fire her, so they must have liked other things about her."

He raised his dark eyebrows as he looked straight at me and took another swig of beer. I thought about asking what he meant, but when I opened my mouth, he waved his hand.

"I didn't consider her the best vet, though she mostly was okay. But one thing she was particularly good at was getting a guy all hot and bothered by suggestive comments or even touches. Nothing completely wrong, but, like I said, suggestive."

"With you, too?" I burst out, then felt my own eyes widen in embarrassment. My glass of beer immediately drew my attention once more. Heck, we were dating. It shouldn't be too inappropriate for me to want to know this.

"Actually, yes. She joined the staff after I did, and I admit I found her attractive. She came on to me—well, we came on to each other. I realized I wasn't the only one who was interested in her, though, so I kept things suggestive but cool. And for a while that worked out just fine. In fact, I found her rather amusing, the way so many of the guys there did. Even our patients' owners were attracted to her."

"But you indicated that she was a reason you decided to leave." Right?

Our server returned with our meals. Sometimes I wished I could choose the timing for such things. Would Reed use this as an excuse to change the subject, or at least drive it in a different direction?

Fortunately, he didn't. We both spent a few minutes removing the extra burgers and giving them, piece by piece, to the obviously delighted dogs who sat up beside us. Then we turned back, regarding each other over the table, both of us holding our own burgers in our hands. I took a bite, my gaze latching onto Reed's deep brown eyes.

He really was great looking. He was sexy. How could I blame any woman, even Raela, for coming on to him? But his attitude toward her was what was in question.

"Okay, back to what we were talking about," he said. I almost stood up and cheered, but waited to hear if he would actually start up where we'd left off. "Yes, Raela was one reason I decided I'd been working there long enough. I flirted with her a bit, yeah, but she flirted with everyone, and she wasn't the kind of woman I wanted to start a relationship with. I also didn't care for the way she seemed to be respected by the vets in charge whether or not she deserved it. I was with her when she almost made a mistake during some dental work on a dog. I caught it and fixed it, but when I started to tell one of our senior vets about it, he just sloughed it off. It wasn't major, but even so, I didn't like his attitude. Of course, she'd been flirting with him, too. Anyway, the upshot of it all is that I started looking for something better, and damned if I didn't find it—right here in Knobcone Heights." Reed's grin was loaded with suggestiveness.

I decided I'd heard all I needed to. "So you're happy here?" I asked, taking a bite of my salad.

"Well, I could be a little happier if we happened to get a nightcap at my place after dinner."

"Me too," I said. I felt certain our nightcap would involve more than additional drinks.

FIVE

UNSURPRISINGLY, I THOUGHT ABOUT Reed later when I was home in bed—and mostly smiled. He'd faced a difficult situation where he once worked and used it as a foundation to catapult his life in a new direction. A better direction. One that had brought him to Knobcone Heights and a veterinary job he clearly loved.

One that had resulted in my meeting him ...

And in my having some really delightful dreams that night.

The next morning when I awakened, I rehashed our enjoyable evening in my mind—and felt glad that I didn't have another shift scheduled at the vet clinic until Monday, and this was Friday. As much as I loved my part-time job there, I really didn't want to wind up seeing "dear Raela" again. Maybe Arvie would make up his mind soon about who to offer the veterinary position to, and the others who'd expressed interest in it would head back to San Diego. Although Raela had made it clear she might not leave any time soon ...

But I was thinking too much about something I couldn't control. The only thing I could control was my own reaction. "Let's go to the Barkery, Biscuit," I told my little dog after I'd gotten dressed and taken her outside. I stayed quiet so as not to wake Neal—first so I wouldn't bother him, and second so I wouldn't have to talk to him about this subject that I wanted to put behind me.

And, in fact, my day at my shops went fabulously well—even though only two of my assistants, Dinah and Frida, were working, partly because I needed all of my employees there the next day for the adoption event.

I did take a little time that day to visit Mountaintop Rescue, to help choose which of Billi's wonderful and needy dogs and cats would visit my shop in the hopes of finding a new forever home. I also contacted Silas Perring, the head anchor for the KnobTV news, as well as Francine Metz, the senior editor of the local small weekly newspaper, the *Knobcone News*. As in the past, both seemed pet-friendly and willing to help publicize Mountaintop Rescue and its adoption events—including those held at my Barkery.

So now word was out, not just in Knobcone Heights but also in some of the surrounding communities, like Lake Arrowhead. Would a huge stream of animal lovers converge on my shop to fall in love and adopt a new pet?

We'd had some darned good luck at the past events, so I dared to hope for a wonderful result.

That day at the shops passed quickly, and so did that evening, which I spent at home alone—or at least alone until midnight, when I heard Neal return. Even so, I was already in bed and didn't get up to say good night.

Then it was Saturday. The day started as it usually did, with me baking in the kitchen along with the first of my assistants to arrive—

that day, it was Janelle. She was a pretty woman, with her long, wavy light brown hair pulled back into a clip, and as usual she was wearing her purple athletic shoes. The others got there soon, too, and split up to help in both shops. Our business was good although not overly busy, which was fine with me.

At about ten in the morning, I got all my assistants together in the kitchen to discuss the event that would begin in an hour. They all appeared to feel as excited as I did. Maybe this was because I only hired people who were also pet lovers.

"When will all the animals get here?" Vicky asked. Of course my chief scheduler would have a question about timing.

"Billi said they'd start arriving around ten, so we should see them any minute now."

Sure enough, I heard the bell over the door ring, followed by a chorus of barks—some of which sounded like Biscuit's. I shot a smile at my staff before hurriedly heading into the Barkery.

Billi was there, along with her assistant Mimi, who today again wore her white shirt that said *Adopt today. Love forever.* So was Shea Alderson, apparently taking a day off from his legal work to volunteer at the adoption event. Each of them held the ends of dog leashes—Billi's a small terrier mix, Mimi's a pit bull, and Shea's a medium-sized dog whose heritage I could only guess at, though it seemed to include Lab and boxer. I'd met them all when visiting Mountaintop Rescue the day before, and I'd also seen some of the other pets before, including a few of the longer-time shelter residents.

I hoped every one of these dogs would find new homes that day. As excited as Biscuit was to have visitors, I figured she also wished the best for them. Janelle's dog, Go, did too, most likely. Go and Biscuit both leaped around woofing, Biscuit in her large open crate and Go leashed to it.

"Hi, Carrie," Billi called, a huge smile on her face. Her sense of humor was on display, since she was clad that day in a dark suit that made her appear like the City Councilwoman she was rather than the head of a wonderful no-kill shelter. I figured it would wind up covered with dog hair, but that was a good thing, not a bad one. "We've got about seven more dogs out there and three cat crates. Is it okay to bring them all in?"

"Of course," I said, returning her smile. I glanced toward the counter, where Dinah and Frida stood with three Barkery customers, who also were looking at the dogs. "Can you help out?" I asked my assistants.

"I heard there was going to be an adoption event here today," said one of the customers, a middle-aged lady with short, orange hair. "That's one reason I came."

"Good," I told her. "Are you looking for a new family member?"

"I'm thinking about it," she responded.

"Then think away—and meet some of our town's orphans who are looking for new homes." I gestured toward Mimi and Shea and the three dogs, who were standing on the bone decoration in the middle of the tile floor. We'd removed the tables for today to make more room. Billi was already outside with the other volunteers, preparing to bring the rest of the adoptable pets inside.

I glanced out the front window and saw not only a van parked along the street, but quite a few people converging on the Barkery from the sidewalk. Potential adopters? I hoped so, but even if they were just curious animal lovers, that could still help to get our orphans into new homes.

The other pets were soon inside the Barkery, ready to meet humans. We kept customers outside for a short while as we got things organized, but were still able to open the doors again before the scheduled start time of eleven o'clock.

Even so, I put organizer Vicky in charge of letting people in a few at a time so we didn't get unsafely crowded. I was thrilled, though, that we had such a turnout. And almost immediately I was even more thrilled that a cheer went up from Billi, Mimi, Shea, and the other Mountaintop Rescue volunteers. The pit bull that Mimi had on her leash had already found a new home.

Speaking of feeling thrilled, I was delighted, at around noon, when Reed appeared outside the window. Vicky knew enough to allow him to come in immediately, although the crowd was thinning a bit so the lineup outside was getting smaller. When I'd first mentioned the event, Reed had told me that he was working at the clinic this Saturday but would head over to the Barkery for his lunch break.

Dressed in casual clothes rather than his veterinary jacket, he edged his way toward me around the groups of people kneeling and meeting the pets. "How's it going?" he asked. "Although with this crowd I think I can guess."

"I think you can, too," I said with a small laugh. "Four dogs and two cats so far, and there are still a lot of interested people here—as well as needy pets."

"Are you bribing any of them with Barkery or Icing treats?"

"What do you think?" Reed's grin told me he'd guessed the answer—an unqualified yes.

"Okay if I go say hi?" He nodded toward Billi, who stood at the checkout counter filling out paperwork for the latest adoption.

"Of course."

I gathered that there was now another cat going home and watched the adoption with excitement as Reed and Billi chatted for a moment. Reed and the other vets at my clinic provided exams and any needed treatment to the rescue animals at Billi's shelter for a reduced rate, and I wondered how many of the animals at our event Reed recognized. Perhaps the cat currently in the spotlight?

Even if he didn't know the cat, Reed made a point of caressing the kitty as it moved its head to look into his eyes. "He's a good guy," Reed said to the woman who'd been filling out the paperwork. "I've seen him at Knobcone Veterinary Clinic for a checkup, I believe, but when you're adopting it never hurts to get the animal looked at fairly soon to make sure all's well, and to get the vet's records updated."

"Got it, Dr. Storme," the lady said.

"Got it, Dr. Storme," said another female voice from behind me, but this time the tone wasn't respectful and appreciative but scornful. "If this *wonderful* veterinarian has checked out that cat before, don't be surprised if it has a lot of issues." The word "wonderful" was said disdainfully, which didn't surprise me.

Even before I turned toward the source of the nasty comments, I recognized who was talking—and wondered why she was here.

Dr. Raela Fellner.

I tried to keep my expression neutral as I looked at her. Too bad she still appeared attractive on the outside, with her blond hair pulled back with a clip to further reveal the loveliness of her smooth face. Inside, she clearly remained an unfettered bitch—and I didn't mean a normal female dog.

"Are you here to adopt a pet or buy some dog or people treats?" I asked her calmly.

"No way. I just wanted to make sure that anyone here who dared to take on a pet vetted by that awful veterinary clinic was warned to have their new animal checked somewhere else. Someplace where all the doctors are competent, not just some of them."

"Then you admit that at least some of the vets at the Knobcone Vet Clinic are good ones?" I couldn't help asking, though I wanted to simply kick her out since she'd admitted she wasn't there to do anything appropriate. I knew who she was intending to hurt by her gibes, and he happened to be right there in my Barkery. It was probably because he hadn't stayed in her life to be insulted and hounded by her on an ongoing basis . . . and that was partly because he had no romantic interest in her. Which I could only applaud.

Raela maneuvered past the people in front of her to draw closer to me—and I quashed my internal shudders. I wasn't about to allow her to insult anyone I cared about without making sure she experienced some kind of consequences. But we were being observed by most, if not all, of the people at the adoption event—and I now noticed that the two media folks I'd contacted were present. They must have come in while I'd been talking to a couple of the dogs with Billi. Great. This nonsense would now be made public.

"Oh, that's right," Raela said. "You work there too, as a mere vet tech, and probably not a very good one, either. I asked around and got the impression that your boss, Dr. Kline, is adequate, but probably no one else who works there is."

Of course she'd say something somewhat nicer about Arvie, since she might still harbor a hope that he would hire her. But I couldn't exactly call what she'd said a compliment.

"I think we've all heard more than enough from you." That was Reed, now standing at my side. "Although I would imagine that anyone hearing you and your unfounded criticisms would recognize the source as less than credible."

Yay, Reed, I thought.

"Oh, I'm damned credible," Raela shot back. "I'm a veterinarian too, one who's just about to open a competing animal hospital here. A good one. One where all these people can bring their pets and know they'll be treated a hundred percent better than what they have to put up with at the Knobcone Vet Clinic."

I noticed then that Shea was in a corner of the room, apparently talking with someone about the mixed-breed dog he'd come in with—a dog who hadn't yet been adopted. Should I invite him over here to listen—or even participate in the conversation?

Maybe my veterinary hospital should bring on an attorney like Shea, perhaps to sue this horribly nasty person. Had he and Raela ever met about his representing her? From her attitude at the shelter, I didn't get the impression she'd deign to follow up with him, so maybe Shea was still available to represent my Knobcone clinic.

But had Raela even said or done anything that would warrant some kind of legal action?

I saw Shea glance in our direction and gestured slightly toward him. He must have seen me, since he stood up and joined us.

As much as I wanted to ask his legal opinion, I had no authority from our clinic to do anything that official, even if he could represent us. But maybe just bringing up something law-related, in front of Raela, would quiet her down.

So all I said was, "How are things going from a legal perspective here, Shea? I know the pets are well cared for, and the adoptions seem to be going well. And—"

"And like I said," Raela said, raising her voice, "you'd all better be careful about adopting any animal that's only had a checkup at that scam of a veterinary hospital. Now, if you'd like an exam by a damned good vet, be sure to contact me. And I can tell you which vets are the worst at that farce of a clinic."

Clearly, my law-related question hadn't fazed Raela at all. She glared into Reed's face, smiled snidely, and then strutted out of the Barkery, people moving themselves and dogs out of her way.

The place was silent for a minute. But then the roar of conversations filled the air.

SIX

Fortunately, things at the adoption event had returned to normal nearly immediately. Sort of, at least.

I overheard people talking about that lady who'd burst in and then left. Was she really a veterinarian? Was she really going to open a veterinary practice here in Knobcone Heights?

And every once in a while, I heard muted voices ask if that woman had actually been right that the Knobcone Veterinary Clinic wasn't a safe place to bring pets, either those adopted at the Barkery that day or those already at home.

I kept my mouth shut, and so did Reed. Better that than having people think we were protesting too much, and therefore implying that what had been said might be correct. Instead, everyone working at the event tried to direct those conversations in different directions— mainly, back to the reason people were here in the first place.

Billi, Mimi, Shea, and the other volunteers, as well as my assistants, seemed quite adept at doing this, pointing out cute actions the pups and kitties were engaging in and encouraging people to determine what kind of pet they were most interested in, what size and age. Basically, discussing everything other than what had just occurred.

It seemed to work. Most people at the event edged up to the dogs and cats still available, kneeling on the tile floor to meet them, asking the volunteers questions, describing their own home situations—and sometimes preparing to adopt a new family member right there on the spot. They would get vetted, of course, to try to ensure that their new homes were appropriate and safe and that the new human family members were kind and caring and knew about what was needed to take care of the pet they were adopting.

Watching, ensuring we had plenty of treats—Barkery ones for the dogs and Icing ones for the people—and talking to people, including saying goodbye to Reed when he had to return to the clinic ... well, all that kept me too busy to dwell on Raela's earlier intrusion. At least, not much.

Eventually it was two o'clock, when the adoption event was scheduled to end. A young couple who'd come with two kids, and an older couple who'd recently lost their dog to an illness, pleaded with us to stay open a little longer, since they were narrowing down their choices and really, really hoped to adopt that day.

"Okay," Billi called to the dwindling crowd. "We're going to start packing up the remaining pets to return to Mountaintop Rescue. You're all welcome to come there during regular hours to visit the pets, help socialize them, and, most of all, adopt them, even if today wasn't the right day." She looked toward the two last families, who stood looking at her hopefully near the Barkery checkout counter. "Of course, since you folks seem close to adoption, I'll hang around a little longer, but we can't interrupt business at the shop much longer."

Billi didn't look at me, but she knew I welcomed the adoption event and didn't mind however long it took to find new homes for as many pets as possible. I felt delighted that the majority of the animals who'd started their day here had been adopted.

I watched as most of the people left, although some headed for the counter to buy treats at the Barkery, or went through the door into Icing.

"Good job," said Shea as I stood beside Biscuit's enclosure, petting and reassuring her as I'd done often during the event. No one was going to take her home but me.

"I agree." I smiled at the good-looking lawyer-with-a-heart. I wondered what he would look like in a suit instead of the kinds of casual outfits I'd seen him in at the clinic, the shelter, and here. I also wondered if he, too, was thinking about possibly representing my clinic in some legal action against Raela for her continued insults against it. If so, despite my inability to get officially involved, I would be happy to testify against her.

I wondered what Reed would think about that... despite our discussion at dinner the other night, when he'd seemed to make it clear that he wanted nothing to do with Raela and hadn't ever wanted to get closer to her.

"How often do you hold this kind of adoption event here?" Shea asked.

Our last one had been a few weeks earlier. I figured that Shea had begun practicing law in Knobcone Heights around six to eight months ago, so there'd probably been three or four adoption events since his arrival. I didn't know him well, but it was early last fall when I'd first seen him at Mountaintop Rescue. Yet he hadn't ever come to one of the adoption events before.

"We host these events as often as Billi wants to," I told him. "At least every couple of months now, usually."

There'd been a time, last fall, when I'd wondered if Billi would even be able to hold an adoption event, or run Mountaintop Rescue or her spa, or continue on the city council. She'd been a potential murder suspect then, poor thing.

Of course I could identify with that, since I too had once been a person of interest in a local killing.

But no need to mention any of that to Shea, even though he was a lawyer. It all was past history, fortunately.

"That's great. I've enjoyed coming to the Barkery with my dogs since I arrived here, as well as volunteering at the shelter. Now I know I can sometimes do both at the same time."

I laughed. "Well, thank you for both. It's really great that a lawyer like you can find the time to do either." I didn't really know much about his practice but figured all lawyers had packed schedules.

"I agree, especially since my new firm here keeps me darned busy. But drafting pleadings and all can sometimes be done in off hours, so I can manage."

"Good job," I said, repeating what he'd said to me when our conversation started.

He high-fived me with a smile, then said, "Not that you needed to remind me, but even though it's Saturday I'd better head to the office for a while to work on some of those pleadings. I've just started on a new case—and before you ask, it's still confidential so I can't tell you about it. But I'll do a good job with it, even though it doesn't involve animals."

"It's probably not as interesting as those that do," I said.

"You're right," he replied as he left.

When Shea was gone, I checked with my assistants and confirmed that we'd sold a fair amount of our baked goods that day. Then I edged my way toward Billi, who remained at the front of the

Barkery talking to the elderly couple now in the process of adopting a Scottish terrier mix.

"How's it going?" I asked during a lull in their conversation.

"Really well." A huge grin bisected the woman's face. Then the smile disappeared and she turned back toward Billi. "Right?"

"Right," Billi responded. "Just a little more paperwork, a few more questions, and a commitment from you that I or a member of my staff can visit your home in the next few days, and you're ready to take Dougal home with you."

"Yay!" the husband cheered as the woman clapped, and I exchanged a happy look with Billi.

———

There was additional cleanup to do in both shops that afternoon, but with all my assistants there it didn't take much time. We remained open as long as always, till six o'clock. I was exhausted by then and was glad that Reed and I hadn't scheduled a date. We did talk on the phone, though, when I was home that night, and I appreciated his celebration of the successful adoption event with me.

"When's the next one?" he asked, reminding me of my conversation with Shea that afternoon.

"Not sure yet, but soon, I hope."

"Me too." We wished each other good night, and that was when Neal returned home. Although it was Saturday, he hadn't led any of his beloved hikes; rather, he'd been working at the reception desk at the Knobcone Heights Resort, his usual day job, which was why he hadn't been able to attend that day's adoption event. He didn't need my description of how things had gone, though, since Janelle had already informed him about the event's success.

We chatted a bit about the adoptions as Neal accompanied Biscuit and me outside for her last outing that day. Because he was my brother, I did tell him about the interruption that happened thanks to that female veterinarian Reed had known before.

"You sound pretty upset about that," my perceptive brother said. "Were Reed and she close before?"

"He said they never were, and that getting away from her was one of his reasons for leaving his old job."

Neal was silent beneath the glow of the nearby streetlight, pulling his jacket closed in the cool night air.

"I believe him," I added in a stubborn tone of voice, wondering if I was trying more to convince Neal or myself.

"Reed's a good guy," Neal said. "If that's what he told you, it's got to be true."

I hoped my brother was right. But even if he wasn't, I'd seen how Reed disliked Raela now. Our own relationship hadn't proceeded to the commitment stage, anyway, and I wasn't sure it ever would.

But in any event, I didn't see Dr. Raela as likely to come between us.

———

On Sunday, my hours at the shops were the same as always, starting at five a.m. with the day's baking.

Neal had told me he wouldn't be at the resort that day but had rustled up some of his most loyal hikers and was going to take a short outing that afternoon. Leading hikes was my brother's favorite activity, his paid avocation, and he did it often—sometimes only with locals he knew, but often with tourists from the resort who he'd recruited to join in. He charged the resort visitors more, but since that venue was rather elite and definitely expensive, he figured they could pay more ... and they did.

Neal's hike was probably the most exciting thing that happened that day, although I could only assume this since I didn't get to go along on this one.

But with Biscuit, as usual, in the Barkery, I put in a normal day's work at my shops, with only a couple of my assistants present: Janelle and Vicky. I didn't have a shift at the clinic that day, so compared with the wonderful events of the day before, Sunday was okay but kind of dull. I didn't even have a date planned that night with Reed, since Arvie had scheduled a dinner meeting for the clinic's vets, plus the two Reed had recommended—apparently to help him decide which one to extend an offer to. Arvie wasn't usually that indecisive, which indicated to me that both Oliver and Jon had made a good impression on him. Would he try to hire them both? I doubted it. Maybe the dinner would just be a fun outing for professional animal doctors.

Which meant I looked forward to an evening home alone with Biscuit. But Reed and I did schedule something for Monday night, so I had something to look forward to.

Plus, I had a shift at the clinic in the early afternoon, so Monday was more eventful and more enjoyable than Sunday. I admitted to myself that I was rather concerned about being at the clinic, since I didn't know if Raela was still in town—although from what she'd said at the adoption event, I assumed she was. I hoped she wouldn't stop by again to spit out her spiteful rant full of fury and threats. Sure, if it would help soothe and heal ailing animals, I'd confront her in a second and keep any pet far from her. But if she showed up again to challenge Reed, or either of her San Diego clinic coworkers—in other words, humans who could rant right back at her—then I wanted to stay out of her presence.

Fortunately, all went well at both shops and at my clinic shift that Monday. Looking back, I was probably somewhat complacent. My assistants on duty, including Vicky in the morning and Janelle in the afternoon when I headed to the clinic, all did a great job baking and waiting on customers—and discussing how well the adoption had gone that weekend.

At the clinic, with Biscuit in doggy daycare and lots of canine and feline patients in for regular checkups and no major illnesses or injuries—and a date with Reed to look forward to that evening—well, I dared to enjoy myself and believe all was well in my life and in the lives of my brother and the friends and employees I cared most about.

Ha. I should have known better.

Reed picked me up at seven that night, once I'd closed up the shops and gone home. No dogs tonight. We sometimes brought them along if we were planning on spending our time in the bar at the Knobcone Heights Resort, but not in its restaurant, unless we wanted to eat on the outside patio. The resort was another of our favorite places, and I couldn't hazard a guess at how often we'd eaten there.

We arrived and parked in the lot in front of the various sprawling, elegant buildings that composed the resort. Each building was a couple of stories high, with a sloping slate roof over thick white walls and dark wood-framed windows. Reed and I walked together toward the registration building, which contained the bar and restaurant. My bro was scheduled to be on duty at the reception desk that night, so when we arrived I led Reed past it, waving hello to Neal before we went to eat. Though he was talking with a couple of guests, Neal saw me and gave a slight wave back.

Reed and I entered the posh restaurant beneath the arched doorway. We were of course known by the restaurant's maitre d', Harvey, so though the place was crowded and few tables were available, we were shown to a nice one in a relatively quiet corner. As anticipated, our table was covered with a pristine white cloth.

Our server that night was Stu, a relative newcomer who nevertheless had been there long enough to know the restaurant's procedures. He appeared immediately to place our matching napkins and flatware in front of us. He was young, with short hair and a welcoming smile. Like the other servers, he wore a white shirt with a name tag on the pocket.

"Hi, Carrie. Hi, Reed." Despite the formality of this place, Stu knew us and greeted us as if we were friends. "Would you like the usual to drink?"

My "usual" drink changed periodically but was currently a glass of Merlot from a Napa Valley vineyard, and it was indeed what I ordered that night. Reed enjoyed imported beers, currently a Canadian one.

"Yes, please," I said, and Reed did the same.

Once Stu was gone, Reed looked at me and smiled. "I figured I'd wait till we were here before telling you about the news I just received."

"What's that?"

"Arvie called and said he's made an offer to Jon to join our clinic."

I leaned over the table toward him, trying to read whatever might lie behind his expression. He seemed happy, but I asked anyway. "And that's okay with you?"

"Definitely. Oliver would have been a good fit too, but the more I considered both of them, the more I hoped that Arvie would decide on—"

He broke off suddenly, and the happiness on his face segued immediately to something less readable. If I had to guess, it was a combination of shock and anger. Reed was staring beyond my shoulder, so I turned to see what had affected him that way.

Raela had walked through the arched doorway into the restaurant and now stood beyond the crowded tables, staring into the room.

Not only that, but Dr. Oliver Browning was with her.

Harvey, the maitre d', joined them nearly immediately, blocking them from our view. I looked back at Reed. "Why is Oliver here with her?" I asked, realizing that he was most likely wondering the same thing. But I hoped he would tell me if he actually knew the answer.

"Damned if I know," Reed growled almost under his breath. He started to stand, as if he planned to stalk over and find out.

"Let's just ignore them," I said in a soft but pleading voice. Whatever their reason was, I suspected that any discussion that took place in the restaurant could get ugly. Any discussion anywhere, probably, but especially here, in public, where we were known, and where Neal worked—well, it would be a really bad idea.

"Yeah. Sure." Reed's tone suggested he was being totally sarcastic, but he did settle back down, and I tried to smile at him again. He stared straight into my face as if wanting to look anywhere but at those two, though I knew otherwise.

Then his shoulders stiffened, his eyes narrowed, and I turned once more to see what he saw.

And wasn't surprised that Raela was maneuvering among the full tables toward us, Oliver following.

In moments, she'd reached us. She wore a sexily snug black dress and stiletto heels. The smile on her otherwise pretty face looked so nasty I could hardly bear to look at her. "Well, fancy meeting you here," she said. Then, moving to look straight toward Reed, she said, "I know about the dinner you vets had last night. You should have invited me—and yes, I know that most of you work at your damned clinic, but not all of you."

She glanced back toward where Oliver stood. Could he hear her? Most likely, since even with the hum of conversations around us, her voice seemed to project as if she were on stage and wanted the world to hear.

"Well, it's done with, even though I'm not happy I wasn't asked to join you. I do have some news you'll be interested in, and I could have told you about it then. I'm not going to tell you what it is anymore. But think about it—and you can be sure I'll tell you soon. When it suits *me*." She emphasized the last word as if everyone in the room, everyone in the world, should care about what did and didn't suit her. "But you can be sure it's already a done deal."

She pivoted, then, moved around Oliver, and gestured for him to follow her, which he did. They sat down at a table across the room, where Harvey stood waiting for them.

SEVEN

I LOOKED UP AT Reed from beneath my eyelashes. My mind immediately pondered what I should say to him next. Laugh at the situation and say what a pompous and nasty fool Raela was? Speculate on what she hadn't told him or me—her "news"?

I unfortunately had a good idea of what her news might be. And as soon as Reed had taken a huge drink of his beer, I realized he, unsurprisingly, did too.

"Is that bitch actually opening a veterinary clinic here in Knobcone Heights?" he demanded, as if I knew the answer. Which, unfortunately, I thought I did.

"She's only been here for a few days," I replied. It had been nearly a week, and she'd made that threat when I first met her. *A done deal.* Could she have found and bought or rented a location so soon? Maybe. But gotten it set up as a new animal hospital?

Unlikely. But maybe she could do something makeshift while obtaining needed approvals and getting the place ready.

Still, how would she get patients? Would any pet parents trust her—or such an impulsive situation?

And why was Oliver with her? He might already know he hadn't been chosen for the job at our clinic. Did that mean he'd be receptive to working with a horrible person like Raela?

Reed had said she wasn't considered a particularly skilled vet at their San Diego facility. Was that everyone's opinion—including Oliver's? Or might he be angry enough to jump in to work with her, maybe even mentor her as a vet, to make up for any disappointment he felt for not getting the job offer at our clinic?

And while it was more Reed's concern than mine, if all three of those vets wound up staying in town, what was going to happen to the clinic they'd worked at in San Diego?

Okay, this guesswork was getting me nowhere, especially since I kept it to myself.

Stu returned then to take our orders. I wasn't hungry anymore and suspected Reed wasn't either. I'd planned on an actual dinner, one featuring a chicken casserole, but that now sounded like too much. I retreated to my sometimes usual, a Cobb salad. Reed ordered a tuna wrap—more like a lunch than a substantial dinner.

I half wished we'd simply asked for the check and left, though I was concerned Reed might use that as an excuse to just drive me home and end our evening together on this sour note.

It wasn't likely to get sweeter anyway, but I realized our leaving that quickly might give Raela additional pleasure at the situation she'd caused.

And so we stayed and ate and talked about some of the patients we'd seen that day at the clinic and others who would be in to receive somewhat unusual treatments that week. I also threw in some ideas I had for additional dog treat recipes to create and sample. It was all neutral stuff that was of interest to both of us, and it kept us from discussing what was really on our minds.

The table where Raela and Oliver were seated was near the wall of the restaurant, toward my right and Reed's left. We both could see them, but we managed to mostly keep looking at each other, pretending to ignore those ugly veterinary elephants in the posh restaurant.

I noticed, though, from the corner of my eye, that Raela sometimes turned her head to stare in our direction, as if wanting to remind us that she was indeed here. But if Reed noticed he didn't mention it, and neither did I.

Our food arrived, and I don't recall ever eating as quickly as I did then. Reed too finished his meal in what might be record time. We soon waved Stu over for our check. Reed and I had an agreement that I'd pay for every third or fourth meal when we got together. He still made more money than I did, even with my stores, but though we were dating I didn't want to seem like an old-fashioned princess who expected to always be cosseted and treated. When we visited each other's homes, the one who was hosting that night took care of dinner, too, and we were about equal there.

Tonight was my turn, yet when Reed took the check, I understood and let him pay. Not that it was likely Raela could see what was going on, but it might embarrass Reed, under these circumstances, to be the one who apparently was being pampered.

I'd hoped we would go to Reed's for a nightcap—and more—before he dropped me off, but neither of us was in that kind of mood. I was glad, though, that Neal was home. He accompanied Biscuit and me out for our last walk of the evening after Reed left. Having someone close to me like my bro was always a good thing, and I really wanted to talk that night.

"Maybe she had something else in mind," Neal said as we stood in the chilly night air, beneath a streetlight just down the block from our house, while Biscuit did her business. "Maybe she's just teasing and is about to head home to San Diego—and she and Oliver are just flirting and showing that off to Reed in case it'll make him jealous."

I looked up at Neal, his face shaded as he smiled down at me encouragingly.

"Yes, maybe to all of that, but for her to act so pleased and smug—well, I'll be interested to hear what she tells Reed, and when she tells him."

We returned to the house. It was only eight thirty, not extremely late. I considered calling Reed but doubted either of us really wanted to talk.

I also wondered if he would call Arvie that night to let him know that we had seen Raela and, speculation or not, there was a possibility she was about to provide the chaos and competition to our clinic that she had threatened.

Enough. I decided to be active and learn what I could. I went into my bedroom, sat down on the coverlet on my bed while Biscuit curled up on her fluffy mat on the floor beside me, and called Arvie.

"Well, hi, Carrie," he said almost immediately. "Good to hear from you." Then he asked, "Is everything okay?" Though we had each other's phone numbers, we nearly never communicated this way. I mostly found out at the clinic when they wanted me to come in, and had any discussions about scheduling in person. Arvie and I got together now and then for meetings and meals, but these too were nearly always planned during conversations when we were face-to-face.

So he must not have heard from Reed, I figured. "Not sure," I replied, and described our fortunately brief but unfortunately disconcerting meetup with Raela earlier. I also told him my speculation about what she'd been hinting at.

Arvie was silent for a few seconds. I wondered what my boss was thinking but didn't ask.

If things went wrong at the clinic, I still had my businesses, and they seemed to be doing well. I could most likely support myself fully that way now. But I really liked my part-time job—and the people I worked with there, most particularly Reed and Arvie. What would they do if competition from Raela hurt their business?

Even more important, in many ways, was the question of how our pet patients would fare if they were taken someplace else for treatment—like to a clinic run by Raela, who had apparently been perceived by her coworkers as somewhat incompetent, even if they didn't kick her out.

"Well, it'll be interesting to learn what's really going on," Arvie finally said.

That was an understatement, but I didn't say so. Instead I said, "I'm scheduled to come in tomorrow afternoon for a shift. Maybe we can talk then."

"Sure," he said. "Maybe by then we'll have a better idea of what's going on."

I hoped so … didn't I?

———

But as it turned out, there was no further news from our buddy Raela when I got to the clinic about one o'clock the next afternoon and left my dear Biscuit in doggy daycare.

I inquired of Faye when I got there about how things were at the animal hospital and in her facility, without being more explicit as to why I was asking. Faye looked puzzled as she replied, "Fine, Carrie. But why do you ask?"

"Oh, I'm always concerned." I bent to give Biscuit a hug before encouraging her to run off to the area where other dogs were already playing with one another, Al and Charlie on their knees and ensuring all was well.

I hurried into the clinic, seeing a another vet tech leading a canine patient and her owner into an exam room down the hall. I quickly changed into my blue scrubs and headed to the vet tech room to sign in and find out if anything unusual was on the agenda for that day.

Yolanda was in there, at the computer. Although she was often moody, she was a really good vet tech, and because of that we generally got along fine. She didn't seem any grumpier today than usual, so I figured all was well... or at least I hoped so.

"Anything exciting going on?" I asked.

"Nope. But since you're here, why don't you just head out to the reception area and bring Falcon back for his shots."

Falcon was anything but a predatory bird. He was a pit bull mix, a frequent patient whose owner was highly protective and always concerned that something was wrong if the dog even coughed or shook his head or whatever. At least his being here just to get shots shouldn't be anything too exciting. I'd wait and see, though, in case the owner had anything else to disclose about the pup.

I looked at a different computer to see who the day's patients so far had been and learn what appointments were scheduled for that afternoon. I was glad to note that the vet likely to handle Falcon's exam was Reed. I closed the computer screen and said to Yolanda, "I'm off to get Falcon. See you later." I left the room.

I took my time, since both Arvie and Reed were most likely already in exam rooms with patients, at least according to the posted info. I hoped to talk to each of them without other people around, although if a dog or cat happened to be present and eavesdropping, that would be fine.

I couldn't help taking a deep inhale of breath as I strode down the hall toward the reception area. The air smelled a bit more heavily than usual of disinfectant, though that scent was nearly always there. The clinic and its facilities were cleaned often, like my shops and their kitchen. I liked that smell here. I always had, from the time I'd become a vet tech.

But of course I liked the aroma of my baked goods a whole lot better, even the meaty and other unique scents of my healthy dog biscuits.

I wondered, not for the first time, if a kitchen should have been set up at the clinic—for healthy munchies and other homemade food for pets with special needs. But when I suggested it to Arvie before I wound up starting my Barkery, he hadn't wanted to either use the space or add another venue within the clinic that would need to be kept completely clean.

I quickly reached the door into the reception area and opened it. I first saw that Kayle was behind the front desk again, and I smiled and nodded at him.

Funny. The look on his young face appeared strained and uneasy, and he held a phone in his hand. I was about to ask if anything was the matter when I turned slightly and realized what had triggered that expression.

Raela was there, dressed in white veterinary scrubs, a large tote bag over her shoulder and her blonde hair pulled back. "So this is how it is, folks," she said to the half dozen people sitting on the waiting room chairs, dogs or cat crates at their feet. "I can understand why you're here, since this was the only place in town—*was* being the operative word." She held a stack of what looked like flyers in her hands, handing one to each of the pet parents. "But I've just opened the Heights Veterinary Care Clinic down the street. You can check the website to learn about my excellent credentials and read a lot of good reviews. You may be stuck here today, but this can be your last time."

Only then did she stop and aim her gaze at me. She'd clearly known I'd arrived but had chosen to present her spiel so I could hear it, too.

"Well, hello there, Carrie." Her voice was as smooth as if she'd coated it with whipped cream. "Fancy meeting you here. I suspect you and the others won't be here much longer, though."

I still stood in the doorway, my hand on the knob, and I clenched it to avoid running into the room and punching the brazen, horrible woman in her grinning mouth.

But suddenly I felt hands at my shoulders, thrusting me off to the side as the door opened even wider. I turned quickly—and saw Reed enter the room at my side.

I'd seen him angry with Raela before, but the word *anger* didn't begin to describe the fury on his face. It nearly obliterated the features I considered handsome. Now Reed appeared to be like some kind of raging creature that was too wild to be treated in our wonderful clinic for pets.

"Get the hell out of here, Raela," he shouted.

"Well, hello, Reed," she said, standing still and tossing an even bigger smile his way. "I was hoping I'd run into you here." She handed him one of the flyers. "Like I said, I had some news to tell you, and I can't think of a better time to tell you than now."

EIGHT

I wanted to shout at this brazen witch, too. Tell her where to go—and I didn't necessarily mean to whatever place she'd chosen for her supposed veterinary clinic.

But I could see the curious and uneasy stares of the half dozen pet parents and the resultant movement of their dogs and cats near their feet. I most certainly didn't want our attitudes to be the trigger that hurled them toward Raela's new facility. Some of the people were even studying the flyers, so it wasn't too much of a guess to think they might consider giving the new place a try even if they'd been happy here.

I held out my hand to Raela for a flyer. "Congratulations." I forced myself not to sound too sarcastic.

"Well, thank you." She handed me a piece of paper, and I glanced at it briefly. The clinic's name was surrounded by photos of several dogs and cats and some hearts, which I supposed was meant to indicate that her patients would be loved and cared for. She had audaciously included a tagline saying that it was the best veterinary facility in town. She could say anything without living up to it, of course. And as I'd wondered before, she surely hadn't had time to obtain all the licenses and approvals necessary to open her facility as a legitimate veterinary hospital.

The address was on Hill Street, as was our clinic, but the number indicated that it was way past Mountaintop Rescue, maybe near the supermarket that was just out of town. There weren't a lot of buildings out there. I wasn't too familiar with the area and couldn't picture just where this was.

Raela had also included a few reviews on her flyer—good ones about her as a vet, not about her new clinic. They were probably false, but the minimal identification of the reviewers indicated that they were based on her prior work in San Diego.

"Does everyone have a flyer now?" she asked, ignoring the fact that Reed stood beside her, glaring at but not touching her—a good thing. All the people in the room seemed to be holding one of the flyers. I wanted to snatch them back and burn them but held myself still.

"Good," she continued. "I'll leave a few more here—but not a lot, since I doubt they'll last very long." Her grin was large again, and after laying some of the papers down on a table between a couple of the waiting room chairs, she reached up to pat Reed on the cheek before oozing her way out the front door.

I hurried to place myself beside Falcon, who sat on the floor beside his owner, Joan. She looked as puzzled as the rest of the people here.

"Everything's okay, folks," Reed muttered, waving a hand without meeting anyone's eyes. He then went back through the door to the inside of the clinic. I took that to mean that everything should now continue as usual, and I should get back to work.

I laughed a little and said to the crowd, "Well, it appears that Knobcone Veterinary Clinic is about to have some competition. We're the best as well as the first, of course, and will stay that way. You can be certain of it."

I held out my hand for Falcon's leash, and Joan handed me the end. "He just needs shots today," she said.

"We'll give him a quick exam to make sure he's healthy, too." It was our regular practice to at least ask questions to make sure there were no changes in the pet's behavior at home. Today we might even go into more detail.

Today, we'd want to look even better than the best.

On my way toward the door, followed by Joan, I stopped briefly and whispered to Kayle that the flyers on the table needed to disappear, as Raela had figured they would.

Then I took Falcon and his mom to the examination room where Reed now waited.

Fortunately, he'd calmed down. "Well, that was interesting, wasn't it?" He didn't wait for Joan to answer. "Now tell me how Falcon has been doing. Eating well? Any problems?" He pulled out his stethoscope and listened to the dog's heart. The rest of the exam, and the shots, seemed to go well, as it usually did.

In fact, the rest of my shift seemed completely normal—except for seeing the quick conversations that others who worked at the clinic engaged in. And I did get an opportunity to say hi to Arvie, a couple of patients after Falcon.

"You were there," he said in a low voice, after following me as I showed a cat and her owner out to the reception area once more.

"Yep," I said quietly. We now stood in the quiet hallway near the closed door to the lobby.

"I know you told Kayle to get rid of those flyers, but he just hid them, so several of us got a chance to look at them. Nothing outstanding there, except the hype about being new and claiming to be the best in town. But advertising and promotion always says that."

"True," I said. "But in this case, I think the person making the claim will go out of her way to make people think it's true."

"Maybe. Well, look, I intend to have a short meeting about how we should handle this—late tomorrow morning, maybe. Would you be able to come?"

"Sure. Just tell me a time and I'll do all I can to be here whenever you say."

The wrinkles edging my boss's eyes crinkled as he smiled at me. "I always knew I could count on you. And I just might be asking you more questions on how to promote a business. You've been doing well with your bakeries, and we might need some advice on how to keep our vet hospital at the top in everyone's estimation around here."

"You know I'll help as much as I possibly can." I gave him a quick hug, then hurried back to the reception area.

———

The rest of my shift was relatively normal, although a couple of the owners who'd been there when Raela put on her show asked questions, like what it had all been about. I just said we'd met that veterinarian before and she'd said she might open her own clinic in town. Though I thought about doing it, I didn't mention Raela's bad reputation with her former coworkers. That might have simply seemed spiteful, and, besides, I only had Reed's word for it. I did, however, urge people to stay with us and suggested that, if they considered trying her out, they should wait till other locals had used her and given her some kind of positive ratings.

"That would be in the best interest of your pet," I emphasized. And I figured that since pet parents love their fur-kids, they would heed this and not go running off to the new place—assuming all at our clinic continued to go well.

A while later, as I got ready to leave, I stopped in at Reed's office but he wasn't there. I hadn't seen him in any exam room for a while either, although that didn't mean he wasn't still around. I figured I'd get in touch with him later, not to meet up, necessarily, but just to talk.

And to make sure he was doing okay.

———

Biscuit and I walked back to the shops, and the atmosphere felt a lot better there than it had at the vet clinic. I didn't tell my assistants the details of what had gone on during my shift, but a couple of them—Dinah, then Janelle—took me aside to ask if I was okay. I wasn't sure whether I appeared upset or worried or … well, maybe I just was not my usual self.

They both had ulterior motives for checking, of course—Dinah because she was always conducting research, and Janelle because of how close she was to my brother.

I told them generally what had occurred but kept my tone and attitude light. They knew me well enough to see through that, but they didn't press for more information.

Vicky was the only other assistant working at the time. She asked a few questions too, after some eavesdropping on my conversations with the others, but all she did was express confidence in our existing veterinary clinic. I appreciated that.

Eventually it was time to close the shops for the night. All three of my assistants helped ensure that only the items that would still be fresh tomorrow remained in the cases, segregating out those a little less fresh to donate to the vet clinic and Mountaintop Rescue, or to the down-the-mountain charity.

It occurred to me that this was a benefit Raela's new vet clinic wouldn't have: my special and healthy dog treats. Unless she decided to buy some of mine, which was a worrying thought.

Biscuit and I were the last to leave. I buckled her into her harness on the backseat of my car, then realized I was in dire need of groceries. I could use some more frozen dinners for nights like tonight when I anticipated eating alone and had no desire to do any cooking. Neal ate those kinds of meals sometimes, too. Plus, I wouldn't mind having some pre-cut salads around so I didn't have to put any effort in that, either. And—

Well, it was a cool enough evening that I wouldn't worry about Biscuit baking in the car. The windows would be slightly open, of course, but I wouldn't leave her in there very long anyway. My foray into the grocery store would be short.

Which it was. But as I returned to my car through the crowded parking lot, I allowed myself to wonder about why I'd really come to the supermarket tonight.

I was going to take a detour rather than head straight home.

I was going to continue driving along Hill Street, farther out of town—to where Raela's new veterinary clinic was located.

Okay, that was the real reason for this excursion. I admitted it to myself. No one else needed to know about it.

After sticking my bags in the trunk and giving Biscuit a big hug of greeting, I buckled my seat belt and pulled out of the parking lot, making a left turn. I didn't remember the full address of her clinic, but after glancing at the number on the front of the grocery store, I realized that the address on the flyer had indicated it was a couple blocks away.

Sure enough, when I reached that block, I saw that a building resembling a small house had a makeshift sign on its front window: *Heights Veterinary Care Clinic.* The outside didn't appear particularly snazzy or professional, and I didn't see any off-street parking or other amenities.

I pulled into a gas station parking lot across the street and just sat there, my car idling and Biscuit stirring in the backseat.

I stared at the building. There was a faint glow coming from the front window, as if a light was on somewhere inside. Was someone present, or had the light simply been left turned on? If it was the former, I assumed it would be Raela. What was she up to at this hour? Doing something to fix up her new veterinary clinic?

Of course, I was looking for issues. Raela's clinic might have already been fully set up inside to do exams and lab work and even surgery, for all I knew—although I would certainly worry about any pet undergoing care in a place that hadn't been adequately remodeled and filled with items necessary for complete care. And I still had doubts Raela could have obtained all approvals this fast.

I couldn't exactly sneak in to find out what it was like. Maybe I could come up with something that would make me seem like caring competition without giving the vets and others at my own clinic reason to mistrust me. Or—

I drew in my breath as I watched the front door open and saw who strode out.

Reed.

NINE

I THOUGHT ABOUT DASHING out of my car toward him. Or staying inside and honking my horn to get his attention.

Or doing nothing except staying where I was and watching him—which was what I did. His car was parked along the street, though I hadn't noticed it before. He got in and drove off.

Reed had been far enough away that I couldn't completely read the expression on his face, but from what I could tell, it looked more blank than angry. In other words, I couldn't tell what he was thinking. That wasn't unusual, although I could generally figure out his mood.

Biscuit stirred in the backseat. "You're right, girl," I told her. "We should go, too." Although an urge to cross the street and visit the new vet clinic tugged again at my mind—to look it over and assess it. That would mean I'd need to see Raela. She had to be in there, since Reed had been. But even if checking out the place was a good idea, just happening to drop in after Reed's visit didn't seem right. Raela might surmise that I was following Reed and add that to her list of things to harass him about.

And so I headed home, following Reed at a discreet distance until he turned off to head for his house in a more elite section of town.

Biscuit and I soon reached our home and I pulled into the garage. Neal's car wasn't there, which wasn't surprising. I didn't know, though, if he would come home that night or if Janelle and he were spending it together at her place.

I unhooked Biscuit from her tether and held her leash as she took advantage of the brief outing. Then I got the bags of groceries from the trunk and we went inside.

I ate part of the pre-cut salad I'd bought, and microwaved one of the frozen dinners. Of course Biscuit got her meal first, then settled on the living room floor beside the fluffy white sofa where I sat to eat. Her dark, begging eyes remained on me, but I didn't give her anything. Not then.

I chose to eat in the living room so I could keep the TV on in the background, hopefully moving my attention away from my quizzical thoughts. Did Raela have any patients yet? How modern was her clinic? Did she have any vet techs or other assistants? Was Oliver really working for her now?

And what the heck had Reed been doing there? Had they talked? Argued? Resolved their differences? And whatever it was, would he reveal it to me?

Good thing I'd also poured myself some wine. I vowed to only drink one glass, though. Otherwise I might inhale the entire bottle, and although that might send me to bed sooner, I didn't want to even anticipate the kind of headache I could have upon awakening.

The news that evening was a bit boring, and there were no shows I particularly wanted to see. I left the TV on, though, as comforting background noise while I took my plate and wine glass into the kitchen. Biscuit's eyes appeared full of hope again—still—as she followed me. "You need to earn your treats," I told her, as I often did. Which wasn't always the case, especially when I used her as a guinea dog—er, pig—for a new dog treat recipe.

I decided to watch a sitcom—not because it was a favorite show of mine, but it might keep my mind occupied enough to help me fall asleep later. I returned to the living room with a glass in my hand—water this time.

And yes, I'd given Biscuit a nice, healthy dog munchie before leaving the kitchen.

I'd settled down to watch the show when my phone rang in my pocket. I pulled it out. It was Reed. Was I surprised? Yes. I'd figured that no matter what had happened earlier, he wouldn't want to talk to me, not that night at least.

"Hi, Reed," I said immediately after muting the TV. I chose not to ask how he was doing. Not directly, at least. "How is Hugo tonight?" We both identified a lot with our dogs, so I figured if Hugo was doing okay, so was Reed.

"He's fine. And Biscuit?" His voice wasn't curt, nor was it sweet or sexy or—well, best I could tell, he was speaking as if we were friends but not necessarily close. Distant, I guess. I could have just been reading that into it, of course—or so I told myself.

"She's doing well. So ... how is your evening going?" *Like, wouldn't you rather be spending it with me?* Especially if his mind was focused on the place he'd visited after work and how it looked.

And was he going to tell me about it?

The answer was yes. I found myself smiling slightly, maybe a bit sympathetically, as he said, "My evening's okay, though it could be better. Look, you might think I'm nuts, but since Raela was nasty enough to drop off flyers with the address of her new place on them, I just had to go check it out."

"Oh? Wow. Really? What did you see?" *And why the heck did you go inside?* I knew a lot of possible answers to the last question but didn't ask it. I might learn the answers as we talked.

Had it been curiosity? Anger? Interest in Raela professionally—or otherwise?

I wanted to encourage Reed to talk while keeping to myself my awareness that he'd been there. I settled back on my sofa, wishing now that I'd allowed myself just one more glass of wine.

"It's a small clinic, so she's not likely to have many vets on staff besides herself and Oliver. And, yes, before you ask, he was there too and said he'd all but committed to sign on with her, though he planned to go back to San Diego to talk to the bosses there before making a final decision. She's already had the basic equipment installed and said she's spoken with resources such as labs in the Lake Arrowhead area who can analyze blood tests and such."

"So it's possible she'll give our clinic some real competition."

"Yes, damn it." Reed didn't yell, but he sounded as if he was speaking through gritted teeth. "She didn't say so, but as we talked she again made it clear she was rubbing the idea in my face—the face she wants me to fall on so I'll quit being her competition, since we're no longer friends, as if we ever were friends. Even so, if I thought she was any good as a vet, if she could treat animals as well as she should—medically, and with compassion and care—well, I'd be a lot more likely to accept her as a competitor." He paused for a few seconds, then added, "I told her I'd do anything to make her give up this idea—for the protection of all the animals who might become her patients."

I heard pain in his tone now and asked sympathetically, "And what was her response?"

"She laughed. Told me to wait and see what it felt like to be out-veterinarianed, to lose patients who would all flock to her in droves, or at least their owners would. She'd give them discounts and other benefits as well as guaranteeing that all who could be healed would be."

"Guaranteeing?" On top of everything else, I felt shocked. No one can guarantee anything in medicine except to put all their effort into providing the best care possible.

"Yeah. I called her on that, and she said that when she lost patients she'd just make it clear they couldn't be healed, so she wouldn't be lying."

"But to give their owners hope like that..."

"She's not only incompetent but also cruel." Reed's voice was no longer the cool, emotionless one he'd started out with, and I almost regretted, for his sake, having this conversation.

Even so, I asked, "Can't you report her to the Veterinary Board?" The California Veterinary Medical Board was the state's official organization in charge of veterinary licenses and procedures and maintaining professional standards—including investigating and punishing vets who harmed animals because the care given didn't meet those standards.

"Not until she does something wrong, other than make threats." Now Reed sounded defeated. I wished there was something I could do right away to cheer him up. Which would probably require doing something right away to close Raela and her new vet clinic down.

Not something I would likely be able to do. And maybe no one else here in town could do it either.

I would ponder it, though, without saying anything to Reed. No sense in giving him any hope.

"Well," I finally said, "Arvie told me he was holding a meeting tomorrow with the entire staff to talk about the Raela situation. Do you know when he's scheduled it for?"

"I think it'll be around eleven in the morning, but I'm sure someone will call you to confirm."

In other words, not him. Well, that wasn't one of Reed's duties as a vet, to communicate this kind of info to a vet tech. Plus, at the moment we were speaking to each other more as coworkers than as a man and woman with a possible romantic interest.

"Fine," I said. "So I'll most likely see you tomorrow."

"Right," he replied. "Good night, Carrie." And then he hung up.

———

I got an opportunity to say good night to Neal, too, just as I was going to bed. I'd already taken Biscuit out for the last time that night and had changed into my PJs, so I spoke very briefly to my tall, casually dressed bro in the kitchen, where he was getting a bottle of water to take to bed—although I did mention Reed's visit to the new clinic to him.

It was occupying too much of my mind to just ignore. And maybe my brother's interest and sympathy helped to clear that mind of mine at least a little, since I did get some sleep.

I woke up even earlier than my alarm the next morning, though—something that rarely happened since it went off early enough for me to get to my shops around five a.m. or so, and start baking around six. Biscuit knew this schedule too, and seemed to like that I let her run loose in the Barkery till almost our opening time of seven o'clock. Or at least I read that in her happy gait and waggy tail.

I wondered how Biscuit would do if Raela were to treat her for some illness … and shuddered at the idea. Even if something went gravely wrong and the Knobcone Vet Clinic closed thanks to that woman, I'd find somewhere else to take Biscuit. Somewhere I trusted the vets.

I sighed as I went into the shop kitchen, scrubbed my hands, and got ingredients ready for some of my favorite healthy carob dog treats. I tried to concentrate on cooking and managed to keep going even when Frida, my first assistant to arrive that day, began baking Icing goodies. I very happily talked to her about the latest non-bakery treats she was creating at home, since she loved all kinds of cooking. Her fiancé was a manager at the supermarket I'd stopped at the night before, which was the reason they'd moved here. As a graduate of the Art Institute of California, Frida had worked as a chef while living in LA, and now created her own gourmet people food in her off hours.

Our conversation therefore was all about food and creativity, nothing about dogs or doggy care—or a new veterinarian in town. And that helped the time go faster.

Soon, we had all the initial goods of the day either in the oven or on trays to be put in the refrigerated cases in each shop—all baked and stored separately, of course. At a little before seven, I went into the Barkery specifically to take Biscuit for another walk before confining her in her large, open crate area.

Time to open up. And business started out well in both shops.

I had to focus on my goods and customers and business. I hardly thought at all about what was going on regarding my vet clinic … or the other one.

Until Kayle called me. It was about eight thirty and Dinah had arrived to help out too, so I went over to work in Icing. When my

84

phone rang, therefore, I had no problem stepping to the side of the shop and answering.

"Are you available at eleven o'clock for the meeting here at the clinic?" Kayle asked.

My shifts were usually in the afternoon, but this meeting was anything but ordinary. "Sure," I said.

"See you then."

———

Things at both shops were fairly busy at ten forty-five as I prepared to hurry to the clinic. But Dinah was there to help Frida. Even if I'd had to close one of the shops for an hour or so, I was going to go to that meeting. I was glad, though, that closing was unnecessary.

I brought Biscuit along with me. Our walk across the Knobcone Heights town square to the clinic was as fast as I could make it without our running. I wanted to be there for the beginning.

Which I was, even after dropping Biscuit off in daycare. We all were crowded into Arvie's office, although Yolanda had been charged with checking the reception area to make sure all the humans there knew their pets would be seen soon. Still, calls had been made to delay appointments during that time, and a sign hung on the door saying that the clinic was closed for a half an hour, starting at eleven.

Surely a half hour would be enough time for us all to learn what the anticipated future of our clinic would be with the new competition in town—whether or not it was competent competition.

Dr. Paul Jensin sat beside Arvie, on his side of the desk, and I wondered whether this less-senior but highly devoted vet now wished that he, like Dr. Angela Regles, had decided to retire or run away.

Then there was Reed. Somehow we were seated beside one another. The staff of veterinarians and vet techs here wasn't huge, and they probably all knew that Reed and I had been seeing one another, so maybe there was an unspoken agreement to ensure that our seats were together. Or maybe it had just happened randomly. I'd arrived first, and Reed had sat down second—and now we could have held hands if that had been appropriate. Which it wasn't.

I wasn't surprised that our newest vet, Dr. Jon Arden, was on Reed's other side. After all, they'd been colleagues in San Diego, and Reed was the reason Jon had come to interview with us.

Although I now wondered if it had been a really dumb idea, under the current circumstances.

Arvie began the meeting. "I imagine you're all aware that Dr. Raela Fellner, a former veterinary coworker of Reed's and Jon's, is opening a new clinic here in town." He raised one of the flyers Raela had brought. "There's been some question about her motives and her competency and more. We know she has already started trying to convince the owners of some of our patients to go to her clinic instead. She's probably bad-mouthing us—or at least Reed. Here's how we're going to handle this."

For the next few minutes, Arvie made it very clear that everyone at Knobcone Veterinary Clinic would rise above what it appeared that Raela intended to do. We would continue to do a superior job of caring for our patients, both to prevent and to treat illness and injury. We would, where appropriate, pat ourselves on the back and suggest that the pleased owners of pets we cared for do the same, letting others know what a great place this is.

"And we will not stoop to the level that Dr. Fellner appears to be approaching. Unless we have specific examples of how she has committed malpractice, we won't suggest that she's an incompetent vet. Do you all understand?"

Everyone got it, even Reed. His smile was grim, but he nodded along with everyone else.

"You okay with that?" I asked.

"I have to be," he responded.

The office door was suddenly thrust open. Yolanda had gone out to check on the reception area again, so I wasn't surprised—until the sometimes cantankerous tech seemed to leap into the room, an expression of surprise and horror on her face rather than grumpiness.

Talk about horror. I felt it probably even more than she did when I saw who followed her into Arvie's office, which already seemed barely large enough for our staff. Suddenly it seemed completely cramped.

Two people whom I'd unfortunately gotten to know over the past year—starting when I'd been a major suspect in a murder and continuing when I'd helped friends who later became suspects in other murders clear their names—now entered and looked around: Detective Wayne Crunoll and Detective Bridget Morana.

"Ah, good," Wayne said. He was dressed in a white shirt and dark pants with an official belt around his waist and looked officially on duty. The same went for Bridget. "It appears that a number of people we want to touch base with are right here." He aimed a nasty smile at me—but I quickly realized that he wasn't looking directly at me, but at Reed.

What was going on?

I found out too soon. "I'd like to inform all of you"—but his stare remained on Reed—"that there has been another homicide in Knobcone Heights. An apparent murder."

He stopped then, as if anticipating that someone would demand to know who the victim was. If so, he wasn't disappointed.

Even before he spoke, my heart had started to sink. I thought I knew who it had to be. And I was right.

"Who are you talking about?" Arvie demanded.

"Another veterinarian," Wayne said. "A newcomer to our town. Dr. Raela Fellner."

TEN

I PARTICIPATED IN THE collective gasp and murmurs of the group. Probably none of us liked the woman. In fact, most who'd met her probably detested her.

But that didn't mean any of us would have killed her … did it?

Yet why else would these detectives have come here? I suspected they were planning inquisitions for at least some of us.

I couldn't help it. I glanced up toward the face of the man sitting beside me. Of everyone here, even including Jon, Reed had known her best and possibly liked her least. But kill her?

Surely not.

I hoped.

And what was going on with our nice quiet town? So many murders in so little time.

A myriad of questions began flooding my mind, but I figured this wasn't the best time to ask. As it turned out, my opinion didn't matter. Arvie stood up and begin demanding, "What happened to her? How was she killed?"

And who do you think did it? was the next question that came to mind. But I figured I'd be glad for now if the two detectives started out by answering Arvie.

"She was found this morning," Bridget said. Detective Morana was middle-aged, older than her colleague, and had bushy eyebrows and a chilly stare. Most of the staff here knew her, since her cat Butterball was a patient at our hospital. They knew Wayne as well because his dachshunds Blade and Magnum—whom he claimed belonged to his wife, though I saw him with them often, even at my shops—were also our patients.

"Where?" Arvie demanded. "And again, how was she killed?"

"We're not at liberty to divulge what we know so far," Wayne replied smoothly. "The investigation is only just beginning, so we don't have answers yet anyway. But we do have a lot of questions. I'm glad to see so many of you here—unexpected, but we'll take advantage of it by informing you right away that we want to talk to each of you. We are aware that there was some friction between the employees here at the Knobcone Veterinary Clinic and Dr. Fellner, thanks to her opening a new and competing animal hospital. We'd like to interview everyone here to learn what you knew about Dr. Fellner and her contacts in town."

And interrogate several of us who might have felt some antipathy toward the woman who'd wanted to put our clinic out of business, I thought.

Uh oh. Would I be considered a murder suspect again? I certainly hoped not.

But I also wasn't thrilled to imagine that some people I cared about might be at the top of the suspect list. That seemed to happen much too much.

"So here's what we'd like to do," Bridget said.

The two detectives hadn't moved from their positions near the doorway, blocking it so no one could get out. Given a choice, I might have run out shrieking… or not. But I did admit to myself that my emotions were already fraying.

Another murder. One I couldn't ignore.

I realized then that Bridget hadn't stopped speaking despite my momentary lapse of concentration on what she was saying. And when I began listening again, I wished I hadn't.

"Yes, we recognize that you have patients in your waiting room already and more coming in," the detective continued, apparently in response to Arvie's complaint about her demand to start interviewing us right away. "If you'd like, you can designate a liaison between us and the pet owners so we can work out which of you to interview, in what order." Her gaze seemed to stop at me.

Me? I couldn't even stay at the clinic very long after the meeting. I didn't have a shift scheduled, and I had to return to my shops.

Yet I—unfortunately—had likely spent more time with these detectives than anyone else here. They might listen to me, at least a little bit.

Maybe I could even help my fellow clinic staff members in some manner, smoothing over what would undoubtedly be closer to interrogations than interviews, or at least help to schedule them in the least intrusive order, whatever that might be.

"I'll be glad to help out," I heard myself say. "I can tell from the computer what the patient schedule is today, and I'll work with that, at least for now. But I can only stay here at the clinic for another hour or so."

"Good enough," Wayne said. "Though it'll be best if we interview you first. Our discussions today are preliminary and likely to be short anyway."

"I'll talk to the pet owners who are here and ask if anyone would like to be rescheduled," Kayle said. He was good at smoothing the ruffled feathers of pet birds—and their owners, and others—when he staffed the waiting room, so that was a good idea.

Maybe I shouldn't have volunteered. But Wayne's stare had more than suggested that he wanted me to. At least he hadn't demanded that I do so for the rest of the day.

"Fine," he said now to Kayle. "Please show us to an empty room where we can start—and after we've spoken with you, Carrie, we'll want you to give us a printout of the order we'll be talking to the others here."

Which was interesting in itself. I had to assume that Raela had been killed sometime the night before, or early that morning. For the detectives on the case to immediately devote themselves to speaking with one group of people … why?

There was something important that they already knew that they weren't revealing to us.

What was it?

———

We all soon rose—Reed included. Like most of the other vets, he didn't have his white jacket on yet, not at this meeting. I noticed that his shirt was an attractive light green color.

"You okay with this?" he asked me, his voice low.

That was what I should have been asking him. I didn't know yet when exactly the detectives would be interviewing him, of course. If Raela was killed the previous night, the cops probably didn't know a whole lot at this point about her new clinic and the specific nature of her conflict with us, or at least not as much as they were likely to find out soon.

Especially from everyone they would be talking to here. Most likely no one was unaware of the reasons Raela had shown up at our clinic and knew about her complaints, especially regarding Reed.

"Sure, I'm okay," I said to Reed. "I just wish I could be in the room when they talk to you." I glanced toward the detectives. Fortunately, their attention was on Arvie, who spoke with them near the door. I hoped he was just asking questions rather than talking about the staff's opinions on Raela, or who liked her least.

"Why?" Reed asked. His smile was wry, as if he was joking. "I know you've come to think of yourself as an amateur detective. But we're friends. I hope you're not intending to throw me in front of this particular bus. I imagine I'm going to be the chief person of interest, or whatever they prefer calling the suspect they want to toss in jail immediately."

Instead of smiling back in any way, I glared at him, hurt surging through me. "Why on earth would I want to put any blame on you?" Because of his attitude toward the murder victim? Sure, Reed had disliked her. But … but he was Reed. He saved lives, not took them.

Although he might believe that keeping Raela from treating any sick animals would in fact save lives.

I banished that nasty thought from my head as I continued, "You may be the one who argued with her most since her arrival, so I won't be surprised if these detectives leap on you as their main suspect. But surely they know that the person who appears to be the most likely killer is often not guilty."

"You've certainly taught them that lately," Reed said, his tone ironic. "Well, I doubt they'll let you be present, although I'll ask for a lawyer if they start asking questions that seem at all accusatory. That's what I should do, right?"

"Yes, and I might caution others to do the same thing. Not in the detectives' presence, though."

I noticed out of the corner of my eye that Wayne was walking toward me around the seated crowd. Time to start my interrogation, I figured. Did I need a lawyer? After all, I hadn't liked Raela either. I'd just have to see how things went.

"And Carrie," Reed said, his voice almost a whisper in my ear. "I know I pushed you not to get involved the last time someone died, to make sure you stayed safe and all. But—well, I definitely want you to stay safe. But if things go as I'm afraid they will—well, maybe you could use the experience you've gained to find the real killer so that I won't get charged with Raela's murder." He looked me straight in the face then, his beautiful dark brown eyes sad and pleading.

Heck, this was ironic—especially after the last situation, where he'd eventually backed down and recognized that I was going to try to figure out who the killer was whether he liked the idea or not.

But of course I would help him.

I only hoped he was innocent.

———

The empty room assigned for our inquisitions—er, interviews—was the office formerly occupied by Dr. Angela Regles and about to be occupied by Dr. Jon Arden. It was a couple of doors away from Arvie's and nearly as large as his, although Arvie had chosen to keep his office fairly empty. Yes, he had a desk and several chairs, but other than the computer, the room contained hardly anything else.

Dr. Regles's old office had all of that, and, in addition, a file cabinet and some end tables, as if it were a hangout not only for its veterinary occupant but also for other people—pet owners, techs, other vets, whoever. I had almost never been invited in there, and when I was, it was to discuss a particular patient.

Since I was the one who actually worked in the clinic, I preceded the two detectives into the office and planted myself in the chair behind the desk, letting them maneuver around the other chairs and tables and sit down facing me. Never mind that they undoubtedly considered themselves in charge. I wanted to take control—at least as much as I could.

"Okay, Carrie," Wayne began. We were on a first name basis since I'd been doing their job for a while—or at least solving the murder cases they worked on. And I seemed to always have the most contact with Wayne. The expression on his face at the moment appeared almost amused, not appropriate for a murder investigation. I kept my look as solemn but interested as I could.

"You've become quite a successful amateur sleuth," he continued, "so I'll ask you right up front: who do you think did it?"

"Even an amateur sleuth needs more information than just hearing that someone has apparently been murdered." I sat back, crossing my arms and looking from Wayne to Bridget. She, at least, appeared serious.

"I'm not surprised you want more details," she said, no expression in her tone. "Well, I'm sure you won't be surprised to hear that what we want from you is to learn what you know. I gather you met Dr. Fellner, correct?"

"Correct." I could have gone into a dissertation about how Raela had burst into the clinic and started badmouthing Reed and his skills and ours and more, but this was their meeting. The detectives could ask me questions, and I'd answer as well as I could without pointing potential fingers at anyone.

Including myself.

"So tell us about it," Wayne said, bursting the bubble I was building around myself. But only partially. I still needed to be careful.

"What do you mean?" I asked.

"I mean, tell us how you met her, what the circumstances were, how she got along with whoever happened to be around, that kind of thing." Wayne no longer appeared amused, and his tone approached belligerent. He leaned forward in his chair and pulled a pen and small notebook from a pocket, as if he wanted to jot down everything I said.

If I told him all of my perceptions, he probably would have noted everything down. But I told him only the facts of what I'd seen regarding the interactions between Raela and the vets around our clinic. I also mentioned the flyers she'd handed out in the reception area and her related comments, without offering any opinions.

"So there were three veterinarians here with a history with Dr. Fellner," Bridget said when I'd finished. "And none appeared to like her."

"That's what I understand, but their irritation with her didn't give me a sense that they wished her any harm—although I gathered they did want her to return to the San Diego office where they'd all worked."

"Mmm-hmm," Wayne said. Sure enough, he was jotting down something on that little pad. I wasn't sure whether I'd seen him do it earlier. "Well, that's not enough reason to arrest anyone. I'm sure you're glad to hear that, since I gather you and Dr. Storme are good buddies ... or more."

So they *were* focusing on Reed. Or was I jumping to a conclusion?

"Now, is there anything else you can tell us?" Wayne continued. "Like, who do you think could have murdered Dr. Fellner?"

"If it's too soon for you to have any good suspects, it's surely too early for an amateur like me," I said. "But if you really want my help, you could tell me how she was found and how she died. Maybe that will help me put things into perspective and recall something else important that will help you."

I was really pushing things, and I didn't expect I'd get any response except laughter. Me, help them? And them give me any genuine information?

Hah.

Except ... over the next few minutes, after the two detectives shared a glance, Wayne actually did give me a brief summation of the little they knew so far.

It turned out that Oliver Browning had been the one to find Raela's body in an exam room at her new clinic. He'd gone there at around nine that morning to talk to her briefly, since, Wayne said, he intended to return to San Diego that day. I assumed that must have been to talk to the powers-that-be at his clinic there before making a definite decision as to whether to move to Knobcone Heights.

Had Oliver argued, then or previously, with Raela? Did he have a motive to kill her? Wayne didn't get into that, even if he had more information or an opinion about it.

In any event, although I hadn't liked Raela, I still felt sorry that she'd died, especially so abruptly.

Wayne went on to mention that the first thing Oliver had done was call 911. He then apparently tried to resuscitate Raela but failed.

That was all they told me about the discovery of Raela's body— except for the most interesting, and most scary, bit of information. They said that the county coroner was in the process of doing an autopsy on the deceased vet, checking whether the cause of her death was a lethal injection of the drug commonly used for animal euthanasia.

The detectives provided no detail about why they suspected, or knew, this little detail.

But it was undoubtedly why they'd come here, to the original veterinary clinic in town, where some of the employees had a potential grudge against the murder victim—and all of the employees, unlike the general public, probably had access to that kind of drug and would know how to use it.

ELEVEN

WAYNE MUST HAVE BEEN reading my thoughts. "Hey, you're a veterinary technician. I bet you could have thought of that—and would have the skills to do it."

"I thought you weren't here to accuse me," I countered. I didn't need to mention how many people at the clinic possessed the knowledge that I did, some even more. Nor did I remind him that a hypodermic needle as a possible murder weapon had arisen during the first murder case I'd become involved in.

I assumed that the drug used to kill Raela was probably pentobarbital. To euthanize a poor, ailing dog, the dosage didn't have to be huge—but pentobarbital was also used in some states as the drug of preference for lethal injections of humans sentenced to the death penalty.

Of course, the medical examiner had not had Raela's body very long, given that she'd just been found that morning. Even if there had been other evidence at the scene indicating that a euthanasia drug was used—like a hypodermic needle, empty vials of the poison, or a prick in her skin—they would still have to finish the autopsy to confirm whether or not the drug was in fact what killed her.

Or so I assumed. The detectives were just starting their inquiries and also making assumptions, which could change.

"So is there anything else you're aware of that we should know, Carrie?" Wayne asked.

"Not now," I said.

"But you may think of something in the future." That was Bridget. "May we assume that you're going to stick your nose into this investigation, Carrie?" Her expression appeared tolerant and vaguely amused by the idea—except for the flash in her light brown eyes.

"I'd rather not, of course," I replied. "But like the other times, if you wind up believing that the culprit is someone I care about and I know you're wrong, then—"

"Well, I'm sure we're going to be seeing a lot of you, then," Wayne interrupted. "I'm naming no names, not even yours, but I think you can understand why we need to check into your fellow vets and vet techs, just in case. And I assume you care about at least some of them."

Oh, did I want to wipe that grin off his face.

Especially since I knew exactly who he was going to consider his most likely suspect.

And all I could do for the time being was hope I would be able to find enough information on someone else to clear Reed.

———

My interrogation was pretty much over. I could breathe again.

But who else around here could?

Since I'd been named as the detectives' primary contact for at least an hour, I hurried to the reception area, hoping Kayle would still be the one working there.

He wasn't. Instead, Yolanda governed the place, which, unsurprisingly considering the delay, was crammed full of pets and their owners. Some people talked to one another, and though I didn't attempt to eavesdrop—much—I could guess that at least some were discussing having to wait … and why.

Did any of them know anything about last night's murder? I couldn't exactly ask, and I didn't have time just to sit there and listen.

Instead, I hustled up to the desk where Yolanda was the greeter. As usual, her black hair was pulled back into a bun, which somehow emphasized the attractiveness of her face.

Now, though, she aimed a frown at me. "They're done with you?" she asked.

"Right. And I need to get the detectives the schedule they requested."

"You're lucky. Kayle likes you, so while you were being questioned he checked with all of us and figured out who could best talk when."

She handed me a piece of paper containing a proposed schedule, presumably created on the computer and printed out.

"May I have another one?" I asked.

"I printed several, of course. One for each of us. That one's the detectives', and here's yours." She shoved another copy at me.

"Thanks." I glanced at the page. "Does everyone here know when they're to be interviewed?"

"Not precisely, though we're all pretty much aware of the order."

The order seemed to me to run from the most likely suspect to the least—starting with Reed, and ending with sweet, energetic

Kayle. I noticed that Yolanda's name was near the bottom, which made sense. I couldn't think of a motive for her to murder Raela.

Which might mean I should keep her at the top of my suspect list, considering the way things had gone in the past.

"Great," I said. "I'll let the detectives know." And on my way back to their office, I'd find Reed and make sure he was aware he was up next.

Yolanda seemed to read my mind. "In case you're wondering, Reed is in treatment room four with a dog who came in with a severe wheezing issue. I'm not sure how long he'll be there."

By design? The vets didn't necessarily get to choose which patients they saw, although owners could request certain vets. In any case, until the animal arrived, it was hard to tell how long any exam or treatment might take.

I wasn't going to ask if Reed did this intentionally. Instead, I glanced at the sheet again and asked, "How about Arvie? Is he available?"

This time Yolanda's grin seemed more triumphant. "I've already let him know the situation, and he's in his office waiting to be told to go talk to the detectives. You going to tell him he's up next?"

"Sure. Thanks. And … " I glanced around the waiting room. "I need to head back to my shops soon, but I'll hold off a bit since we're so busy here."

"And so you can see Reed." Yolanda glanced at the computer as a patient with a golden retriever on a leash followed Kayle into the reception area. "Looks like someone's exam is over," she said. "Kayle will figure out the bill and determine which patient is up next. You available to help out then?"

"Sure." I only hoped that whichever patient it turned out to be, I wouldn't have to spend a whole lot of time on the case.

"And by the way, the owner didn't designate which vet to see, and the next one up is our newbie, Dr. Jon."

"Great. It'll be interesting to work with him." And perhaps question him. Jon was one of the few people who'd known Raela for a while. He had apparently disliked her, too. Enough to kill her?

I'd certainly rather it be him than Reed.

Kayle took over the reception desk. He was fine with me helping out with the next patient of the day—which was also my only patient of the day.

First, though, I hurried down to Jon's future office to give the printout to the detectives. Bridget was on the phone, and Wayne was pacing the room. "Sorry," I said. "Here's the proposed schedule, but it's already changing. Reed is in with a patient now so I'll go tell Arvie to come and see you."

Which I did. He didn't look thrilled, but he did remark before leaving his office that at least he'd be getting this over with.

Sure, as long as the detectives didn't decide to pin the murder on him.

Especially since it was *detectives*, plural. I'd usually only been questioned by one at a time. I wasn't sure whether they considered this latest murder more challenging, or more interesting, or what. Not that it really mattered to me.

I walked Arvie, who was in his official white veterinary jacket, down the hall. "Good luck," I said.

"Were they hard on you?" he asked, his aging face even more full of wrinkles than usual.

"Not especially. I think they're just looking for information before zeroing in on someone as their chief person of interest."

"Well, let's hope they don't zero in on anyone here." Arvie waved at me, then shoved the office door open without knocking.

I had a feeling that my boss would do a darned good job of standing up to the two cops.

————

Of course, the interview I would most have liked to sit in on was Reed's. Kayle, still at the desk after I finished helping Jon with his patient, told me that Reed was currently in talking with the two detectives.

The patient, a French bulldog named Bully, had lost most of his appetite, according to his owner. Or at least he wasn't eating as much as he used to. Turned out he had some pretty messed-up teeth. Jon had prescribed a teeth cleaning as soon as possible, which would require that Bully be anesthetized during the procedure—and the likelihood was that poor Bully would lose a few teeth. I felt bad for Bully but knew he'd be better off after he was treated.

I also felt bad for myself, since I hadn't found an opportunity to ask Jon any questions relating to Raela. Nor had I had a chance to talk to Reed before his interrogation. I felt the worst for Reed, although I couldn't predict how the detectives would deal with him.

I needed to know how things went, though. Somehow I'd find a way to get together with Reed later, quiz him about his interview, and be there to sympathize with him if the session was as grueling as I feared it would be.

And so, as I headed for doggy daycare to retrieve Biscuit, I texted Reed. Told him he was coming to my house for dinner that night, he and Hugo. I didn't give him a chance to say no—although of course I recognized he could.

After that, leaning on the wall just outside the daycare center door, I called Neal. I was pleased but a bit surprised when he answered right away, since when he was on duty at the resort it was sometimes hard to reach him.

"Don't come home tonight till eight or later, okay?"

"Hey, sis, you don't usually kick me out. What's going on?"

I told him. He'd already heard rumors, at least, of the murder of the visiting vet who'd tried to become more than a visitor.

"I wondered if you'd get involved with this one. And let me guess. Reed is somehow involved."

"The cops might think he is. They're talking with him right now, in fact. I've invited him over for dinner and want to hear everything they ask—and everything he knows."

"And you'll fill me in on it later?"

"Maybe."

"Well, I don't suppose there's any use in my telling you not to get involved in figuring this one out, is there? Not with Reed a probable suspect."

"Unfortunately, you got it."

I heard some scrambling of canine feet near the doorway and figured someone was coming through, so I stepped back. Sure enough, Faye came into the hallway holding the leash of a pit bull mix I'd seen there before.

"Hi, Carrie," she said. "Are you coming for Biscuit?"

I nodded, then said into the phone, "I'll talk to you later, Neal. And I think Janelle has a shift at the shops this afternoon, so I'll make sure she's okay with hanging out with you tonight somewhere other than at our place."

"Her place is fine." I heard the smile in my brother's tone.

"I'll bet it is," I replied, then hung up.

As I walked into the daycare facility, Biscuit was in the middle of the room playing keep-away with a squeaky ball and a couple of other dogs around her size. She noticed me immediately, dropped the ball, and raced over.

"You didn't need to stop that quickly," I told her, "but I'm glad you did." I retrieved her leash from the shelves near the desk and let assistant Al know we were leaving.

I half expected Reed to either text me back or call during the walk to my shops. After all, he'd probably already been with the detectives for half an hour, and for them to question everyone at the clinic, they had to keep the sessions fairly short.

But I didn't hear from him.

Maybe he was mad at me. Or maybe he simply didn't want to talk to anyone about what was going on.

Surely they hadn't arrested him … not this soon, at least.

It was only early afternoon, and I was used to coming back to the shops fairly late after a shift at the clinic. That was because my shifts tended to start sometime after lunch.

I wasn't hungry, so I didn't stop for lunch. I figured I could treat myself to one or two of my own people treats if I needed to eat something.

When I walked into the Barkery with Biscuit, Janelle was there, waiting on customers. There were quite a few of them, which was a good thing. But I wanted to let her know about my brief conversation with Neal.

I got an opportunity to do that about fifteen minutes later. I'd popped in at Icing, saw that Dinah and Frida had everything under control, and then went back into the Barkery to help Janelle. The crowd had thinned, and everyone there was still deciding what they wanted.

I motioned for Janelle to join me near Biscuit's enclosure. But telling her that I wanted her to keep my brother company that evening somewhere other than at our house seemed pointless now, since I still hadn't heard back from Reed.

I told her this, my voice low, as I described the misery of the day so far—and the horror of another murder causing it all.

"You poor thing," Janelle said, giving me a hug. "And—well, I'll want to talk more about it with you when you have time, but not tonight. Are you and Reed . . . well, should I assume that the cops are talking to both of you?"

"Yeah," I acknowledged, figuring I could give her more details later. But if Reed wasn't going to make himself available to talk that night, I certainly didn't want to be alone. And so I started to tell Janelle that my plans could change and I might treat Neal and her to dinner.

She cocked her head, clearly confused. "I think we need to talk even sooner. Are you—"

My phone started ringing in my pocket. I pulled it out, apologizing quickly to Janelle and saying, "I need to take this."

For it was, in fact, Reed.

"Hi," I said, not sure what tone to take.

"I got your text." Reed's voice sounded raspy. "Good idea. I really need to talk to you tonight. Hugo and I will be at your place around six thirty. Is that too early?"

Since I closed the shops at six, we usually didn't get together till closer to seven or even later.

The fact he wanted to see me earlier worried me.

At least he wasn't in jail.

Not yet.

"Six thirty will be fine," I said, wondering suddenly what I had in the house that I could cook for us quickly.

I would figure something out. I told Janelle the latest develop-ment, and she assured me that she and Neal would hang out some-where else that night.

The most important thing was to learn what was going on with Reed.

TWELVE

BISCUIT AND I STOPPED on the way home to pick up a people dinner. I decided on something that Reed and I had both enjoyed previously: food from a delightful Chinese restaurant.

And one of the main reasons for stopping at that restaurant was that there was a liquor store next door. After ensuring that Biscuit was still okay in her harness in the backseat of my car, I ran in for a bottle of a Napa Valley wine I particularly liked—and bought two bottles, just in case we really got into it that night. Instead of driving home semi-plastered, Reed could always sleep on the sofa if Neal came home later…

As I pulled into my driveway a short while later, Reed was just parking on the street. Good timing. Biscuit and I waited while he helped Hugo out of the backseat, and Reed took the two bags I'd brought from my car. We all entered my house through the garage, and Reed soon placed the bags onto the beige granite kitchen counter.

At first he seemed to stare at the bags as if waiting for them to say something or fall over or somehow keep his attention.

"Are you okay?" I asked softly.

"Not sure." He paused. "Could we open one of those bottles of wine?"

My brief laugh was anything but happy. "Of course." I opened one of the counter drawers and brought out my favorite corkscrew that always did a good job—fast. Rather than handing it to Reed, I opened the bottle and then got a couple of wine glasses from one of the upper wooden cabinets.

In a short while, Reed and I were in the living room sitting on my white sofa, both holding wine glasses filled with the shiraz I'd bought. I watched Reed. I again admired his light green shirt tucked neatly into his dark trousers. The planes of his face seemed deeper, making him appear gaunt, and his dark late-day shadow contrasted even more than usual with his pale skin.

All sorts of questions inundated my mind, but I waited for him to start talking first.

Which he did, by asking me a question. "What were those detectives like when they interviewed you?"

Reed's gaze was quizzical, his dark eyes narrowed as if he were in pain, and he seemed almost to wince as he spoke, as if expecting a blow.

This wasn't the Reed I knew … and possibly loved.

I didn't necessarily want to answer his question till I'd heard how the detectives had acted while interrogating him. Somehow, he must have read this in my expression, since he added, "I'd imagine they weren't particularly kind to you, but probably not as demanding as they were with me. They teased at first, then goaded and accused me, but they didn't talk about arresting me … yet."

"Tell me more specifically, Reed. Please." I spoke softly, putting my glass on the coffee table and reaching for his hand.

Hugo must also have sensed the emotion in his alpha's mind, since he got up from where he'd been lying near the table to come sit with his head on Reed's leg. Biscuit just watched as she remained lying near me.

Reed clasped my hand even harder. "You know, Carrie," he said, "We've been dating for months now, during three situations where you worked on solving murders—a weird state of affairs each time. Though I worried about you, I never completely understood what you must have felt like—first when the cops thought you were the killer, or even later when you were helping people you care about prove their innocence. I watched, but I didn't, well, feel it."

"I understand," I told him. "It's not something people generally get involved in unless it's their job, and I never intended to, either. But to the extent I did get involved—yes, I felt it deeply." I paused. "Please, Reed, tell me more about your session with the detectives."

He'd already indicated that Wayne and Bridget might be focusing on him, not that I was surprised. But they were acting that way with nearly everyone. Even so, I didn't want to potentially make Reed feel any worse by describing my back and forth with those two. Had I liked it? Not particularly. But I also felt that although they hadn't removed me from their extensive and potentially growing suspect list, I wasn't at the top.

But Reed could be. And once more, I couldn't help thinking his position there might be justifiable.

He took a long sip of wine. Then, turning enough to be able to meet my eyes, he said, "They talked about you first thing. Said they were aware that you and I were friends, and that they'd appreciated your help in finding answers in the past in the odd series of murders that have gripped Knobcone Heights. They asked what I knew about those situations, and—well, you know that I wasn't generally pleased about your involvement, since I was concerned about your safety. But I made it clear that I was proud you helped to find the right answers."

I could only smile fondly at that—especially since with each case, Reed had seemed to try harder to get me not to become involved. And I actually would have preferred not to, but the circumstances seemed to force me into it each time.

The detectives had recognized the possibility of it happening again this time, when we'd talked. Maybe if they focused on a suspect I didn't care about, I'd be able to back off.

But Reed's next words indicated it would be impossible.

"That was when Detective Crunoll started laughing, though he didn't sound like he was having fun. He asked me if this was why I'd killed Raela—because I figured you'd investigate the situation and you'd determine how to pin it on someone else."

I drew in my breath in shock.

Of course, I'd long doubted that Wayne appreciated how I'd uncovered the killers before, and I knew he didn't want me involved this time, either. And here I was, involved again whether I liked it or not. I had to try to find the actual murderer because Reed was a suspect … though I recognized that it could in fact be Reed. I might not trumpet this thought to the cops, let alone the world, but never would I manufacture evidence or do anything to convict an innocent person of a crime, if that's what Wayne was suggesting.

I sucked in my lips, trying to figure out how to say what I needed to next. "I'm at a bit of a loss here," I finally said. "First of all, the idea that I'm somehow already involved, that I'm investigating … I hadn't intended to before, and this time—well, there are several people involved that I care about and if one of them is the killer, I'd prefer not to know it, let alone prove it. Especially when it comes to you. But I'd never, ever, make things up. He had to have been joking."

"Maybe. Very funny, isn't it?" Reed spoke with no emotion. His expression was blank. The only indication that he felt anything at all was how he lifted his glass and all but chugged what was left of his wine.

"I'll have to talk to them, make sure Wayne didn't really mean it."

"Sure." Reed paused. "I know it doesn't look good for me, Carrie. I was the one who argued most with Raela. I didn't like her, and I didn't even attempt to hide that fact."

I nodded slowly. "True."

"And I can understand why I'd be a major person of interest in investigating her murder."

I allowed myself to keep nodding but didn't respond.

"Now, here's more detail about how my interrogation went." I noticed that Reed was calling it by its correct name now, rather than "interview" or something else more benign. He proceeded to describe how the detectives had gone from almost teasing about his knowing me and how I might get involved to digging in and demanding he share all the details he could in the short time about how he knew Raela.

Reed had even asked at one point if he should have a lawyer, present, and they'd said it was up to him.

"Maybe it was foolish," he told me, "but I just said I didn't do anything to harm Raela and since they shouldn't arrest me, I wouldn't hire a lawyer. I know that doesn't convince the authorities of anyone's innocence. I've seen similar stuff on TV and in the movies. But it seemed appropriate at the time."

"I understand," I said. "What was their reaction?"

"They just kept at it. And when I began to think I'd been pretty dumb and should tell them I'd changed my mind and wanted a

113

lawyer, they said the interview was over, that they had to get on to the next interview, and they let me go."

"That's good," I said, with at least a small amount of relief. Had Reed convinced them of his innocence?

Or did they just want him to think so?

"I went back to my office for a little while just to calm down and start thinking like a vet again, and then I saw a few more patients."

He lifted his glass again—his empty glass. "Here, let me refill these," I said, since mine was nearly empty, too. I went to the kitchen to grab the wine bottle.

I figured Reed would follow me, but only Biscuit did. When I returned to the living room, Reed was bending over, hugging and stroking Hugo as if he really needed the contact.

I considered drawing close to him and hugging him to show how much I cared. But he straightened up and grabbed his wine glass from the table where he'd put it, and I filled it again, as well as mine.

"So where do you think things will go from here?" he asked after taking another swig.

"I don't know," I said honestly. "Even if I asked Wayne and Bridget, they wouldn't tell me who their prime suspects are—although their comments do suggest you're one of them. But the situation is so new I doubt they have enough evidence to pin it on anyone yet, which might be good for you. I know they'll keep investigating, though. Interviewing more people, maybe. Unless, of course, there's something particularly telling about the evidence they already have."

"Right. I gather they believe Raela was given a shot or two of pentobarbital, which was why they're focusing on those of us at the clinic. We have a supply there and we all know how to use it."

"That's what I gathered, too," I said.

We both paused. My mind kept going over the possibilities—and I was glad Reed didn't ask what I was thinking.

Because I did still wonder whether, in fact, it could have been him.

Maybe my expression said so. Reed put his wine glass down and rose. He put out a hand toward me, and I put my glass down as well and grasped his hand.

He pulled me closer, and I was suddenly in his arms.

He was shaking. I pulled back and saw moisture in his eyes before he again drew me close.

"I know it looks bad, Carrie," he rasped in my ear, "but I swear I didn't do it."

"I know," I lied. I only hoped he was telling the truth, and that that was the reason for his emotion.

"And I'm sure you never thought you'd hear this from me," he continued. He pulled back and looked me straight in the eye. "I remember full well how much I tried to keep you from getting involved with solving that last murder. I was worried about your safety. I'm still worried about your safety—but as long as you're careful and don't put yourself into any dangerous situations ... Carrie, I'd really appreciate your looking into this murder case and finding out who actually did it."

THIRTEEN

I supposed this wasn't completely unexpected. The last time I'd gotten involved with looking into a murder, Reed had eventually segued from trying to get me to back off completely to accepting the fact that I'd keep on doing my own kind of investigation—though he'd continued to tell me to be careful.

Somehow, I figured, Reed must have come to respect what I'd done. Or at least recognized my sleuthing abilities enough to want to use them to his advantage now, if it was possible.

And I hoped it was.

I looked at him over my wine glass, which I lifted as if in a toast. "Here's to the cops finding the right bad guy first—but if they don't, then here's to my figuring it out."

"I'll drink to that," Reed said. We clinked glasses and each took a sip, with the dogs stirring on the floor near our feet.

Surely Reed encouraging me to look into the situation this time meant he was innocent … didn't it? Of course, he was a smart guy.

Maybe he figured that he had to say something like this in order to convince me he hadn't done it, even if he had ...

Darn. Enough of this. I took another swig of wine, then said, "And now I think it's time for us to eat some of the great Chinese food I brought home. Okay?"

"Sure," he said. "Let's do it. I think I actually have an appetite now."

We went into the kitchen, where I pulled out plates and flatware. We each scooped our own food out of the boxes and warmed it as we wanted in the microwave. I'd chosen mu shu chicken and stir fried veggies. Plus, I'd gotten two fortune cookies.

I wasn't ready to look at those yet.

Just before we were ready to sit down at the table, my phone rang. It was Neal. "How are things, sis?" he asked.

"Okay. How are things with you?" Like, are you coming home any time soon? But I didn't ask that aloud.

"I'm probably staying the night here at Janelle's," he said as I watched Reed take his seat, both dogs following as if prepared to beg for any treat at all. "How would that work for you?"

I wasn't sure what was going to happen the rest of my evening, if Reed would stay or go. I still preferred not spending the night alone, but I also didn't want to ruin Neal's evening if Reed chose not to hang out here.

"That works fine," I said. We traded a few more vague comments about his evening, though I knew how close Neal and Janelle were getting.

"Was that Neal?" Reed asked as I hung up.

"Yes. He just wanted to let me know he won't be home tonight." *So will you spend the night with me?* That was another question I thought of without voicing it.

Fortunately, I didn't have to. "I'd like to stay here tonight, if that's okay with you," Reed said. "I need some company of the human kind." He nevertheless reached down and patted Hugo's head. His dog maneuvered as if he was trying to nuzzle a treat from his person's hand, although none was there at the moment.

"Sounds good to me," I replied, relieved. We might have been feeding each other's angst, but we might also be able to help each other deal with it.

After we finished eating, it was time to feed the dogs. The kibble I kept for Biscuit was nice and healthy, of course, and Hugo had eaten it before. I also gave them some premium canned food, and followed it all up with a treat from the Barkery that I removed from the cookie jar shaped like a doghouse that I kept on the counter. There was no trouble with getting either pup to enjoy dinner.

Then it was time to go for our walk. It was dark now, but the streetlights in my neighborhood made it easy for us to see the sidewalks along the slightly curving street. I occasionally just let Biscuit into the fenced dog run at the side of my house, but I believed we both preferred walks, so we did that more often.

And tonight, we were in good company.

We soon returned to the house. Inside the front door, Reed took me into his arms and we kissed—warmly, but not hotly. Would we get more involved tonight? I wasn't sure, but I knew I'd treasure it either way.

"Hey," he whispered into my ear, and I waited to hear him whisper something seductive … or sweet nothings. "Did we get any fortune cookies tonight?"

That certainly wasn't what I'd expected, and I laughed. "Yes," I said, "we did."

We returned to the kitchen and I picked up the cookies from where I'd placed them after taking them out of the bag. I held them out to him.

"You choose." He was acting as if these cookies' messages would actually matter.

But he could use some good luck now, so I certainly hoped that his fortune at least suggested it could happen.

I picked one of the cookies but waited till Reed had cracked his cookie open before reading my fortune. "What does yours say?" I asked.

"You tell me yours first."

"Okay," I said. Mine turned out fairly benign, a typical fortune cookie quote. I read it aloud. "*Smile. It will make you happy.*" I pasted a huge, toothy smile on my face and then said, "Yours?"

Reed held up the small slip of white paper. The look on his face could have been a smile—or a grimace. "Well, I hope this is right," he said. He read the fortune aloud: "*Things are never as bad as you may think they are.*"

"Hey, we should think things are good," I said. "We're healthy and free, have wonderful dogs and wonderful careers, and even if one or both of us are murder suspects—"

Reed interrupted, shaking his head. "At least neither of us is under arrest."

"Right!" I exclaimed. *Yet*, imposed my mind. I didn't say it, though. Instead, I said, "I'm tired. Let's go watch some news, then go to bed."

"Sounds good to me." Reed stood up and held out his hand. "At least let's hope for some good news."

———

We did go to bed soon afterward. It remained a snuggly, quiet night. I guessed that neither of us was in the mood for any drama—even the fun kind. But I was glad to spend it with Reed, and when I woke early the next morning I was glad he was still there.

I watched him for a minute while he still slept beneath my lavender coverlet. He looked so much better than he had last night, relaxed. Whatever his dreams might have been, they apparently hadn't made him feel worse.

Maybe his unconscious mind was focusing on that fortune he'd gotten: "*Things are never as bad as you may think they are.*"

In any event, though I hated to wake him, I needed to start getting ready to go to my shops. Reed knew the routine, and I believed I knew his, too. He'd take Hugo back to their house, shower, and grab his breakfast there. A little later, he would head to the clinic to begin his day as a vet. While I baked dog treats and people treats and sold them.

I'd see him later, though. I had a shift at the clinic scheduled that afternoon.

I started to slowly make my way out of the bed, trying not to wake him yet. But as usual, I saw Reed's eyes pop open, even as both dogs started moving off the fluffy dog beds on the wooden bedroom floor.

"Good morning." His voice was raspy—and sexy.

But the time for those thoughts was over for this visit. "Good morning," I returned cheerily. "It's about that time."

We both got up, showered, and dressed, then again took our dogs for a walk, still in darkness broken only by streetlights at this early hour.

We talked only about the new day and the fact I'd be seeing him soon at the clinic, and that we'd need to check our calendars to see when and where to get together next.

A little while later, we both left in our cars, heading in different directions: Reed toward his house, and me toward downtown Knobcone Heights and my shops.

I couldn't help wondering what the rest of the day would hold for both of us—particularly him.

———

I was the first to arrive at my shops that day. I placed Biscuit in the Barkery to run around till we opened and hurried into the kitchen. I did some preliminary scrubbing, washed my hands thoroughly, and then got out the ingredients to start baking what were maybe my favorite dog treats, except for the carob ones—one of the first recipes I'd developed for our dog patients at the clinic. These were cheese-favored biscuits to which I'd added crushed yams. Mmmmm. I loved sampling them myself.

I'd gotten a batch formed and on the baking sheet when I heard someone's key in the back door. I knew who it would be. Dinah was scheduled to come in first.

Sure enough, it was her.

"Hi, Carrie," she said as she pulled off her blue jacket. Then, being Dinah, she added, "So what have you learned since yesterday about what happened to Raela?"

Today she was wearing one of the Icing T-shirts. I generally asked my assistants to alternate between promoting the two shops. The black knit shirt I was wearing now, though, was one of my favorites, although so far I hadn't made it available to my staff. I had come up with the logo that was on the pocket: a heart, with lettering on the top that said *Barkery*, in the middle said *Bakery*, and at the bottom said *Icing*. I'd changed the design a couple of times but thought this one would stick.

Without new information to relate to my research guru, I just said, "I haven't gotten into it much since then." But a thought dawned on me. Dinah was a genuine pro at eliciting information. "I'm thinking about really digging into it, though. I haven't come up with any kind of plan, but if you have any suggestions, please let me know."

The smile on her round face was massive. "I figured you'd do that. First, it's another murder for my amateur sleuth boss to solve. Second—well, I gathered from all I've heard that the most likely suspect is Reed, and I knew you'll want to help him. Unless, of course, he really is guilty." The now-innocent look on her face didn't soothe me or make me feel any better.

"I believe in Reed," I said. Which was true. But that could also mean I believed he could be guilty, though I wouldn't tell her that.

"Tell you what. I'll try to come up with some research and interrogation ideas. Maybe we should talk first, though. Who all's going to be working today?"

I'd checked the schedule earlier. Vicky and Janelle were coming in, though not Frida. I told Dinah that.

"Great. Let's figure out a time to go to Cuppa's for some coffee and discussion, okay?"

Cuppa-Joe's was one of my favorite places in town, a coffee shop and cafe owned by two people who were very dear to me. I loved the idea, and Dinah and I decided to head there around ten thirty, assuming the others appeared on time and that business at the shops didn't require us to hang around.

I looked forward to it.

In the meantime, every time I wasn't baking something or waiting on customers, I let my mind chug along on figuring out a plan for my definitely amateur, but hopefully fruitful, investigation.

FOURTEEN

TEN THIRTY TOOK QUITE a while to arrive, or at least it felt that way. We had a steady stream of customers in both stores, which was good, but no large crowds—and having only a few people to wait on, with or without their dogs in the Barkery, tended to make time go slower.

But Janelle and Vicky arrived on schedule as usual, and their presence further slowed down time as they efficiently waited on customers, handed out a few samples now and then, and checked to ensure that our products remained plentiful in the display cases. Less for me to do that way, but I liked it.

I looked forward to my outing, not just because I wanted to talk to Dinah but also because I couldn't wait to see the Joes—Irma and Joe Nash, the couple who owned the coffee shop. They were more like parents to me than my actual parents, who were so involved with their new families that they didn't pay much attention to the offspring of their first marriage.

I realized, while making the date with Dinah, that I'd hardly visited the Joes over the past several weeks, just popping in now and then to say hi and sometimes get a cup of coffee to go rather than spending time with my dear friends like I usually did.

I couldn't really remedy the visiting part today, but at least I'd get to see them and hopefully would change my bad habits from now on.

Plus, I'd get to see Sweetie, their adorable gold-colored dog, who appeared to be part toy poodle and part terrier and resembled Biscuit a lot. Sweetie had been available at a Mountaintop Rescue adoption event and was scooped up by the Nashes, making me feel highly relieved that the—yes, sweet—little dog had found a new and loving home.

At about ten o'clock I started checking on everything to ensure I'd feel comfortable about leaving, although it wouldn't be for long. But Vicky, in Icing, made it clear that Dinah and me being gone for an hour or so would work out just fine.

And Janelle, in the Barkery, stepped out from the counter where a few people were discussing what dog treats to buy and gave me a hug. She then led me into a corner where it would be harder for anyone to hear and said to me, "We'll be fine here while you're gone, Carrie. Honest."

Janelle understood my concerns probably more than anyone—since she, too, had been a murder suspect not long ago.

"I know you'll do a good job," I assured her.

"But you're a worrywart, and you've got important stuff on your mind—like Reed."

"Right. Like Reed. And murder … again."

Her laugh was sympathetic. "You'll figure it out. I'm sure of it. And I think Dinah's a good person to bounce ideas off of. So go and have as good a time as you can."

I made a conscious decision to go along with what Janelle said. At exactly ten thirty I went into the sweet-smelling kitchen, where Dinah was getting some plates of peanut butter doggy treats ready to take into the Barkery, and said, "Are you ready to go?"

She grinned, lifted one of the plates, and said, "Soon as these are out there on display. Care to carry one?"

I did. And as soon as they were in the glass-fronted display case I got Biscuit on her leash, said goodbye to Janelle, and waved to Vicky in Icing. Then the three of us left.

My shops were on Summit Avenue, facing the town square. Cuppa's was on Peak Road, right on the other side of the square. It therefore didn't take us long to get there.

We had Biscuit with us, but instead of going straight to Cuppa-Joe's patio, I walked right into the restaurant. I knew the corner where Sweetie would be confined and wanted to say hello to her—and let Biscuit do so, too. Both the Joes were inside, sitting at a table near the counter that contained multiple urns of coffee, and they stood as soon as we came in.

"Carrie!" Joe called. His voice was strong and carried through the crowded room. In his sixties, Joe had gray hair with a receding hairline, as well as deep facial divots. He was one wonderful older man. "So are you back in town?"

I knew he was joking, but I still felt bad I hadn't been there for a while. "My mind is," I said. "Sorry I haven't visited lately."

"You're here now," said Irma, who'd drawn close and now hugged me. She bent and hugged Biscuit and even hugged Dinah when she

126

stood up again. She was as old as her husband but didn't look it, always dressed up and lovely, with hardly any lines on her face. Today she wore a frilly yellow blouse tucked into tan slacks, and her brown hair looked perfectly styled but a little longer than usual.

Joe looked down at Biscuit. "Would you all like a table in here today?"

"One outside under a heat lamp will be fine," I said, looking at Dinah, who nodded. As if in explanation—though we were truly supposed to sit outside with a non-service dog, per local law—I looked around. Nearly all the tables in the room were occupied, though there were no dogs except Sweetie and Biscuit. I leaned a bit toward Joe and said, "Dinah and I have some stuff to discuss that I'd really prefer no one hear."

"About that latest murder and Reed, I'll bet." Joe was definitely astute—and he always kept up with what was going on in town. Plus, he knew me.

"Could be," I said noncommittally, but the slight smile I aimed at him told him he'd hit it head on.

"Okay, follow me and we'll find you a nice, comfortable, private location." He winked at me and grinned at his wife. "Right, honey?" Then he looked back at me. "But you know, of course, that even if we seat you far from everybody else, you're going to have to put up with us joining you now and then for a few minutes, got it?"

"Oh, gee, I don't know about that," I teased with what I hoped looked like a horrified expression on my face, which morphed immediately to a big smile. "I guess we'll just have to deal with it."

"You sure will, with Joe," Irma said. "Now with me, I might just need to check to make sure everyone on the patio is doing okay—and decide to sit down for a while with you."

"Only if you can put up with my sticking you in a story some-where," Dinah said solemnly. Of course, the Joes knew my full-time employee was a part-time writer, so that didn't scare them—I hoped.

Soon Dinah and I were sitting out on the fenced-in patio beneath one of the warmers. It had just been turned on, so I felt a little cool, but not too bad. We were approached immediately by my favorite server, Kit, who aimed one of her toothy smiles at us. She was in her mid-twenties, cute, with curly blond hair and pink cheeks. As with the other servers, she wore a knit shirt that had a steaming coffee cup logo on the pocket. Today that shirt was black.

"Welcome, stranger," she said to me. Uh-oh. Even the wait staff had noticed my absence.

"Since I'm now a stranger," I said, "I guess I have to tell you every detail of my order." I tried to appear grumpy but figured I wasn't very successful.

"Well, I think I can tell by how you look exactly what you want." Kit told me I'd want coffee with cream. Oh, and some cheese and crackers to munch on since it wasn't quite lunchtime.

I laughed and agreed and let Dinah place an order of some kind of loaded latte.

"Oh, and a bowl of water for Biscuit," I ended.

"Absolutely. Be right back." And Kit hurried away.

Finally, it was time to talk to Dinah.

My mind had been attempting to focus on the discussion I wanted to hold, both to get my thoughts moving in the right direction and to get Dinah's opinion, but I hadn't really been able to concentrate.

But I would now. "So," I said, "I really appreciate your helping me figure out what to do next."

She'd rested a spiral notebook on the table that she must have extracted from the large purse she carried. A pen was poised over a blank page.

"In other words, investigate the murder," she said. "It's what you do."

"Yeah." I sighed. "Though kind of unwillingly."

"You've helped yourself and you've helped some friends," she said. "And since this time the guy on top of the heap of suspects is Reed—well, of course you need to investigate."

"Of course," I agreed just as Kit returned with our coffees and snacks. I didn't see the Joes outside yet, which was a good thing since Dinah and I were probably going to get to the crux of this conversation pretty quickly. I thanked Kit and she left. "Okay," I said. "Here's the thing. I looked into those other murder cases randomly, without starting off with much of a plan, and they kind of developed. I may still do that this time around, too, but if your writer mind has other suggestions, it will be great to hear them."

"Well, I think you always had a bunch of alternate suspects in mind besides the person the police were apparently focusing on. Can you do that now?"

"Of course, and that's what I thought of first. The most logical people to suspect are those who knew Raela before—and locally that does include Reed, but also the two other veterinarians who were in town. They all worked together in San Diego. I don't know if Dr. Oliver Browning will stay in town, though, since Raela had apparently been planning to hire him at her new practice. I need to talk to him to find out if he's taking it over or what."

Dinah jotted something in her notebook. "Fine. That should be first. Who's the other person?"

I told her about Dr. Jon Arden, and then relayed how the cops had also interviewed all the veterinarians and vet techs at my clinic.

"Well, you need to do that, too, but since they're your coworkers you'll probably need to be discreet about how you approach them." Dinah bit at her full lips as she wrote down something else.

For the next fifteen minutes we just talked back and forth and traded ideas. I felt as if my thoughts were finally beginning to gel. I wondered if I should always run my thoughts by Dinah to get them into some semblance of order.

I also realized that the major reason I'd felt so discombobulated this particular time around was that I was so afraid I would not find someone who was a better suspect than Reed.

But I had to do it. Or at least try. And I had formed a fairly good idea of how to approach it when the Joes finally came out of the coffee shop. Someone was with them: Shea Alderson, the lawyer. The Joes stopped to say hi to people at the several other occupied tables, but Shea approached us.

Over the past few days, I hadn't thought much about this dog lover who also happened to have a law license. But it occurred to me that I might be able to get some information, and even advice, from him once I started zeroing in on the people who might have had a motive to kill Raela. Of course, Shea had met her, so that by definition made him a suspect. Had he ever taken on her legal representation? Even if he had, it would probably have given him reason to want her alive and paying.

I motioned for him to join us. Dinah had met him at the adoption event at the Barkery and didn't seem to object.

"Hey," Shea said, "good to see you here. I just left my office for a quick coffee break, but now I regret that I didn't go home to get Buffer and Earl, too." He reached down and patted Biscuit's head. My pup had come over to sniff him in greeting. "Everything okay with you?"

I knew that was just a friendly question that I didn't need to answer truthfully. And in fact things were okay with me, at least at that moment.

Even so, that gave me an opening. "I'm fine, more or less. But like a lot of people around here, I'd like to find out who killed Raela. Did she ever talk to you about representing her in her opening of that new clinic?"

"We did talk. I even helped her out a little. But if you're asking if I killed her, guess what my answer is. I'd never kill a client, even a minor one. No profit in that." He laughed, and so did I.

Soon the Joes joined us, too. And for about another half hour—much longer than I'd anticipated staying—I was able to cheer myself up, even as my thoughts kept percolating and organizing ideas for how I would actually dive into this investigation.

We only talked about the new murder in town in generalities, though. The discussion then evolved into us telling Shea about the other recent cases and how odd it was that there were so many murders in such a small town. And, oh yes, I'd tended to snoop into them, not by design but from concern for the people involved.

Shea seemed amused but didn't offer any legal advice. Just as well. I doubted it was against the law to do my own sort of investigation as long as I didn't disrupt the real cops on the job or do anything to damage any evidence.

Eventually, the discussion ended. I wasn't the one to stop it, though. Shea pulled out his cell phone, looked at it, and said, "Hey, guys. Sorry. I didn't mean to hang out here this long but I certainly enjoyed our conversation. Time to get back to the office, though."

"And we need to get back to the shops. But it sure was great seeing you," I told the Nashes. "And I promise I'll be back soon."

"Anytime," Joe said, and Irma nodded.

As I rose, so did Shea, as well as Dinah and Biscuit.

On our walk back to the shops, Dinah asked, "So, do you know what you're going to do next?"

"Snoop," I said. "But if you're asking whether I actually have a plan in mind—well, that's a work in progress."

FIFTEEN

OVER THE NEXT FEW hours, I didn't have a lot of time to get that work in progress progressing. The shops were busy for a midday on Thursday, so it was a good thing that Dinah and I were back to ensure we had enough product and wait on customers in both shops.

But whenever my mind got a spare second to think, it was busy on the topic Dinah and I had discussed.

As a result, I had a plan for when Biscuit and I left for my shift at the clinic. I decided to drive there that day, since I intended to take a detour.

And so, at about half an hour before my three o'clock shift was to begin, I talked to each of my assistants individually and became fairly sure, despite the delightfully large crowds, that I could get away and still feel comfortable that both shops were adequately staffed.

I took Biscuit for a quick walk, hooked her into her backseat harness in the car, and drove alongside the town square to Hill Street. There, I made a right turn rather than the left I usually took toward the Knobcone Vet Clinic. I was instead heading for the

Heights Veterinary Care Clinic—to learn if the building still remained, after such a short time, a veterinary hospital.

And if so, I wondered if Oliver would now take over as the veterinarian-in-charge. Of course, I'd heard he wanted to go back to San Diego before making a decision, but depending on the degree to which Raela had gotten the hospital designed, licensed, and funded—assuming she'd at least gotten the process started—maybe he now thought it made sense for him to step in and keep the new facility open.

If so, could that have been a motive for him to murder Raela?

But that seemed both obvious and extreme ... right?

In any event, my mind had so far targeted Oliver as a prime suspect, so I really wanted to find and talk to him. And this seemed at least a possible place to start.

Traffic that day was slightly heavier than the usual stream of cars in Knobcone Heights, so it took me a little longer to pass the supermarket and reach the building that was now—maybe—the competing vet clinic.

I parked across the street and wasn't at all surprised to see the property circled by ugly yellow crime scene tape. Maybe there was no access into the building even by Oliver, let alone me. Even so, I checked to make sure that Biscuit was comfy with the windows partially open in the coolish March air, then got out of the car and locked it. I carefully crossed the street and walked along the sidewalk.

A few other pedestrians had stopped to stare at the site, and I did the same thing. A bunch of people who looked like crime scene investigators were walking in and out of the building on the other side of the crime scene tape, but I didn't see anyone who might have worked there the one day it had been open.

Nor did I see my detective buddies, or anyone else in suits or cop uniforms.

"Anyone know what they're doing?" asked a gawker, a high school aged kid who had an eager expression on his fleshy face.

"Someone got killed there," replied a blasé-looking guy who seemed only a few years older than the high school kid. "Don't you watch TV enough to recognize a crime scene?"

What were either of them doing at the clinic instead of attending school? Not my business—even less so than the scene we were all somewhat glued to.

The boys now started attempting to outwit each other with their knowledge of fictional crime scenes they'd watched for fun, and I wanted to shut them both up. Instead, I just raised my eyebrows and observed without saying a thing.

I wondered, since I saw no indication that Oliver or anyone other than the crime scene crew was around, if my suspect was still in town—and, if so, whether he might be in custody already for the crime. But I wasn't going to find that out standing around, if at all. At least not now.

It appeared unlikely that I would learn anything else there either. More important, it was time to head to my own part-time job before I arrived late. I'd at least get to see Reed and Jon, and I could ask whether either of them had heard from Oliver.

That would give me a good excuse, in fact, to take Jon aside and ask his opinion on what happened and who did it ... while assessing the possibility that he was the guilty party.

And so I crossed the street once more and opened my driver's side door, enjoying Biscuit's enthusiastic greeting in the back. Then I drove down the street and found a parking lot to turn around in, since I had to head the other way.

We arrived at my clinic only a few minutes later and I parked in the back lot. Then I took Biscuit inside to doggy daycare.

Faye was, as usual, there and in charge. I signed my dear Biscuit in and handed Faye her leash. Then I inquired almost as a matter of course, "Anything new here that I should know about?" When I asked this usually, I meant had there been any new dogs left there to be cared for.

But Faye responded as if I'd asked about rumors and gossip related to the murder of the new vet in town. Her assistants were in the middle of the room playing with some dogs, but she whispered even so. "Things have been odd. Tense," she hissed. "Some cops have even come in and asked questions here." Her gesture encompassed the whole facility. "I'm hearing that a couple of the vets have been questioned a lot more since the other day. I just wish…" Her voice trailed off.

"What?" I prompted softly.

"That Dr. Angela hadn't decided to leave. Or even if she did, that Arvie hadn't decided to hire a new vet. Or…"

"Yes?" Was I going to have to keep encouraging her to talk? Clearly Faye felt uncomfortable with what she was saying, but she did say it after my prompting.

"Or that Reed hadn't suggested some of his old friends interview for the job. Maybe if they hadn't come here, Raela wouldn't have either."

"Amen to that," I said, then realized I probably shouldn't have said it aloud. Oh well. Faye and I were buddies. And I did, in fact, wish that things had remained as they were before at my wonderful clinic, rather than having this pall of suspicion hanging over at least a couple of the people who worked there.

Including one I particularly cared about.

"Anyway," I continued quickly, "I'd better get to work. Biscuit's in good company here as usual." I bent to give her a hug, then left.

I stood in the hallway for a minute after I'd closed the door behind myself, breathing slowly and trying to let my thoughts loose. I had to go do the normal things like changing into my scrubs and signing in. Those came first.

The rest—well, I had lots of questions but would have to see how things worked out regarding who I could interrogate—er, talk to—next.

Jon was at the top of my wishful agenda. Maybe Reed, in case he had more information, particularly about where Oliver was and how I could get in touch to chat with him.

Maybe even Arvie, to get his ideas and find out if he had heard anything from the cops or otherwise about the future, or lack thereof, of the other very new clinic in town.

And whether the cops were talking to him as a suspect for that very reason. Not that Arvie would hurt anyone, even a threatened competitor. But maybe the authorities, who didn't know him as well as those who worked with him, wouldn't be certain of that.

"Good. You're here." I heard a male voice behind me and turned to see the person I'd just been thinking about, Arvie, right behind me. "We've got an emergency case coming in, a dog. Auto accident. I've got Jon already primed to help out but we'll probably need you, too, if the injuries are as bad as the owner described in her phone call."

"Of course," I said. "I'll go get ready right away."

I would have to wait to have the discussions I'd been pondering. Taking care of patients' health always came first—and I could only hope now that we could ensure the poor, injured dog's comfortable survival.

———

The dog's jaw, ear, and front leg on the left side were hurt but not too badly, and after the examination and x-rays, Arvie, assisted by

Jon, determined that there was nothing worse going on—fortunately. The six-year-old dog had been in the front seat when his owner had rear-ended another vehicle and the air bags had deployed, so things could have been a lot more severe.

The dog's name was Remus and he was part German shepherd, part Great Dane, and who knew what else? If he'd been smaller, he might have been injured even worse. But he was going to be okay, though he would need time to heal. He was bruised and scraped and in pain, but fortunately no bones were broken.

I'd helped by holding him as best I could on the examination table, to ensure that Remus didn't jump or fall off as the vets checked him over. He was clearly scared being in a vet's office and definitely hurting, but he didn't attack anyone—a really good dog.

I of course had to concentrate while we examined Remus, but my mind still managed to ponder how I could have a conversation with Jon afterward.

Eventually, I was sent out to the waiting room to summon Remus's owner, a middle-aged man. He'd been the driver and was clearly also hurting, but he'd insisted on rushing Remus to the clinic rather than spending time in the hospital himself. He, too, was bruised, his face mottled.

"You can come in now, Mr. Harbin," I told him, and he immediately stood up from the chair where he'd been sitting thumbing through a magazine and avoiding the curious and sympathetic looks from the pet owners around him.

A discussion ensued about treatment, which would include antibiotics and pain killers for a while, as well as how Remus should be walked in the short run, including limiting his exercise. Mr. Harbin was also told, for future reference, that harnessing dogs in the backseat of a car sometimes helped to avoid these kinds of injuries.

He was told to bring Remus back in a week for a reevaluation. After the meds were provided, the hurt owner and dog were sent back to the entrance to pay and get on their way.

"A shame," Jon said after Mr. Harbin left, his brown eyes seeming to reflect the poor dog's pain.

"But he should be fine," Arvie pointed out. "That's the important thing. Thanks for your help, both of you."

Which was a dismissal. Although we did have some other staff on call for cleanup duty in the exam room, I usually did it myself. Not this time, though. I followed Jon out the door.

"I'm so glad Remus is going to be okay," I said as we reached the hallway. "I'll bet, as a vet, you've seen car accident cases a whole lot worse than that." Unfortunately I had, too, but I figured this might get our discussion going.

Jon turned and looked down at me, his expression sad. "That's for sure. It's one of the reasons I'm a lot fonder of pets than their owners. Sometimes dogs unexpectedly rush out onto the street in front of cars, sure, but more often than not the situation could have been prevented by the owners. Same goes for when they're both inside cars and accidents occur." He shook his head. "Sad."

Arvie then exited the exam room we'd been in, and Sheldon, one of the janitorial folks, slipped inside. As a part-timer, I didn't see Sheldon or his counterparts much, but I felt sure they were handy to have around. Arvie undoubtedly made sure they knew how to sanitize the locations as well as a vet tech could—or at least I hoped so.

"How long will you be around today, Carrie?" Arvie asked as he started to slip by us.

I glanced at my watch. I'd been there about an hour already. "About another hour and a half," I told him.

"Good. Let's hope the rest of our patients just need standard exams and such." Arvie hurried down the hall in the direction of his office.

"I agree with that," Jon said and began to follow.

I immediately caught up with him. "So, how have your first days as a vet here been?" I asked, searching for a way to get into what I really wanted to ask him.

Jon stopped again and looked at me. "Not exactly as I'd anticipated," he said. "For one thing, I'd no idea that one of my former colleagues would follow and create such turmoil—and, on top of that, that she'd wind up dead."

Yes! He'd gotten us onto the topic. "Oh, I know," I said sympathetically. "Even if you weren't close friends, the situation must be difficult. But—well, the fact that she'd opened a competing clinic … how did you feel about that?"

"Not good. I was concerned about the animals who'd become her patients. But maybe she'd change, here. And she did apparently hire Oliver, and he's a really good vet. I'm glad I got this job, but he's probably equally qualified."

Okay, should I ask Jon if he'd had a reason to murder Raela, or should I stay on the subject of Oliver? I decided the latter would work best for the moment, and maybe I could slip in the former.

But the reception area door opened and Yolanda came into the hallway, holding a cat crate and followed by a woman who was probably that patient's owner.

Darn. An interruption. And it became more of one when Yolanda said, "Exam room three, Doctor?"

"Fine," Jon said and started following them.

I managed to remain with him, though I figured if a tech was needed it would undoubtedly be Yolanda.

And while it was yes to the first, it was no to the second. Yolanda said she had to get back to the front desk, so I remained with Jon for the exam.

The cat hadn't been eating and had diarrhea, so Jon had to ask questions and get me to run blood tests and more, including getting a stool sample to check—not the most fun thing about being a vet tech, but I was used to it.

It turned out that what I found was at least part of the problem: hookworms. Yuck. But the clinic had plenty of the kind of medication that would get rid of them.

And soon this kitty and her mom left, and I was once again alone with Jon.

"I was wondering," I said. "Have you heard from Oliver? Does he intend to try to keep the new clinic running now that its founder won't be around?"

"I don't know. We're having dinner tonight and I think that'll be a topic."

"Really?" Should I invite myself? If so, alone or with Reed? I decided on the latter, even though I wasn't sure what Reed's opinion would be. But he'd been friends with both these guys. And if I was able to start a conversation about who they all thought might have done away with their former co-worker ... well, I might wind up concluding that it couldn't have been any of them—or focusing on one of them as my main suspect.

"You know, I'm planning on eating with Reed tonight at the Knobcone Resort," I continued. "Would the two of you be able to join us there?"

Surprise seemed to register on Jon's face, then pensiveness. "Why not?" he said after a long moment. "I'll check with Oliver, and unless he objects, let's do it."

"Great. I'll check with Reed—and same thing on my end."

But one way or another, with Reed or not, I was already planning on that dinner.

I nearly immediately was given another assignment, this time with Arvie. But after he'd given the next patient a clean bill of health during an annual exam, my next assignment was with Reed.

It was another annual exam, this time for a cat. And when all was once more pronounced well and the kitty and owner departed, I got a moment alone with Reed in the examination room.

"We're having dinner together at the resort," I informed him.

The look he leveled on me was both longing and heated. "I'd rather you and Biscuit just come to my place."

"We'll do that again soon," I said, "but tonight is another step toward fulfilling the extracurricular assignment you've given me."

He looked puzzled—until I told him who we were eating with.

"Thanks," he said. "But—"

"Be careful," I said in unison with him.

SIXTEEN

I SPENT A WHILE at the shops after my shift at the clinic was over and Biscuit and I had returned to them. I was glad my assistants could stay until closing time. They did the bulk of the work, and I treasured them.

I did wait on a few customers, though—particularly some who visited often. I wanted to make sure their experience today was as wonderful as always, despite the distractions that I was trying to keep in a corner of my mind.

One of those customers was Sissy, probably the town's most loyal aficionado of our red velvet cupcakes—the recipe I'd bought along with Icing from my good friend Brenda Anesco. Brenda also had given me her slogan, "Make them sweet and make them good." I kept it in mind for everything I baked and sold in Icing—though only the "good" part fit the Barkery.

Another of our long-time Icing lovers, Cecilia Young, whom we referred to as Cece, came in that afternoon, and I was glad to see her.

Then there were Barkery fans, both dogs and their owners, who also showed up frequently. I for the most part let Janelle wait on them that day, particularly since her real career was as a professional photographer and she often made arrangements with customers to take photos of their dogs—and people, too. She'd told me she was hoping to take a few days off soon and concentrate on using her camera, so finding subjects to photograph was one of her current goals. And it never hurt for her to mention this in the Barkery.

So the rest of the day went by busy and fast, but I was glad when closing time finally rolled around. As usual, I got help closing both stores, and soon Biscuit and I were on our way again. I took my pup home, walked and fed her and then left her there, since I suspected our dinner party would want to eat in the Knobcone Resort restaurant rather than hang outside with a dog—even though all of my companions for the night had to be dog lovers, or why would they be veterinarians?

But were any of them people haters—or at least, haters of one particular person, enough to commit murder? I hoped I'd have a better sense of that by the end of the evening.

Reed picked me up at home around six forty-five. Both of us were dressed fairly casually for an evening that might turn out to be momentous—or I hoped so, at least. He wore a light blue sweater over slacks, and I had on a yellow blouse tucked into black jeans.

"You look good," he told me as he walked me to his car.

"You're just complimenting me so I'll want to do something nice for you tonight—like clear you of a murder."

He laughed as he opened the passenger door to his car. "Yeah, I wish, although I still hope it wasn't Oliver or Jon."

And I hope it wasn't you, I thought, but I said, "Well, let's hope we can clear them of suspicion." And get their suggestions about who else could have hated Raela enough to dispose of her.

We soon arrived at the entrance to the resort's parking lot. I'd already checked with Neal. Yes, my brother was working that night until seven thirty at the registration desk, but no, he unfortunately couldn't validate our parking ticket.

Reed found a spot close to one of the buildings that housed the hotel rooms, and we walked together toward the registration center. As soon as we entered, I headed toward the right, as usual, so I could wave at my bro, who sat behind the main desk with a couple of other people. He waved back.

As I turned, I saw Les Ethman walking toward us. Les, like Billi, was a member of the City Council—and a member of one of Knobcone Heights' most elite families. In fact, the Ethmans owned this resort.

Of all the Ethmans, Les was definitely the nicest. Although I was currently getting along with all of them, I'd had some bad moments in the past with some of Les's relations—including when I'd been all but accused of the murder of one of them.

"Hi, Les," I called, waving at him.

"Carrie. Reed. Good to see you here." Les was fairly elderly, with silver hair and lots of lines on his face. The edges of his eyes turned down, like those of most other members of his family. He was wearing a suit that night, and I figured he must have conducted some city business earlier. "Are you here for dinner?"

I nodded. I glanced at Reed, wanting to invite Les to join us, but that wouldn't have been a good idea.

"Wish I could invite myself to join you," Les said, as if reading my mind, "but I'm off now to meet a couple other members of City Council." Aha. That explained the suit. "Let's do it another time, though."

"Absolutely," I said, somewhat relieved. He was a good guy, and he was owned by an adorable bulldog named Sam, whose medical needs were handled at our vet clinic. "Let's do it soon."

Les walked off, and Reed and I headed toward the left side of the rear of the lobby, where the restaurant was located.

I started to tell the maitre d' that we were meeting a couple of people, but Reed said, "They're right over there."

Sure enough, Jon and Oliver were near the entry but off to the right, seated at a table that, fortunately, was large enough for us to join them. Presumably we were welcome.

I wondered if we'd remain welcome after our discussion started.

The men, too, were dressed casually. Jon wore a gray Knobcone Heights T-shirt and jeans, and Oliver also had a T-shirt on, a black one that didn't hype anything. Of course they shared a profession with Reed, but veterinarians were clearly individualists. Certainly these guys were.

Neither of them was as good-looking as Reed, though—but of course I was biased. Jon was just slightly shorter than Reed and a lot thinner—not much in the way of muscles that I could discern, even though he had to be strong enough to lift large dogs. And Oliver was shorter and thinner than either of them, plus his hairline was receding.

I wondered if studying their appearances would give me a clue about what was inside the head of each of them. But just staring wouldn't yield much in that department.

I approached their table, through the substantial crowd, with a smile on my face, knowing Reed followed close behind. "Hi, guys," I said enthusiastically. "Good to see you." Which wasn't untrue, since I had lots of questions for them that I would attempt to get answers to—though probably more subtly than just belting them out.

"Hi, Carrie, Reed. Welcome!" Oliver was the first to greet us, which I found interesting considering his possibly tenuous relationship with this town. But he'd been Reed's friend before either had arrived in Knobcone Heights, so I shouldn't be too surprised.

"Glad you could join us," Jon said, standing as Oliver had. Interesting for him to say that, though. I'd have thought neither would really like the idea of our joining them—except, again, because of their relationship with Reed.

But welcoming me? I wondered why. Or maybe they were just nice guys.

Both already had drinks on the table in front of them, and Oliver reached for his glass of beer as we all sat down, Reed right beside me. Jon, across from me, had some kind of clear hard liquor combo with ice in it—gin and tonic, perhaps, since a lime slice hung over the side. He, too, took a swig, and I envied those guys for an instant. But I needed more than alcohol to keep myself relaxed enough to do what I intended.

I was glad to see a server approach our table nearly immediately. I was even gladder to see it was Stu, who'd been our server the last time we were here—a nice guy.

Reed and I gave our orders quickly, including for food, since the others had already told Stu what they were having. Reed and I both chose beers for our drinks—mine imported from Mexico and his from Germany. I decided to order one of my favorite dinners, chicken

Kiev, and Reed asked for a burger and fries. Both of us also chose side salads.

When Stu left, I decided it was high time for me to start the conversation I wanted.

"So, guys," I said, "I realize this is a more-than-sensitive subject, but at least some of you have talked about Raela with me before and I want to do so again. I hope that's okay with you." I didn't wait for their reactions but turned to Oliver. "I heard you were the one who found her." It wasn't a question, but I was curious to see his reaction.

The shadows on Oliver's narrow face seemed to grow deeper as his hazel eyes sparked at me with what looked like rage. Was it because I'd brought up a subject that wasn't far from anyone's mind around here, or because I'd done so in a manner that mentioned his involvement?

"Yes," he said in a sadder tone than I'd expected. Guilt—or genuine mourning? "I was still in decision mode about joining her new practice and was planning to head back to San Diego," he went on, looking down at his wristwatch as if to check the time. "And that would have been right around now. But under the circumstances I figured I'd better stay in town."

"I assume those circumstances include commands from the local cops, right?"

Oliver smiled sadly, his apparent ire of a few seconds earlier already gone. "You got it. But that's not all. I don't know legally what's going to happen to the new clinic. Raela had just opened it and though it didn't have all the equipment or staff I'd like to see, and I'm not sure if it had necessary licenses ... well, I'm wondering if I should do what I'm sure she'd have wanted and stay here to run it." He looked straight into my face. "Assuming I'm not arrested for her murder.

That's what you're thinking, isn't it, Carrie? We've heard about you and how you solve this town's murders. And since I knew Raela and was considering working for her, I bet you think I'm a suspect."

"Gee, I thought you were a veterinarian, not a mind reader," I responded with an overly bright smile. To keep this going, I wanted to stay on their good sides—even if I did dare suggest I believed one or both of them could be murders.

Both? Had they conspired? Heck, I really didn't know what the motivation had been for the murder, despite my attempts to come up with several possibilities. Anger? Jealousy? Something else I hadn't thought of since I really didn't know who'd done it?

"Oh, we veterinarians all have some mind-reading abilities." Since we hadn't been served our drinks yet, Reed, at my side, lifted his water glass as if toasting his colleagues. "After all, we can't exactly ask how our patients are feeling, or where and how they hurt, so we have to determine that by looking into their eyes, not just at wounds or tests like x-rays. That skill transfers somewhat to humans as well."

"Hmm," I said. "Vet techs share that skill, too, at least a bit. We have to tell the vets in charge what our patients have related to us so they can get the best care possible."

Stu returned with our two glasses of beer plus a basket of rolls for the table. I thanked him and got ready to get even more pushy, but Jon took control of the conversation.

"Okay," he said, raising his glass in a toast. "Let's drink to Raela. May she rest well wherever she may be, and let those who are expert investigators know who really sent her there." He looked tellingly at me, as if he was making sure I understood his underlying message: it wasn't anyone at this table.

"Hear, hear," said Reed, and we all took sips of our drinks.

"So okay." I put my glass back on the table. "I'm glad I have all three of you together again. You've got to realize that since you were the only ones in town who knew Raela until a very short while ago, you're likely to be the primary persons of interest to the cops—and, yes, to me. I'm far from being an expert investigator, but I've had a little luck solving murders lately, whether I like it or not. And now that there's been another one—and someone I care about is a potential suspect—"

I looked at Reed, whose cocked head and small smile made me want to leap toward him and pound the truth out of him regarding whether I should continue to include him as a suspect. But now wasn't the time for that.

"—you can't be surprised if I ask all of you to convince me that I can stop suspecting you," I finished. "I'd like to consider you to be potential resources, especially if anything comes to you about who else might have had a reason to dislike Raela. Right?"

I hadn't drawn my gaze away from Reed yet, and now he looked both amused and—if I was reading his expression right—fond of me ... and probably more.

But this wasn't the time for that either. I turned toward Jon, who I believed had more of a motive to dislike Raela than Oliver did. Oliver must have at least liked her somewhat, since he'd been considering accepting a job offer from her.

It surely had been too early in their business relationship for him to decide to murder her to get control of the brand new veterinary office—hadn't it? But there could have been other reasons, if Oliver had been the one to do her in.

Our salads arrived then, making me wish, as I had before in other situations, that I had some control over when plates were plunked down in front of me and my dining companions. The interruption wasn't welcome at all—at least not by me.

I nevertheless dived pluckily into eating my greens and radicchio with honey mustard dressing and watched the guys begin their salads as well—while also grabbing rolls from the basket on the table and passing around pats of butter.

As we all settled down to eating, I again looked at Jon, then from him to Oliver to Reed and back again. "So, doctors," I said, "why don't we address directly the elephant in the room, or the pall hanging over this table, or whatever you want to call it. I realize you've all spoken with the cops, probably the detectives I've had the pleasure—or not—of interacting with before, who are now trying to solve the murder. I'm sure you've all sworn you're innocent. Hopefully, you all are. But just in case—do any of you want to admit to the murder? You can always claim self defense or some other kind of mitigating circumstances. Or should I move all of you to the bottom of my suspect list?"

I was grinning through all of this, as if maybe I was kidding … or not. And since, at that moment at least, they were my primary suspects, I hoped one of them would claim full innocence but somehow give a sign—a look, or a clenching of fists, or a huge swig of their drink—that they were lying.

But none of them did.

"I don't think you're going to get any big confessions here tonight," Reed finally said after several seconds of silence.

"Well, I could hope," I said. "Would any of you like to point a finger at one of the others and say why he's the killer?" I again looked around the table, blinking as if, once more, I was hopeful of getting an actual response. By now, though, I realized I was just playing games. None of them was going to confess. Still, pointing fingers could be fun … and might actually lead me in a direction that would help me figure out whodunit.

Only I hoped that the others wouldn't point to Reed—or provide some kind of motive or anything else that might make me suspect even more that it could be him.

But no one pointed, and since we'd all finished our salads, those plates were removed by a busboy as Stu started passing out our entrees—another interruption at a critical time.

But this time I didn't think the distraction was going to keep anyone from doing anything helpful.

We were soon eating again, talking about how good the food was and how the tables around us that emptied were soon filled with new patrons.

Nothing about the subject that I felt sure we were all thinking about, at least a little.

In a while, though, Oliver surprised me by saying, "Look, Carrie, I don't know why you're an amateur sleuth, if that's what you are. But we understand why you'd like to figure this one out." He looked from me to Reed and back again, and I couldn't help smiling a bit ruefully. Was I that obvious about how much I cared for Reed? Was he being obvious that he cared for me, too? Had Reed even told his friends that we'd been seeing each other as more than co-workers at the Knobcone Clinic? Or was Oliver just basing his opinion on the glances I'd traded earlier with Reed?

No matter. Our relationship did seem to be growing, and I liked it that way—and rather hoped it would develop soon into something even more.

Now, though, Oliver said, "We'd all like to figure it out, mainly because, like we said, the three of us are the main suspects, and understandably so. But I'm convinced that none of us did it."

"Me too," said Jon, and Reed expressed his agreement as well.

"But what we can and will do," Oliver said, "is let you know our thoughts about who actually did it and why—if we come up with anything. Right, guys?" He looked at the others, who nodded.

Good idea—maybe. "So do any of you have anyone in mind right now? Or a motive, even if you don't know who did it?" I had to ask, of course.

We spent the next few minutes discussing possible motives, even something as simple as Raela rubbing someone the wrong way more drastically than she had the members of this group.

Oliver mentioned Arvie and Paul Jensin, who both might have really resented someone opening a competing veterinary clinic in Knobcone Heights.

"I've thought of them, of course," I said. "But I know them both well enough to figure they'd need a whole lot more of a motive than that to actually hurt someone. After all, they're devoted to saving lives, even if it's lives that aren't human."

We kept up this conversation for a short while till it eventually petered out, with no clear motives or definite suspects being named.

"Well, we've all been thinking about it, I'm sure," Reed said, "and we'll continue to. Like Oliver said, if we come up with anything, let's be sure to tell each other—discreetly, of course. And most especially we should tell the one among us who has a history of solving these kinds of cases." He grinned at me, and I couldn't help recalling how he'd tried so hard, not long ago, to keep me from sleuthing.

But that was before he'd become a prime suspect. I got it.

And I also knew I would continue to do my own form of prying and investigation till, hopefully, I'd be able to clear his name.

Assuming, of course, that it deserved to be cleared.

SEVENTEEN

So I DIDN'T GET to clear Reed of murder that night despite what I'd said earlier—not even in my own mind. At least not completely.

But we finished our meals and our drinks and stopped talking, at least for a while, about what had happened to Raela and how. Instead, we discussed some recent trends in veterinary medicine, some new pharmaceuticals that appeared to be nearly ready for national distribution, and other things relating to their full-time profession and my part-time one.

Which was fine with me.

When we were done, we got our individual bills from Stu since we'd told him first thing that we would need separate checks. I wasn't about to let any of the men try to treat me, since they knew full well that I considered them murder suspects, or at least had initially. Including Reed, though I kind of hoped he thought I'd seen the light and cleared him in my mind.

For the purpose of getting along with him as well as I wanted to, I decided to let him assume that no matter what the rest of the world might think, I believed in his innocence.

And that was, in fact, what I wanted to do.

After we all paid and walked into the lobby from the restaurant, I was somewhat surprised to see Neal and Janelle standing there.

"Oh, good, you're through," Janelle said. "Neal thought you might be. Will you join us for a drink?" She nodded toward the resort bar, which was located off the other side of the lobby.

I was curious about this invite, but first glanced toward Reed. He, in turn, had looked at me, and we both smiled at one another.

"Sure," I said, and he nodded.

But what about the other two? Were they also invited? Apparently so, since Janelle and Neal now leveled their gazes at the veterinarians.

"Sure," Jon said at the same time Oliver said, "Why not?"

Why not indeed? If Neal and Janelle just wanted an update on what I'd learned in my informal and unprofessional investigation, they could have just asked me when we were alone. So what did they want tonight?

Reed and I stayed back and brought up the rear of the small group as we followed Janelle toward the bar. As crowded as the restaurant had been, the bar practically made it seem unoccupied. The many tables, mostly small squares of wood veneer with chairs on all sides, all had patrons sitting around them, drinks either in hand or on the tables. The stools facing the bar also had a lot of customers filling them. The TV over the counter was on and tuned to a soccer game, though I wasn't sure where the game was being held.

Despite the crowd, the fact that Neal was Neal and also an employee of the resort resulted in a table for six being made available nearly immediately. It was near the rear door of the room, which opened onto a patio from which a stairway led down to the lake. And that meant we got a great view of the lake, although at this hour what we saw were reflections of lights from the resort below and the homes on the lake's far side, as well as a few boats on the water here and there.

We sat down, and soon a server I didn't know approached our table—a woman who didn't seem a whole lot older than the legal drinking age. But she was efficient and took our orders. Those of us who'd just eaten all asked for repeats of what we'd been drinking before. Neal and Janelle both requested glasses of wine.

Then there we were, in a bar whose noise was hyped even more by the cheers for the game being played. I still didn't know whether the teams were US or foreign, but apparently at least some of the bar patrons were enjoying the competition.

I glanced up at the game to check the team names and score, but instead saw, at the far side of the room, two people at another table whom I knew. Billi was sitting across from Shea. They were looking at each other, so I doubted they'd seen us come in.

Interesting. Of course, Shea volunteered at Mountaintop Rescue. Was that what they were talking about? Or did Billi have legal troubles, either at the shelter or at Robust Retreat, or as a city councilwoman?

Or ... were they interested in one another?

Or all of the above? I didn't know about Shea's personal life at all, but I was aware that as interested as Billi had been in Jack Loroco, Jack hadn't been around much over the past few months, ever since he and Billi were cleared as murder suspects. Maybe their mutual interest had lessened and Billi was receptive to seeing someone local—a lawyer, no less.

Well, I was hardly going to maneuver through the crowd to interrupt their discussion merely to satisfy my curiosity. But I made a mental note to ask Billi sometime soon, on one of my many visits to Mountaintop Rescue.

I remembered that I hadn't mentioned Shea during our earlier conversation. He remained on my suspect list for Raela's murder, but I still couldn't think of any motive for him, even though he'd apparently given Raela some legal advice. Besides, she was killed by a very veterinary weapon. Not that I was eliminating the non-veterinary world from my consideration, but still…

I purposely hadn't mentioned Arvie either, although he had access to that kind of weapon. But no way could he have done it, even if he theoretically had a motive.

Our drinks were served and I wasted no time taking a substantial slug of my beer, only then drawing my gaze back to those at my table.

I'd half-heard the conversations going on—about Neal's job at the resort and which of the vets were working at the Knobcone Clinic, and an inconclusive discussion about the newly opened clinic.

Nothing specifically—yet—had been said about Raela's murder. But I suspected that was what was on Neal's mind, and possibly Janelle's, too, given her experience as a murder suspect.

Finally, Neal caught my gaze, and I soon learned the reason behind this little get-together.

"Hey, all of you," he said loudly enough to be heard above the noise, "who's going to tell me who killed that lady vet? You all knew her, right? I've heard about her murder from lots of sources, including gossip here at the resort and in the local media, and I want some answers." He leaned over the table and began looking from one of the vets to the next, finally stopping his gaze on me. "I won't ask you, since I know that if you'd figured it out, you'd have gotten the person arrested already."

I couldn't help laughing, even as I saw the expressions on the other men's faces. This wasn't too different from what we'd discussed over dinner, but it came from someone who was a stranger to them—and who'd mentioned the media.

The media. Not too long ago, I'd met with some of the local news sources about a murder case. I hadn't watched much TV or read any papers since Raela's murder, but I did wonder what Silas Perring, the main news anchor at KnobTV, whom I'd last thought about while publicizing the pet adoption event at the Barkery, had reported this time. Any potential suspects mentioned? I'd have to check.

Same went regarding Francine Metz at the *Knobcone News*. Had anything interesting been in that paper yet? It was another potential source for me, even if it was just for speculation and gossip despite the paper purporting to be a responsible journalism organization.

In any event, I wanted to know why my bro was so interested. He'd had some interest in the other recent murders, but he hadn't seemed quite as curious as this.

Perhaps he was just helping Janelle—or someone else? Did one of them have a suspicion about someone else and want to help that person out?

Okay, this was all just speculation. I'd have to ask him. But how should I handle this discussion—for the second time—tonight?

As it turned out, Neal made that decision for me by admitting why he'd gathered us to discuss the subject. He lifted his glass in a toast and said, "Here's to getting this latest murder figured out damned fast so I don't have to worry about my sister."

Really? As we all toasted and took sips from our respective drinks, I watched Neal—as he watched Reed. Stared him straight in the face, as if trying to read what was in his mind.

And then I got it. Neal actually was worried about me, more than he'd been when I'd snooped into the earlier murders.

This time, the killer might be close to me. Perhaps too close.

If it was Reed.

I believed now that Reed was at the top of Neal's suspect list and that he wanted a good reason to move him down, or to learn something that would otherwise make him feel sure I wasn't in any danger—especially if I continued to insert my nose where it didn't belong and try, once more, to solve a murder.

Maybe Neal hoped to get a sense that Reed's former coworkers had more of a motive than he did? Or just get some kind of vibe from Reed that whoever it might be, it wasn't him? A vibe Neal could believe.

Oh, how I'd like to feel that, too.

Of course, Neal hadn't been that worried when his own main squeeze Janelle was high on a suspect list. But then, he could just have backed away.

He probably figured I wasn't going to just walk away with Reed in the spotlight in this murder. And he was right.

I quickly realized that I was the only one who hadn't lifted my glass. I remedied that and we all toasted to solving the murder. Again.

And then my brother tried to move the conversation the direction he'd suggested, not too different from my initial attempts at the restaurant. "I assume none of you is the killer, right?" His gaze now started on Reed and moved to the other two men.

All of them were scowling now, clearly tired of the subject. I was, too. This wasn't the way to get the answers we all wanted—or that at least some of us wanted.

"You can definitely assume that," Oliver responded, then took another drink. That answer didn't exactly indicate that all of them were innocent.

"Can you think of anyone else who might have wanted to harm your former coworker?" Janelle asked. "Like someone else you've worked with at your San Diego clinic?"

Again, nothing new here. I considered, as I had earlier, how to end this conversation and start another one, but at that point Oliver and Jon rose simultaneously, both pulling out their wallets and leaving money on the table as if they'd choreographed this reaction.

"Sorry," Jon said. "I think it's time for us to leave. Good night."

We all said good night back. And that was that—almost.

"So which of them did it?" Neal asked, after they were gone, in a normal tone like he was discussing the weather. People around us wouldn't necessarily have known what he was talking about unless they'd been eavesdropping, but it still made me uncomfortable.

Even so, I looked at Reed. If either of us could answer, it would be him.

"Let's hope that neither did," he said.

"Even if it would clear you?" Neal asked bluntly.

"Well, if that was the case, then sure, feel free to pin it on one of them." Reed's grin seemed full of irony as he rose. "I'll be right back. I want to say good night to them."

Which he'd already done along with the rest of us. I wondered what he would really say to them, but I figured I'd better stay with Janelle and my brother.

When Reed had left, I looked at Neal. "You didn't really think any of them would admit to it, even if they were guilty, did you?"

"No. And I also figured you'd have asked them the same question, maybe even tonight."

I couldn't help laughing. "Oh, you know me so well, bro."

My gaze met his, then Janelle's. "So do you think they're all innocent?" she asked.

"You know who I want to be innocent," I replied. "But it's still too soon for me to reach any kind of conclusion."

"Well, sis"—Neal raised his glass to me once more—"one of the reasons we're here is so I could find a way to let you know the other little bit of information I got today that might help your investigation—or hurt it."

I felt my eyes widen in surprise. "What's that?"

"It helps to work at the reservation desk," was his initial cryptic response, but he quickly explained. "I booked a reservation starting tomorrow for a guy named Dr. Mickey Krohan. Since the contact info he provided indicated he was from San Diego, I couldn't help being a bit curious. I checked out his ID and Googled him, just for my own information. Turns out he's the head veterinarian at the San Diego Pet Care Center."

EIGHTEEN

VERY INTERESTING. DID DR. Krohan's coming here mean anything more than that he was trying to figure out what was going on with his current, former, and potentially-current-and-former-at-the-same-time staff members?

I'd have to find a way to meet him and hopefully discuss the situation with him—and get his opinion on whether any of his veterinary employees could have killed his other former veterinary employee. I told Neal and Janelle this. "I have to assume he'll be speaking with the cops and possibly visiting the animal hospital that Raela just opened. He'll surely also come to our clinic. Not sure if I have a shift there tomorrow but I'll have to work one out. I—"

I shut up, then, since Reed had returned from seeing the others off. He sat down and picked up his glass, taking the last swig of his drink.

"So did you say good night to your friends?" I prompted, hoping he'd tell me more.

"Yes. But before you ask, we didn't make any arrangements about when to get together again, though I'm sure we will. I'll at least see Jon at the clinic tomorrow. Did I hear that you want a shift there, too?"

I wondered how much he'd heard. I nodded. Heck, it shouldn't be a problem for him to know that his former boss would be visiting Knobcone Heights—would it?

I decided to consider the information a bit more before revealing it. "Yes," I said, "I do. Partly just to keep up my sleuthing—for your sake." That was enough of an explanation for now.

"I'll work it out. We can talk about it in the morning."

So were we now parting for the night? I could get a ride home from Neal, but I wanted more time with Reed, possibly alone time. But I didn't exactly want to say so, here—not without some bland explanation like we needed to talk about what we'd learned.

Which, as far as I knew, we didn't.

"In the meantime," Reed said, "I think it's time to get going. Don't you?"

I would have, if Billi hadn't come over to our table just then with Shea following her. "Hi," she said. "I saw you here earlier but you looked occupied, and I was having a conversation with Shea, too, that I wanted to finish. But can we join you now for a drink?"

I'd drunk enough for the evening, but I liked the idea of meeting up with my friend for at least a short while—and maybe finding out the reason she and Shea were together. "Sure," I said without checking with any of my companions. Reed sat back down next to me.

"Sorry, but we've got to leave," Neal said, giving no explanation. I figured he and Janelle also wanted time to themselves this evening.

"Have a nice night," Reed said, and I shot a smile at him. Of course, this latest disruption made it even more likely that he and I wouldn't get any alone time together.

We said good night to Neal and Janelle, and Billi and Shea sat down in two of the four now-empty seats at the table. The server must have been watching, for she came over immediately.

Ah, what the heck? I ordered another one, and so did Reed. I knew he could handle it even better than me, but he was driving. Good guy that he was, he also ordered some chips and salsa for us to share at the table. Food should help all of us stay sober, I figured. Plus, the drinks had been imbibed over a couple of hours now. Should be no problem. And I would only nurse mine.

I didn't know how much Billi and Shea had had, but both of them ordered soft drinks. Smarter maybe.

Or maybe they needed to keep their minds alert just to interact with one another.

"So … is everything okay at Mountaintop Rescue?" That was an interest I knew they had in common, at least somewhat.

"Oh, there are a couple of things regarding our adoption contract and ability to check on our former inhabitants that I wanted to talk to Shea about," Billi said. She shot him a glance that suggested to me that she'd had additional reasons to be in contact with him, but that was their business. She wore a pretty but not especially elegant charcoal dress that went well with her loose, dark hair with its golden highlights. She wasn't in city councilwoman mode, I figured, but wanted to look good with this handsome attorney.

Shea wasn't professionally dressed, either, but his blue button-down shirt still gave him the appearance of being partially in lawyer mode. His medium brown hair was brushed more over his forehead than I'd noticed before, and he had more than a slight beard shadow that evening.

"I had a couple of suggestions," Shea said, "but for the most part it sounds as if all is going great at the shelter. I certainly enjoy volunteering there. And that adoption event at your store, Carrie—well, it worked the way all those kinds of events should, or at least it looked that way to me."

I grinned at him. "I agree. Now, if we could do it every week, we'd get a lot of orphaned animals new homes—and I could hopefully sell a whole lot of Barkery and Icing goods, too."

"Everybody wins," Reed said, and he reached over and clasped my hand where it rested on the table beside my glass.

I liked the feel of his hand on mine, but I wondered why he was doing this. Did he feel threatened somehow by Shea and the way he looked at me? It was friendly, sure, but that was all.

And I felt sure of this when Shea leveled a much more interested gaze back on Billi.

———

Neal wasn't home when we got there. I figured Reed would just drop me off anyway—I needed to walk Biscuit, and he had to go to his place to take care of Hugo. But he parked along the street and came inside with me.

Biscuit greeted both of us. First thing, I decided I needed to share Neal's information with Reed about the impending visit of his former boss. Reed seemed surprised and pleased, although he did express concern over what his former boss might want—especially with all that had been going on with some of the vets who'd worked for him.

Then we had a nice discussion, a somewhat frank one, about how what was going on was affecting both of us—the time it was taking, the stress it imposed on our lives. Reed thanked me for looking into the murder but also emphasized, for my safety's sake, that no matter what he'd said before, maybe I should just back away and not get any more involved in attempting to solve this murder, not even to help him.

Or hurt him, I couldn't help thinking, even as I told myself that that was enough. I had to make myself assume Reed was innocent until I found something that proved him guilty. That was how things were supposed to go even with real suspects, right?

But, oh, did I want to absolve him, particularly in my own mind, as we ended that evening. Reed joined Biscuit and me on our walk, then came back inside.

After I'd unleashed Biscuit in the hallway at the entry, I turned to find Reed standing close enough to heat my side nearest to him, but not touching me. Yet.

He looked down at me, his dark eyes sad, his mouth pursed before he began talking. "I can't stay, Carrie, and not just because of Hugo." He reached out and grasped both of my upper arms. "I'd love to just drag you into bed till we both forgot all that's going on, but the way things are, that might mean we'd never get out of that bed." He shot me a wry smile. "I wish I'd never even thought about getting one of my former colleagues to move here and take Angela's place, but I guess we all can come up with lots of stuff in our lives that we wish had never happened."

"Not many things have these kinds of consequences," I said with a wry smile of my own. "And every time I've stuck my nose into one of these investigations—"

"Well, you couldn't say that about your own situation, I'm sure. When you were accused, it was because of an argument the victim started with you when she was triggered by the opening of your shops. And I'm sure you've never regretted opening your shops."

"True."

"But the suspicions about me are based on my argument with Raela, or series of arguments, which went on for a long time—"

"And the reason for these arguments are related to your own career, which you treasure, right?"

Reed pulled me closer. "You're pretty observant, aren't you, Carrie? Along with smart, ambitious, loving…" He suddenly bent his head down and kissed me. Not just any kiss. A long, sexy one that also seemed full of other emotions to me.

What had he just said? *Loving.*

Then I wasn't the only one considering it, was I?

My mind was muddled as we stayed in each other's arms, our mouths searching yet our hands not engaging in anything.

Not now, at least. Though the idea certainly crossed my mind many times.

But Reed was the one to finally pull away. "I've got to go," he said sadly. He retained a light grip on my arms and looked once more into my eyes. I restrained myself from standing on my toes and kissing him again. "But look," he continued. "When all this is over, well, I want for us to spend some time together. Quality time, maybe even away from Knobcone Heights. Or you and Biscuit can come stay with Hugo and me for a while."

"Why?" I couldn't help asking.

"I want to talk to you about … well, about our future. But for now—" He bent, gave me one more quick kiss on the lips, and then pulled away. "Assume you've got a shift tomorrow afternoon at the usual time. That way you can see what's going on at the clinic as well as meet Mickey Krohan. I'm sure he'll stop by. He can be a nice guy, but he's a bit of a tyrant when it comes to ensuring that his patients are treated right, and that things are going well at his veterinary hospital, which is probably why he's here. But—well, we'll just have to see how things go."

Reed's tone had turned more remote, and I could tell he was distancing himself from me in more than the number of feet between us as he started toward the front door. He opened it, bent to pat Biscuit goodbye, and waved at me.

"See you tomorrow." And then he was gone.

It was okay. He didn't need to stay with me that night, and not until Raela's murder got solved.

And however that would happen, it surely would get Reed off the hook. It had to.

I really, really wanted to experience alone time with him again. To talk to him again.

To figure out my own future, and whether it included him. Which it couldn't, of course, if Reed was arrested and convicted of a murder. A murder he certainly couldn't have committed.

Not someone as sweet and caring as he was, and not just regarding his veterinary patients.

No way could I believe, after our date tonight and all Reed had done and said this past week, that he could possibly be the one who'd killed Raela. That was, at last, resolved in my mind.

But as I started toward the living room with Biscuit at my heels, ready to turn on the television and watch some hopefully unrelated news, that mind of mine started separating itself yet again from my emotions.

Surely Reed's words and actions couldn't have been a ruse.

Could they?

NINETEEN

I SLEPT OKAY THAT night, even though my last thoughts before dropping off were of Reed and how I could clear him, and how hard I'd work to do it... though I wouldn't accuse someone else and amass "proof" against that person just to save Reed.

After all, genuine evidence implicating that as-yet-unknown person should be available somewhere, since Reed didn't commit the crime.

I woke up with some of the same thoughts but got ready quickly, walked Biscuit, and headed to the shops a few minutes early.

I needed something sweet in my life right then—and not just recollections of the kisses I'd shared with Reed. Nevertheless, I decided I'd start by baking some of my favorite Barkery munchies for dogs, just because they were my own recipes, before jumping into the sweet Icing goods.

As a result, after leaving Biscuit loose in the Barkery, I began baking some of my cheese biscuits as well as those containing beef and yams and liver. The aroma of the kitchen definitely started off dog-treat-related rather than people-treat-related. In other words, delicious but meaty.

Frida was the next to arrive, and I got her to work on Icing goods, which of course made her happy, too.

And things progressed well that morning, with lots of products ready for both shops by the time we opened. Dinah and Vicky arrived soon after, and then Janelle.

I purposely didn't remind Janelle about how recently we'd seen one another and where—or what we'd discussed. Not that I believed she wasn't already thinking about it all, too.

Both shops were fairly busy, which wasn't surprising since it was Friday. Locals often stocked up on both kinds of treats for the weekends, and a few weekend tourists arrived early. Which was why I tended to have all four of my assistants working on Fridays. It turned out to be a good idea that day, and I had no trouble slipping away for my afternoon shift at the clinic.

Biscuit and I walked there. I carried a couple of bags of leftover dog treats, one for the clinic and one to take to Mountaintop Rescue later. I could hopefully touch base with Billi and find out what exactly she'd been discussing with Shea.

We entered the back door, as usual, to go to doggy daycare, where I checked Biscuit in, this time with Charlie. As I reached the doorway into the vet clinic hallway, I heard some raised voices.

Oddly, it reminded me a bit of when Raela had visited a few days earlier and caused an uproar, particularly when she'd argued loudly with Reed about how wonderful a veterinarian she was. But I knew that whatever was happening, it couldn't be Raela's fault this time.

I opened the door and saw Reed there—not a surprise—along with Jon and an older fellow I didn't recognize. A patient's parent? No, considering all I'd heard so far about Reed's ex-boss from San Diego coming to town, I had to assume that this was Dr. Mickey Krohan. But what was he yelling about?

I stood there for a moment to listen and saw Arvie doing the same thing, down the hall beyond them.

"It's all your fault she's dead," the man yelled at Reed. "First of all you quit our wonderful hospital, and then you decided to ruin it by inviting some of the remaining best vets to leave."

Did that mean he'd considered Reed one of their best vets? Even if he had, I was sure it wasn't making Reed feel any better.

"I don't know what kind of relationship you and Raela had before you left, but I figured something went wrong and that was the reason you quit. But you had no right to recruit anyone from our clinic to come here. And to tease Raela that way, and for her to wind up dead—"

"Excuse me," I said, noting that both Reed and Jon were clenching their fists as they attempted to break into the guy's rant. I simply walked up to him, stared up at his face, and put my hands on my hips. "Let's take this someplace private, shall we?" I wasn't sure when one of the other techs might lead an owner and pet through the hall, but no one needed to see—or hear—this.

Dr. Krohan was older than his two former employees, though not quite Arvie's age. He was apparently attempting to look like a member of a younger generation, though, judging by his short light brown hair and beard. He wore black-rimmed glasses and a glare that he aimed at me as if he wanted to spit fire, though he had shut up at least for now.

"Who are you?" he demanded.

"Oh, I work here. And who are you and why do you think you can disrupt this clinic by yelling that way? Wait a minute. Don't tell me now. Dr. Arden, can we take this into your office?" Jon's office was just a slight bit closer than Reed's. I started edging myself toward the San Diego vet, and, as he began moving backward to get away from me, I edged him sideways toward that part of the hall.

As the three men silently, if unhappily, obeyed my demand, I glanced back down the hall toward where Arvie stood. "Thank you," he mouthed, then headed toward the door to the waiting room. I hoped none of the patients and their owners would have to wait too long to see a vet, but this situation needed to be faced and stopped right away.

In a minute, we were all in the office. Jon sat down behind the desk, and Reed and Dr. Krohan sat facing him. My arms still crossed, I stood near the door.

"Okay," I said. "Please introduce yourself and tell me why you think you can come in here and yell like this."

The vet actually obeyed. "I'm Dr. Mickey Krohan," he said, then explained his role as head vet and boss to Reed, Jon, and Oliver—and Raela—back in San Diego.

"Then Dr. Browning also worked for you there?"

"That's right. And after Dr. Fellner quit my clinic and came up here to start her own, I had to come up. She got murdered! I need to find out exactly what happened."

But when, exactly, had he come to Knobcone Heights? When he'd first heard Raela moved here, or after she was murdered? He wouldn't have had to stay in town, after all. He might have come up to see what was happening and decided that if he couldn't convince Raela to return, he would get back at her in some other way—like by killing her.

So I now had another suspect. One with veterinary skills. One I didn't care about at all. Great!

I wasn't going to point that out, but I would see if Krohan had any other ideas I could follow up on—in case I was focusing on him solely because I'd just met him and wouldn't feel bad if he was the killer.

"So what have you learned so far about what happened?" I asked. "Who do you think did it?" Judging by his rant before, it seemed Krohan believed it was Reed. But for now I wasn't buying that. And, again, I needed more suspects to check out.

"I don't know," the vet said, surprising me. Not Reed? For an instant, the guy looked defeated. "I thought it was going to be easy to come here and see my former employees and point fingers at one or more of them as Raela's killer. But I actually liked all of them, at least before they left. And though I know that Reed and Raela had some kind of feud going, I just can't believe he would do that." He glanced at Reed. "Besides … " He looked down at his mottled hands, which he'd placed in his lap.

"Besides," Jon said gently, beside him, "you were glad when Reed left because that gave you an opportunity to see if you could develop something with Raela, right? At least that was how it looked to the rest of us."

Dr. Krohan gave a deep sigh, still not looking up. "She was a pretty woman, even if she wasn't the most skilled vet on staff. I did like her, and I think for a while she liked me, too. But it hurt when she followed you guys up here to interview for the job." He looked at me, as if he knew I was the one checking into all the possibilities.

"And before you ask, I cared about her too much to sneak up here and kill her just because she'd decided to leave me and our hospital."

Of course he could say that. But as with so many people whom I'd spoken with over the past many months, denying that he was a killer didn't mean that I, or anyone else, had to believe him.

"We get it," Jon said, and Reed just nodded. "Anyway, it's good to see you, Mickey. But as I'm sure you know, we all have to get to work saving animals. How long are you staying? Could we meet later for dinner or drinks or something?"

They made arrangements that made it clear I wouldn't see Reed that night. No one invited me. But that didn't mean I wouldn't get an opportunity to talk to their ex-boss again sometime.

After all, thanks to my brother, I knew where he was staying.

"I need to get to work now," I said, then addressed Krohan as he stood near his chair. "If you're in town for a while, be sure to stop at my shops. They're right next to each other, and one of them, the Barkery, sells special, healthy dog treats that I developed while working here as a veterinary technician."

To my surprise, he actually appeared interested. "Really? Yes, I'll have to visit. I very much believe in healthful eating for my patients. And I should be around at least for a few days. I've already hired a couple of additional veterinarians at my clinic, so I'm able to stay away for a while." He looked at Reed and Jon as if daring them to chide him for hiring someone else.

They just smiled and finalized their arrangements to meet later that evening.

And me? Well, I spent the next hour or so being a vet tech, helping Arvie, Reed, and others with some of our pet patients. But that day I was happy to leave when my shift was over. I needed a different venue, a friendly face, and some good conversation. Therefore, Biscuit and I were heading to Mountaintop Rescue.

TWENTY

I STOPPED FIRST TO change clothes, then pick up my leftover Barkery goods from my locker. I didn't need an excuse to visit the shelter, but I wanted to do my part to make the residents there as happy as possible until they found their forever homes.

I picked up Biscuit next, and we walked to Mountaintop Rescue in the warming March air. I smiled as I opened the front door to the administration building. Yes, I heard dogs barking. It was almost impossible not to, anywhere at the shelter, unless one arrived late at night when they were all sleeping—and even then, hearing someone enter, many of the residents awoke and acted like watchdogs.

Today, as usual, Mimi sat behind the tall desk in the entry. Her doggy shirt read *Rescue Dogs Rule* and had a drawing of a grinning Chihuahua on it.

"Hi, Carrie. Hi, Biscuit," she said right away. "How are you today?" Her smile moved from the two of us to the bag of munchies I was holding.

"We're fine—and you can see the reason why we're here." I moved to place the treat bag on top of the desk. "Another reason is that I'd love to see Billi. Is she available?"

"She's in her office. Let me check." Mimi picked up a phone from the desk and pushed a button.

I walked, with Biscuit, toward the door leading to the back area where the rescue dogs were housed. I couldn't see much from there, but I wasn't able to go farther with Biscuit with me.

In a minute Mimi called, "Yes, she'd like you to come up to her office, okay? It's fine to bring Biscuit."

"Great. Thanks." I gently pulled on Biscuit's leash and we started walking up the stairs to the upper hallway. There, we went past a couple of doors until we reached the one to Billi's office. As always, I couldn't resist smiling at the sign identifying whose hangout this was: *Councilwoman Wilhelmina Matlock, Boss of the City, Canines, and Cats*. I smiled, knocked on the door, and stepped in.

"Hi, Carrie," she said. She came over to us and knelt on the gold-decorated area rug to greet Biscuit with a hug, then rose again. She was wearing nice-looking slacks and pricey-looking athletic shoes, but her T-shirt was a standard beige Mountaintop Rescue one. Her long, highlighted brown hair was pulled back in a clip, emphasizing the loveliness of her face. "Glad to see you—and I think I can guess what brings you here today."

"Leftover treats," I responded, although I knew that wasn't what she meant.

"And maybe some gossip. I get it. Have a seat." Billi gestured toward a chair facing her desk, and she went around to her own chair on the other side.

I always noticed how clean and professional her elegant wooden desk looked. The desk was clearly paid for by Billi herself, who as a Matlock had no budget restraints to manage. She was one of the most organized people I'd ever met, and she had even more careers than I did.

We started by yet again praising how well the recent adoption event at the Barkery had gone and discussing generally when the next one would be. Then Billi said, "Okay, you want to know why you saw me having a drink with Shea, right?"

"Gee, what makes you think that?"

She laughed. "Because I know how nosy you are. Anyway, as I mentioned, he and I were discussing legal issues related to the shelter's adoption contracts. I had questions concerning a couple of adoptions that I might want to rescind. I'm not sure the dogs involved are getting the kind of care the adopters promised in the contracts they signed. Shea may be a volunteer here, but that isn't all he does. He comes in handy."

"Glad to hear it. And does he maybe have another reason to be here … like helping the manager with her personal life?" I raised my eyebrows as I grinned.

"Could be. Jack and I are still seeing one another, but he hasn't been in town a lot lately so we're less serious than we were for a while. Shea's a nice guy, even if he's a lawyer, and his love of animals certainly helps." Her turn to grin. "So how are things between you and Reed?" Her grin faded quickly. "Is he still considered a suspect in that vet's murder?"

"You know the case isn't solved," I said. "And until it is, I'm afraid he'll be on the hot seat, since he'd argued with her."

"So you're still involved, too—trying to solve it." It wasn't a question, of course. Billi knew me too well.

"That's right. I just wish … " I let my voice trail off. There were actually a lot of things I wished for, right then, not the least of which was that Raela hadn't been murdered by anyone. Not that I'd have liked her still hanging around, especially with her new veterinary clinic. But even so, things would certainly have been a lot simpler than they were now—we would just have had to work harder do a better, more economical job than she did treating pets.

Billi and I had become close enough friends that she read my thoughts. "You wish this latest murder hadn't happened, but you still worry about how things would have gone with Raela running a competing veterinary clinic. Am I right?"

I laughed. "Are you ever!"

Billi leaned forward toward me, clasping her hands on her desk. "Well, you're not the only one who was concerned about that competing clinic part. Shea didn't give me any details, of course, thanks to his attorney-client privilege, but he did tell me that Arvie had tried to talk to him about some legal issues regarding the opening of Raela's clinic. Shea couldn't help him since he'd already spoken with Raela."

Really? I shouldn't have been surprised, of course, that Arvie had sought legal counsel. Arvie was one smart guy, even beyond all his wonderful skills as a veterinarian. Of course he'd have been concerned. He'd have questions, legal and otherwise.

But the fact that he'd sought advice about Raela, no matter what questions he asked … Well, heck. I certainly wanted to be able to move my suspicions away from the man I had a relationship with, Reed—but I definitely didn't want them to light on my boss and very dear friend Arvie.

Even so, I'd considered him before and now would probably do so again, more seriously. Darn it. Of all my major suspects so far, I'd really hoped the killer was Oliver, since I didn't know him that well. Or Jon. Our conversations so far had led me to believe that these two vets could be innocent, although that didn't mean they definitely were.

"Interesting," I said. "There probably isn't much Shea could have done, anyway. I will ask Arvie about it, but—"

"Shea and I are having dinner together tonight to talk some more, and yes, you're invited to join us. Reed, too. You can ask him anything you want, though I suspect he'll pull the attorney card and change the subject when it comes to either Arvie or Raela. But you can try. Are you in?"

"I am," I said happily. "Reed has other plans, though." Which actually might be a good thing. Reed didn't need to be involved in this conversation, at least not yet. "At the resort?"

"No, we talked about trying someplace else. I'll let you know."

"Sounds good," I said. That settled, Billi and I changed the subject to rescue animals: those at the shelter currently, and, once more, when we could hold our next adoption event.

As I prepared to leave with Biscuit, Billi received a call on her desk phone. "She is? I'll be right down." She hung up and looked at me. "Our illustrious mayor is here, apparently interested in possibly adopting a dog. Care to say hello?"

"Sure."

I liked to meet everyone interested in adopting a dog. Their new family members would undoubtedly enjoy treats. But Mayor Sybill Gabbon? I didn't know her well at all and rarely thought about her. I'd seen her in the distance occasionally at functions, but the only words we'd ever exchanged were mostly along the lines of "hello."

Billi, of course, knew the mayor and had worked with her, or at least had dealt with her in relation to city business.

This should be interesting.

And it was, for possibly a minute. The tall, well-dressed, middle-aged mayor was leaning on the reception desk chatting with Mimi. Billi stepped up to her immediately, while I restrained Biscuit on her leash. My pup enjoyed greeting most people she met, but that wouldn't be a good idea at the moment.

After Billi greeted Madam Mayor, she introduced me, mentioning the fact that I was a vet tech and owned the Barkery and Icing. I doubted at first that the mayor would be interested, but she greeted me as a valued constituent. And then she turned back to Billi.

"I haven't had a dog for a long time," she said, "but for economic and other reasons, my son Corwin is moving back home in a few weeks. He … well, you don't need to know the details, but he needs more companionship than I can provide. I'd like to meet the dogs you have now, and I'll probably bring him in to choose one when he gets here."

Interesting. I thought I'd heard that Corwin was married and lived in the Bay Area. I wasn't sure what he did for a living.

Well, it wouldn't hurt to have another resident return who apparently cared about dogs.

For now, as Billi started to take the Mayor Gabbon back to the shelter area, I just said, "See you later!" Then Biscuit and I left.

———

I was due back at my bakeries but decided I needed to make a short detour: a brief return to the vet clinic to see if I could ask Arvie a question or two about the legal issues related to Raela's clinic that had worried him—and whether they still did. Assuming he'd tell me about them. And had he hired a different attorney?

Fortunately, Kayle was the vet tech at the reception desk. If it had been grumpy Yolanda, I wasn't sure I'd have gotten her cooperation, but Kayle was a nice guy. There were only a couple of humans waiting, one with a cat in a carrier and the other with a Shih Tzu sitting on her lap.

"Any chance I can see Arvie for just a minute?" I asked Kayle very quietly.

"He should be through with his current patient in a few minutes. I can work you in then."

"Thanks."

I sat down on one of the empty chairs, Biscuit lying at my feet. I actually waited about ten minutes, but I finally got in to see Arvie. Kayle sent me to one of the examination rooms, and Arvie was in there waiting.

My sweet boss was clearly surprised to see me. After all, I'd been on duty only a short while earlier. "Carrie? Everything okay with Biscuit?"

"Yes, I'm glad to say." I quickly told him why I was there: curiosity about the legal questions he'd wanted to ask Shea. "I know it's not my business, but—"

Arvie laughed. "Oh, I know you're trying to figure out who murdered Raela. And yes, I did have some legal questions about how she was starting her clinic—did she have all the right permits and what was her own background and all. Not that Shea could give me any information. I still don't have the answers. And there was nothing especially threatening about her clinic, if you're wondering if I killed her. Which I didn't."

"I didn't mean—"

"I know you're trying every angle you can think of to help Reed, and that's fine. But I think Shea is a pretty competent lawyer, so he probably won't answer any of your questions about Raela, either. I would have tried another lawyer but I never got around to it."

"Oh, well." I didn't mention to Arvie that I'd likely be having dinner with Shea that very night.

I also had questions that Arvie might not have tried to ask the lawyer, questions about Raela's muscling in on the veterinary community here before she'd died. But I wasn't sure what was happening with her clinic—whether Oliver or someone else was in charge or if it had simply been shut down.

I wasn't sure whether Shea would know much about that either, even if he'd had Raela as a client. But I just might find out that night.

Oh, this was another question to ask Arvie. Surely he, among a select few in this town, would know the answer.

"Do you know what's going on with that clinic Raela supposedly opened? I know it's a crime scene, so it's closed at least for some time, but will it reopen? Is there a vet running it, like Oliver or someone else?"

"A living vet, you mean?" Arvie snorted. "I've talked to Oliver, and—well, he and I are discussing the possibility of his working here along with Jon and the rest of us. He seems a bit confused, and I suspect he would rather not run a veterinary hospital of his own. But if he and I don't reach an agreement? Well, I don't know. Maybe he'll go back to San Diego—or not. And if we do reach an agreement, I don't know what'll happen to the lease and equipment and everything that's there."

"I guess that will depend on Raela's heirs," I said, wondering not for the first time if she had any family who would miss her. I hadn't heard, and neither had I asked Reed.

"I guess so," Arvie agreed. He shook his head. "Bad situation all around—but these dratted murders around here always are."

"Yes," I agreed, "they are."

TWENTY-ONE

Now, finally, it was time to return to my shops. I still had an hour before closing time, and when I got there I was pleased to see that both bakeries had customers in them as well as staff who were doing an excellent job taking care of them. There were even a couple of dog customers in the Barkery, including a Doberman mix and a German shepherd.

Biscuit seemed happy to see them. They'd met before, since the dogs' owners were frequent customers at both shops.

Dinah finished waiting on the Dobie's owner, and after a few more nose sniffs between the dogs I put Biscuit into her enclosed area in the corner. Then I approached Dinah behind the counter, ready to ask a few questions. She beat me to it—probably because she knew I was a concerned shop owner who, never mind if things looked well, wanted to confirm it.

"Yes, everything was fine while you were gone. No, we had no disasters. Yes, some of our regular customers were here as well as some I didn't know. Now tell me—did you save any animals' lives at the hospital today?"

I grinned at her. "Thanks for the update. And no, fortunately today things were fairly standard and no lives were at risk."

"Oh, one more thing," said my supportive assistant. "Did you solve that murder yet?"

This time I laughed, perhaps a bit sardonically. "Still working on it."

"You doing any investigation tonight?"

I felt fairly sure Dinah wanted to know if I was seeing Reed. "Of course," I said. "Though too bad my buddy Dr. Storme won't be with me."

Dinah's eyes grew larger, but before she could ask any further questions, another customer reached the counter, pointed into the display case, and began asking about the treats' ingredients. I stifled my laughter but continued to feel some levity at the frustration I knew Dinah must be feeling at not learning more.

But then I considered the fact that yes, tonight I hoped to learn something relating to the murder. But was I likely to solve it with the information I received? And was I really making much progress?

I sighed, ducked behind the counter, and came out with a plate full of sample treats. I needed a distraction, and giving bonuses to my customers could only help.

Next, I headed over to Icing to ensure that all was going well there, too—which it was.

Eventually our crowds began thinning and soon it was time to close both shops.

Dinah managed to take me aside after Frida and Janelle had left. "So, are you going to tell me what's going on tonight, and why Reed won't be involved?"

I laughed. "What, so you can take notes for your latest story?" She opened her mouth again, as if getting ready to say yes, but I interrupted. "I'm just meeting with a couple of people who might have information about what's going on with Raela's clinic. If I learn anything helpful, I'll let you know." Maybe. Although I might edit it first.

"Who would that be? The cops? The vet Reed knew, who Raela hired? Or—"

I lifted my hand and shook my head. "Good guesses, but for now I'll keep you guessing and not say yes or no. Tomorrow's Saturday, so I assume you're working, right?" Though Dinah was my only full-time employee, the two days she usually took off each week were Sunday and Monday.

"That's right."

"Good. I can't promise we'll talk then, but maybe."

She looked disgruntled. "You can be sure I'll push you for answers then," she said.

"Yes, I feel sure of that," I responded.

Dinah left shortly thereafter and I finished closing the stores, which included confirming that all financial information was locked securely in my small office at the rear of the kitchen. Then I got Biscuit ready for our drive home.

I figured I could call Billi on my Bluetooth to find out where we were going to meet for dinner, and when. Not having heard from her yet, I had some concerns that the plans had changed.

They had in some ways, as it turned out, but not in all. Billi wound up calling me nearly the moment after I got into my car. We were still getting together with Shea to eat, but we weren't dining in a restaurant at all. Instead, Shea was cooking at his place.

Interesting. The guy was a lawyer and a dog lover—and he cooked, too. I'd already figured it might be a good thing that Billi wasn't counting on Jack Loroco as her main love interest anymore. Shea might be a good replacement.

Billi told me where Shea's home was—a duplex in a gated condo community that was closer to downtown than my place or even Reed's. I was familiar with it and assumed Shea must be renting there, since I doubted a lawyer would want to remain for long in one of those small dwellings, but that wasn't my concern.

This was, though. "Would it be okay if I brought Biscuit?"

"Sure. I'm bringing Fanny and Flip. They get along fine with his dogs, Buffer and Earl."

I'd met Shea's dogs and so had Biscuit, of course, since he'd brought Buffer and Earl to the Barkery as well as the clinic. No issues there about getting along, either.

"Tell you what. I'll pick you up on my way. Biscuit, too. I should be there in about fifteen minutes. Okay?"

That didn't give me a lot of time to walk my pup and change clothes, but I could do it. "Fine," I said, and we hung up.

Once home, I walked Biscuit along our residential street for a couple of minutes, then hurried inside to change. No need to be formal tonight, so I chose some nice jeans and a plaid shirt. I was ready when Billi called again to say she was just pulling up outside.

I helped Biscuit into the back of the car, where Billi's dogs already occupied a large portion of the seats, but my small pup had no trouble finding a spot on the floor. The dogs knew each other and they all got along fine.

On the way there I couldn't help asking, "So you've been to Shea's before?"

I watched the expression on Billi's face as she drove. It appeared almost defiant, which I found interesting. We were friends. She didn't need to get embarrassed, but neither did she need to argue with me about what she did.

"Yes," she finally said. "And in case you're wondering—which I know you are—we didn't do anything steamy. He just wanted to show me something in an antique law book he had about the rights of women in government."

"Really?"

"Yes, really," she said. "It was from back in the day when women had only recently gotten the right to vote. It was fascinating."

And Shea couldn't have just brought it to Mountaintop Rescue to show her? Heck, it wasn't really any of my business. There could have been timing issues, like he'd wanted to show her immediately after mentioning it.

Or maybe he'd hoped for a steamy visit but it hadn't gone in that direction, at least not at that time.

In any event, along with the questions I hoped he'd answer tonight, I would watch Shea and Billi for signs that they cared for one another. Or didn't.

We soon arrived on one of the nice but not extremely elite residential streets where there were a couple of gated communities. Billi drove up to the entry of the first one and stopped, pulling her phone from her jeans pocket. She made a quick call to Shea, and nearly immediately the large metal gate opened inward. She drove inside, where a row of identical two-story buildings burgeoned on both sides. She turned right and soon parked in one of the spots in front of the left side of one of the boxy, multi-windowed duplexes.

Shea was waiting outside for us. He smiled his greeting, said hello as we got out of the car, and took charge of black Lab Flip's leash. Billi took beagle-mix Fanny's leash and I grabbed Biscuit's.

"Need a walk?" he asked.

Just to be safe I said yes, despite the woofs I heard from inside the home. We all ambled with our dogs past Shea's half-house and along the sidewalk in front of some others, then back again.

After a few minutes Shea led us inside, and of course we were greeted enthusiastically by his yellow Lab mix, Buffer, and his pit bull mix, Earl.

His home appeared to be a standard condo, with wood-laminate floors, a moderate-sized living room, and a kitchen with pale wood cabinets and deep yellow countertops, which was where we headed, The round wooden table was already set for dinner.

The place smelled good—a bit more like my Barkery than Icing, so I figured we were having some kind of meat dish for dinner. This turned out to be true, since after Shea got us seated and poured some claret into small glasses for us, he brought a plate of meat loaf to the table and placed it on a trivet. He'd also prepared a nice, large salad and a small side dish of creamed spinach.

The guy had promise, I thought. For Billi, not for me. I was happy enough with Reed's bringing in chicken dinners or Chinese food or even pizza when we ate at his house, and he never seemed to mind my doing the same if I wasn't in a cooking mood when I got home.

All the dogs were well behaved enough to settle down on the floor near us as we began eating. The meat loaf was tasty and I decided to save a little to treat Biscuit, but not while we were still dining.

And since we humans, too, were settled down I figured it was a good time to start the conversation I wanted to have.

I looked at Shea. He was dressed as casually as when I'd seen him at Mountaintop Rescue, in a dark T-shirt and jeans. His brown hair appeared even more askew than I'd noticed previously, and his expression was serious, as if he'd been anticipating my questions and considering his response in advance.

I considered throwing him something completely off topic to confuse him. Maybe then he'd be more off guard and answer some questions in an un-lawyerlike way. Then again, I needed to talk to him *because* he was a lawyer, and because he'd apparently advised Raela and spoken a bit with Arvie.

Plus, since he'd known Raela, that automatically kept him a murder suspect, at least in my mind. But since she'd been somewhat of a client and not his rival, I still doubted he was the one.

Time to begin. "This meal is delicious, Shea. I assume it's to distract me so I won't ask you anything difficult."

"Hey, I'm a lawyer," he retorted with a smile that lit up his already nice-looking face. "I'm used to answering difficult questions. So, fire away—although I'll tell you right up front, as I have to, that there'll be certain things I won't be able to answer if they violate attorney-client privilege."

"I figured. I'll try to keep it simple. First, you indicated that Raela was your client, right?" If this turned out not to be true, I could ask a whole lot of things that I otherwise wouldn't get answered.

"Yes, she was." He nodded, his face void of any emotions.

Okay, that was confirmed. I'd be cautious how I asked the next few questions. "Did she seek your advice for things she needed to know to open that new veterinary clinic?"

"Yes, and before you ask any particulars—and this is a stretch for me to say—but I can tell you she did consult me about several matters relating to the property and permits, that kind of thing, although the advice I provided was minimal. I can't tell you more." He took a long sip of his wine as if he needed a bit of a boost, and I did the same, glancing at Billi. She, too, drank some wine, saying nothing and watching us.

"Did…did she ask your advice about how to deal with the competition with the other veterinary hospital in town?"

"Maybe, and that's all I can say about that." Shea's tone seemed to be getting sharper, though not overly so. He might have had some emotions relating to being Raela's attorney, but he clearly wasn't going to talk about them. Or her.

I nevertheless asked, "I understand you and Arvie spoke, though I gather you made it clear you couldn't talk much with him. Did you—I mean, did he ask, once Raela was gone, if you could represent him in anything?"

Like, his veterinary practice—or to handle any criminal allegations against him?

"That's something you should talk to Arvie about."

I didn't have the sense that Shea was a criminal attorney, though he could have done criminal work along with his transactional stuff, I supposed. But if Arvie happened to believe he was a major murder suspect, maybe he would have checked with Shea about representation.

Was that the case?

I hadn't asked Reed if he had hired Ted Culbert yet—the local defense attorney I'd had dealings with thanks to the other murders. If so, Ted wouldn't be available to anyone else in this situation. Could Shea, having been Raela's transactional attorney, represent someone who might be a suspect in her murder? Seemed a conflict of some sort to me, but I was far from an expert.

"Okay," I finally said. "I may have more questions, and you may have more non-answers. But just let me ask one additional thing. Well, two, actually. Do you happen to know if the clinic Raela started is still open, or will be after the criminal investigation is over? And if you do know, what's the answer?"

"I can answer those easily: I don't know. I guess we'll all find out eventually. And if it is open, well, I have an idea who the vet there will be. But I'm not even sure of that."

This sounded like Shea could have met Oliver during his representation of Raela. Maybe he'd even worked on some kind of contract between them. That would be interesting. Even if it was true, though, Shea probably couldn't, or wouldn't, discuss it with me either.

Oliver, on the other hand … maybe he'd be able to tell me what was in such a contract, and anything in it that Raela had found important.

And would that help give me more clues about who might have killed her? I guessed I'd find out then … maybe.

TWENTY-TWO

THERE WASN'T MUCH LEFT to say on this topic after that. Or maybe there was, but I figured no one was going to talk about it anymore, especially Shea. I therefore started asking about the current residents at Mountaintop Rescue, a subject I knew every one of us cared about.

Eventually, we all decided it was time to take the dogs out for a final walk while we were together. Shea led the group, pointing out some of the features of the gated community where he lived, including a large meeting facility and a swimming pool that would be closed for at least another month.

"Very nice," I said, and I was somewhat impressed with it for what it was. I didn't live in the most exclusive area in Knobcone Heights, as Billi did, and even Reed's home, closer to me, was in a neighborhood that catered to people who brought in more money than I did. Shea's place was probably in between Reed's place and mine in property value—but my preference was to live in a stand-alone home rather than a duplex in a gated community.

The dogs seemed impressed enough with it. They all sniffed their way around the grass edging the sidewalks and took care of their business in the most appropriate of ways. Shea had come prepared with plastic bags so his neighbors would have no issue with our outing.

We returned to Shea's condo then, and at Billi's car she and I said good night to our host. I bent down to attempt to appear to be adjusting Biscuit's collar so that the other two humans could have a teensy bit of privacy to convey whatever farewells they wanted, including a kiss if they so chose, but they didn't. Yes, I was peeking.

Did they abstain because of my presence, or because that wasn't where their relationship was, at least at this point? Not really my business—though I remained curious.

Billi and I helped our dogs into the back of the car and we were soon on our way. I didn't feel as if I'd learned much that evening, except that Shea might have more information that would be helpful but he wasn't about to impart it to me—most likely justifiably.

Did he have an idea who'd killed his client? I hadn't asked directly, but I figured that if he did, he was more likely to follow the law, or at least common sense, and tell the police rather than a person like me who kept nosing into murder situations without any authority.

"I'd like to see it," Billi said as she turned off Shea's street and onto a wider avenue heading toward my place.

"What's 'it'?" I asked.

"That interloper veterinary clinic-slash-murder scene. I have a general idea where it is but haven't gone by it. Would you mind showing it to me? I know it's out of our way."

"Sure, let's go." I hadn't been there since yesterday. Was it still marked as a crime scene? If not, would we be able to tell from outside whether it was an open business? That might not be clear this late in the evening, but we could at least see if the minimal signage that had been there before was still present.

The dogs were all settled down in the back, so I doubted they'd mind the extra ride.

It took us about ten minutes to get there. We passed my shops and wended our way around the town square, ending up on Hill Street. We then went by some of Billi's territory, including Mountaintop Rescue and City Hall, and beyond them to the building where Heights Veterinary Care Clinic had been opened so very recently, only to witness tragedy that didn't involve dying, injured, or ill pets.

As we started to pass on the opposite side of the street, I pointed at it. "No crime scene tape," I said. Or at least none that was visible under the street lights. "Can you turn around and park for a minute over there?"

I kept my eyes on the place while Billi did as I requested. A light glowed inside the small, single-story structure, as it had the night I'd seen Reed emerge. Had the police left it on—or had someone else?

As Billi parked, I observed that there was still a sign in the window closest to the entry door. I was too far away to read it, though. Did it say this was a veterinary hospital—or was it a For Sale or For Lease sign? I determined to find out.

"I want to check something," I said to Billi. "Can you wait here a minute with the dogs?"

"No, I'm curious, too. I'll join you."

We both rolled down our windows a little to let some air in for the pups in the backseat. They were all sitting up now but were well enough behaved not to try to squeeze out as we exited the car.

Although there were other buildings in the area, they mostly appeared to contain offices, including one or two human medical facilities. I didn't see any retail stores close by, and nothing appeared to be open this late.

I went up the paved walkway to the door and looked at the sign. It gave the name of the veterinary clinic. I peered inside the window behind it—and saw some movement inside.

Startled, I stepped back, bumping into Billi.

"What's wrong?" she asked.

"Someone's in there," I said quietly. I moved once more to see if I could make out who it was—as the door opened.

"Hey, what are you doing here?" Oliver demanded.

I realized I shouldn't have been surprised. If someone was there and it wasn't the police, it made sense that it was either the building owner or the person who might take over the vet clinic. And who would the latter be besides Oliver?

"We could ask you the same thing," Billi responded. She was now beside me in front of the door. "I gather that the authorities are done investigating this as a crime scene, but from what I understand, the murder victim was the tenant under the lease."

"Yes, but—heck, why don't you come in and we'll talk about this, okay?"

We agreed, but I wondered if it was a good idea. Oliver's presence here certainly ensured that he remained at the top of my suspect list. If he'd killed Raela and thought we knew it, our lives could be in danger, too.

"We can't stay long," I told him. "My brother is waiting for me at home. I told him we were driving by here out of curiosity, and—well, I doubt you know my brother, but he's overly protective. If I'm not home in a short while he'll come after me."

Okay, I realized this wouldn't exactly save our lives, but it might give Oliver pause if he was considering doing away with us.

199

And if I saw any hypodermic needles out and about, I'd call 911 right away.

Oliver's sweatshirt made his shoulders look bulky, giving him more of an appearance of strength than I'd given him credit for previously. But heck, he was a vet. He had to be used to manhandling large dogs for their treatment.

The front door led into a reception room, similar to the one at my clinic. This room was a lot smaller, though. It had enough cheap-looking chairs for all of us to sit, and a light was on overhead.

"Okay," Oliver said in a belligerent voice. "Why are you really here?"

"To check to see if this place is going to stay a veterinary clinic," I said. "And since you're here, I gather that it is."

"I don't know," he replied angrily. "I'm glad I now have an offer from Arvie to work at your clinic, but I'm just not sure. I wasn't his first choice, though I like Jon Arden and wouldn't mind working with Reed and him again. But I got fairly excited about the idea of helping to open a new place in this town, with all its wealthy people, including a lot who love pets. But—well, now Raela is dead and I don't know what's going to happen here. I'm thinking about trying to take it over all by myself, to start with. But this place … this place … I found her, you know."

"Yes," I said.

"I'd thought things would be so simple if I accepted her job offer. So great. But now, I just don't know."

This all suggested that Oliver had a reason to want Raela alive. But had that been the case when she actually was alive? They could have argued about his position here. They might have started some kind of relationship even before they'd gotten to Knobcone Heights.

There was a lot I still didn't know, and this wasn't exactly the best time to ask.

"Well, whether to run this clinic or not is certainly your decision," I said. "I'm biased, of course, but I think you'd be better off joining our clinic. For one thing, you haven't found any dead bodies there."

"Yeah, there is that," he said. "It was eerie for me to be here, even after the cops cleaned it. If I stay, I might keep the equipment but rent some other building. Or maybe it would be better if I did start working at your clinic."

"That's what I think, of course," I said. "We're damned good and have a great reputation. Starting from scratch with a new veterinary hospital, here or someplace else, sounds like a real challenge to me."

I said what made sense for him, I realized, but did it make sense for me and the others at my clinic? Maybe, if Oliver was a good veterinarian, sure. But what if he also happened to be a murderer?

"I agree it's your decision," Billi said from beside me. "And it sounds as if you've already made the decision to remain in Knobcone Heights—which, to me, as a representative of the local government, I'm sure is the right one."

"Have you two met before?" I asked then. Oliver hadn't been at the adoption event at the Barkery, nor would he have been at our clinic if Billi brought in one of the rescue animals for a checkup. In case they hadn't, I introduced them, including Billi's wonderful credentials as a city councilwoman, spa owner, and pet shelter manager.

"Wow," Oliver said, sounding suitably awed. "Well, if I practice veterinary medicine at either clinic, I hope to see you there. But now—well, I hadn't intended to stay here so late, but I wound up mulling over all the possibilities while I was checking the place out again. The door wasn't locked, which isn't a good thing. I'll have to let the police know, since they were the last ones in charge here."

"Good idea," I said. I wasn't sure how much equipment Raela had brought in, but I hated to hear of it being susceptible to theft.

Or was Oliver lying about the open door? Was he lying about anything else?

Was he a killer…? Well, when we'd had dinner together, he'd said he wasn't. I hadn't asked him again tonight, even though I was still trying to figure it out.

"I'll take care of that." Billi pulled her cell phone from her pocket. She walked away from us as she held a conversation with someone probably at the Knobcone Heights PD. In a minute she returned. "The police dispatcher I spoke with will take charge of making sure this place is locked, though he wasn't sure whether they had the keys or would need to get them from the property owner. In any case, a patrol car will be here soon to keep an eye on the place."

Which meant, at a minimum, that Oliver was unlikely to be able to return to the clinic on his own—unless he was lying and had the keys himself, possibly having stolen them from Raela when he killed her…

Okay. I was over-thinking this, since I was so eager to be able to prove that the killer was anyone but Reed.

"Anyway, it's time for us to leave," Billi said. "You need to get up early in the morning as usual, right, Carrie?"

"Absolutely," I said. "I don't have another shift at the clinic for a few days," I told Oliver, "so I won't see you there even if you go in to talk to Arvie. But if you need any information from a very happy part-time employee, you can always contact me."

If he did, I might get more of a sense as to whether Oliver could be a killer. Or not. But if he wasn't—and assuming he was a good vet, since Arvie had made him an offer—I'd be doing my part on behalf of our pet hospital.

We said our goodbyes, and then Billi and I walked out to her car where the dogs happily greeted us. We slipped into our seats, but Billi didn't turn on the engine immediately.

"Are we waiting here till the cops get here?" I asked.

"You got it," Billi answered.

A marked car arrived just then, possibly responding quickly since the Civic Center, which included the police station as well as City Hall, wasn't far down the street.

Only after a couple of uniformed cops got out and walked up to the building's door did Billi drive off.

"Well, that was interesting," I said. "But I still have more questions than answers. I haven't been harassed by my usual detective buddies from the police department this time, but I'm thinking about paying them a visit to ostensibly give them some ideas about possible suspects—like Oliver."

"*Ostensibly* because you'll really go there to pick their brains?"

"You got it."

TWENTY-THREE

I REALIZED IT WAS impulsive, but I called Reed later that night when I was just about to go to bed. Neal was home, and he and I had chatted briefly before we'd both retired to our rooms, although he'd gone with Biscuit and me for a short final walk for that day.

I hadn't gotten into detail with Neal about my evening, but that didn't mean it wasn't on my mind. I still had questions about what Shea might have discussed with Raela that could help to solve her murder if he would tell the police about it. Did attorney-client privilege apply after the client's death? Shea would know the answer, but even if it wasn't still in effect, I supposed he might have other ethical reasons not to blab about their legal conversations.

Then there was Oliver—again at the site where he had discovered Raela's body, this time late at night after it had apparently been released as a crime scene. Pondering what to do next in his life was a potentially good reason for him to be there, although he could have been just clasping his hands in glee at what he'd done, if he'd had good reason, in his mind, to murder Raela.

I was confused and needed a friendly conversation before I would be able to sleep—or so I told myself. That was a good enough reason to call Reed, after all, though I had no news to impart that might help him sleep better, such as a certainty that I'd found Raela's killer. A possibility, yes, in Oliver, but I'd already been considering him, and other than the fact that he apparently liked hanging out at the murder scene, there was no new evidence I could hand over to the police.

Still... sitting up in bed, I pressed in the single digit number I'd programmed into my phone to call Reed.

He didn't answer on the first ring. Was he already asleep?

Was he with someone?

Okay, that just popped into my head even though I had no idea who else Reed might hang out with this late, except perhaps Jon. But my concern was that it was a woman, and—

"Carrie! Sorry, but I left my phone in my bedroom when I just walked Hugo. How are you? Where are you?"

He sounded interested, at least, and his excuse seemed rational. Heck, it wasn't really my business if he did have another woman there with him. We hadn't discussed being exclusive with one another, even though it felt to me like we were.

"I'm home," I said. "Just about to turn out the lights and get some sleep. But... well, Billi and I had an interesting evening. I don't want to get into it now, except to make you wonder, though I have no news for you." I didn't want to disclose my plan to visit the cops tomorrow either, but I hoped I would learn something from them that could wind up being useful... or not. "If you don't have other plans for tomorrow evening," I went on, "maybe we could at least go grab a drink together. Okay?"

I felt my teeth grit as I half expected a negative answer—but my grimace turned into a smile as Reed said, "Absolutely. I've been hoping to hear the latest update on your progress in solving the murder, since you're so good at such things. I assume you're still doing it, right?"

"You know me," I sang, as if I was in a really great mood.

"And you're being careful, not putting yourself in danger?"

"I'm trying," I said, recalling my concerns about joining Oliver inside the building that was the murder site.

"Keep trying. Be careful or forget the whole thing, damn it. I care about you, Carrie. I should never have even asked—"

"You didn't need to ask it," I said, feeling all warm inside again thanks to his attitude. "You know me well enough to recognize that I'd have jumped in anyway."

"Yeah," he said, in a tone that somehow sounded sexy over the phone. "I do. Anyhow, see you tomorrow."

"Yep, see you tomorrow." And after hanging up, I found myself relaxed enough to give Biscuit a final pat good night and soon fall asleep.

———

Another early morning wakeup, dog walk, and quick drive to the shops. More baking and welcoming my assistants, followed by greeting a nice abundance of customers.

And all the while I was thinking how to handle the outing I intended to engage in briefly that afternoon.

First, I needed to ensure that at least one of the people I wanted to speak with would be available. Consequently, during a lull in the Barkery around ten that morning, I called Detective Bridget Morana. I could have called her colleague Wayne Crunoll, but although both of them gave me a hard time about the cases I found myself involved in, I had the sense that Bridget was the more professional of the two.

Even though they were animal people, it didn't raise them up much in my estimation, since they seemed to have fun figuring out how to make each situation more difficult for me to look into.

To my surprise, Bridget not only answered her phone but said she would be able to spare a few minutes to talk to me around three that afternoon. Would that work for me?

"Oh, yes," I told her.

And so at two forty-five, I left Biscuit in the care of my assistants on duty—all four of them, since it was Saturday—and drove to the Knobcone Heights Civic Center. I fortunately found parking at a meter along the street; it was more expensive to pay for a space in the official lot. And then I hurried inside the police station, carrying a small bag of Barkery treats. I didn't anticipate seeing Wayne, but I figured it wouldn't hurt to leave him some munchies for his two dogs.

The large reception area was busy, which wasn't surprising. I went up to the tall front desk, where a young uniformed cop acted as receptionist. He nodded when I gave my name and said yes, I had an appointment with Detective Morana. Had she told him to expect me? Or was he just being pleasant? "I'll let her know you're here." He picked up the desk phone.

I turned to look for an empty seat in the crowded room and found one nearby, but before I could sit down, Bridget appeared at the side of the reception desk where, behind it, a door led into the station. She strolled up to me. "Hi, Carrie. Let's go inside."

Bridget was dressed professionally, as she always seemed to be while on duty, in a charcoal suit. She leveled her brown eyes at me in a bland expression, so I didn't hazard a guess about what she was thinking. Usually I got some sense of her mood, at least, by whether or not she raised her bushy eyebrows, which were about the same nondescript shade of brown as her short hair. Nothing like this today, at least not yet.

"Great," I said, just to be friendly, and followed her.

As she led me down the hall I saw more cops, in uniform. We soon reached the conference room where I'd been taken for other meetings here at the station. Bridget opened the door.

And I was confronted with my first surprise of the day. Wayne was in the room, apparently waiting for us. Maybe he wasn't even on duty, since he wore a bright blue shirt tucked into dark slacks. Or maybe he was heading somewhere undercover after this. How would I know?

"Hi, Carrie," he said with one of his traditional ironic grins. "Welcome. Do you have something to tell us?"

As I entered and took a seat at the table in the center of the room, I countered, "I came here to learn what you could tell me."

"Now that could be a problem," Bridget said. "We've gone through this before, but let me remind you—"

"You're the police," I broke in. "You have the authority to question civilians about things relating to open cases, as well as other things. But I'm just one of those civilians, even if I stick my nose into your cases. Am I right?"

"You got it." Bridget's return smile appeared anything but friendly.

"Well," I said, "I think we now have a kind of pattern established. I'll show you mine if you show me yours."

"You go first." Wayne leaned forward with his elbows on the table. Today he had a slight five o'clock shadow on his pudgy face. His dark hair was in its regular short cut. He looked like—well, a determined cop, since he didn't move his gaze from mine as I stared into his light brown eyes.

"No," I said, "you go first." I pursed my lips as if to show him a small degree of belligerence. Nothing threatening, of course. Not with cops. And not for no reason.

He laughed a bit, and even Bridget smiled grimly. "I assumed we'd have a standoff," Wayne began, "and so ... "

Then he drew his gaze away and looked behind me. I heard a noise and turned, too.

Police Chief Loretta Jonas was in the room. She closed the door behind her and walked toward me as I stood up.

"Hi," I said with a grin. "To what do I owe this honor?"

"I think you know."

As usual, Loretta was wearing her uniform, although today, at the station, she didn't wear her dark jacket with its many medals. Instead, she had on a beige button-down shirt. She was in her fifties, with a dark complexion and eyes. The first time I'd met her, I'd guessed that she dyed her medium brown hair, since it was all one shade with no highlights.

Loretta smiled and moved toward me, with her hand outstretched so we could shake.

I tended to like the chief—partly because she had an adorable schnauzer mix, Jellybean, whom she'd adopted from Mountaintop Rescue. Also, I considered her a skilled and dedicated police officer, or at least she mostly seemed that way to me.

Still, at this moment we appeared to be playing some kind of a game. I gestured toward the conference table and sat back down in the seat I'd taken before. All three cops joined me.

Then I began the conversation. "Okay, I figure you're all interested in what I may have found out so far about Dr. Raela Fellner's murder. Right?"

"And have you found out anything?" the chief responded smoothly. Unsurprisingly, she appeared to be in charge.

"Nothing, really, although I've developed some suspicions. How about you? Do you know yet who the perpetrator is?"

"We've developed some suspicions," Chief Loretta repeated with a smile. "How about if you tell us where you are so far? And before we go any further, I do want to incorporate some formalities. First, I want to remind you that, no matter what you may have done or thought in the past, you are not a member of our team in any way. You do understand that, I assume."

All three stared at me, as if waiting for my objection. But I said, "I've just been fortunate enough to be able to help you. I didn't set out to intrude in any of those prior murder investigations, and I certainly don't intend to here. But when friends of mine become suspects and I believe them innocent, I want to help them if I can."

The chief nodded. "I assume that's the situation this time, too."

"That's right. You're aware that I work at the Knobcone Veterinary Clinic part-time as a veterinary technician, and I gather that a person you believe to be a major suspect is Dr. Reed Storme, who works there, too. Correct?"

"Unlike you, we can't reveal who our suspects are." The chief's tone was no longer smooth but sharp, as if attempting to stab into me the reality of professional versus amateur.

Well, heck, I knew that. And clearly I was unlikely to learn anything helpful here, at least right now.

But I nevertheless could provide some information and suggestions that should, if they were smart, get these professionals to open their minds and let some other suspects in.

"Okay," I said. "I understand. But I probably shouldn't say any more either. I mean, I'm just a civilian, and if I start pointing fingers, accusing people as possible suspects, I might be liable to being sued for defamation, right? I don't think that can happen to you." I'd had some concerns about this before, too—but not enough to keep my nose out of those situations either.

"We just want your opinion, not accusations," Loretta said smoothly. "We'd need a lot more than you're likely to be able to suggest anyway. You can suspect, maybe even have an idea of what evidence might exist and where it might be, but you haven't the ability to go grab it. Tell you what. You tell us who you believe at this point to be guilty, and why, and we'll follow up in our professional capacity any leads that appear potentially legit."

In other words, things were different than before. They'd never liked my snooping, but since I'd actually figured out who the killer was in each of the prior cases, they'd come to respect me, at least somewhat.

"But you still won't let me know your opinions, or who you're zeroing in on, or anything like that?" I knew I sounded grumpy, but, hey, I was about to give them something for nothing. Yes, I'd decided to go along with what they said.

"We recognize you still don't know all the legalities," the chief said smoothly. "But we so much appreciate your help, Carrie. You're clearly one smart and interested civilian. And just remember how much pride you felt helping us figure out the killers before."

She was right about that, even though I had no interest in changing, or adding to, my current professions. But if I could help myself, and people I cared about, by being nosy—and now, letting the cops in on my suspicions—then what the heck?

"All right," I finally conceded. "I don't have anything at all definitive yet, but I can let you know where I've been and where I think I'm going."

I looked at the detectives, and the smug smiles on their faces only irritated me more.

"That's wonderful," the police chief responded, standing and taking my hands as if we were now good buddies. "I don't need to be here for this, but Detectives Morana and Crunoll will ask you questions, take notes, and record what you say—and then they'll report to me. Okay, everyone?"

After we agreed, Police Chief Loretta thanked me and left the room.

And there I was—again—with the detectives who'd been sometime thorns in my side ever since my first, unanticipated murder investigation.

"All right," I said with a sigh. "I can only hang around here a short while longer. This is what I've discovered so far."

TWENTY-FOUR

I STARTED OUT WHERE I wanted to, at least. I told them what they must already know I believed. No, what I felt sure about.

"I mentioned Reed Storme for a reason," I began. "You interviewed him along with a whole bunch of other employees at my veterinary clinic, and a lot of those people probably mentioned that Reed had argued with the murder victim. You're also probably aware that I'm dating Reed, so I have a reason to be biased. But even so, I know he didn't do it. Period." I glared from one detective to the other and back again, ignoring the amusement on their faces.

I wanted them to believe me, of course—but also realized they didn't.

Which gave me even more of a motivation to state my other suspicions and the reasons for them, so that the cops, too, would concentrate elsewhere. If they paid any attention to me, at least.

"Okay," Bridget said. "We understand. Now tell us more."

In other words, I figured, they heard me but didn't necessarily believe me—so if I wanted to protect Reed, I'd better point my fingers in a different direction and have some backup for it.

"Right now all I have are suspicions," I cautioned. "The person at the top of my list is Dr. Oliver Browning. I'm sure you know that Dr. Raela made him an offer to work at her new clinic as a veterinarian, but he was still deciding whether to accept this offer at the time when she was killed. I don't know how they got along, but Oliver was the one to find her body, or so he told everyone. I'm sure you're aware that, last night, he was back at the murder location, now that it isn't blocked with crime scene tape. I found him there and we wound up calling this department to keep an eye on the building, since Oliver said it was unlocked when he got there."

"And what do you believe his motive was?" Bridget asked.

"I have no idea whether or not they had some kind of relationship beyond the possibility of working together at her new clinic, but they definitely worked together at the San Diego clinic. They could have felt some animosity toward each other because of their work there, or maybe because Oliver apparently didn't just jump right in and accept Raela's employment offer, or—well, I can come up with other possibilities, too, but don't have an answer yet."

"Right. And some of those possibilities also could apply to Dr. Storme and the new vet at your clinic, Dr. Jon Arden." Wayne was speaking mildly, but his eyes were glued onto mine as if he was awaiting my reaction.

"True," I said, "especially where Jon is concerned. He's one of my suspects also, since there could have been some friction between them regarding her coming to town and opening a competing clinic, or about something I'm not aware of at all. But they did know each other."

"Right," Bridget said. "Anyone else?"

"Well, I haven't really eliminated anyone yet, but I'm not aware of everyone in Raela's life, let alone those who had grudges against her. One possibility is their boss from San Diego, Dr. Mickey Krohan. He's currently visiting here and has probably talked to you."

I was staring back at Wayne and thought I saw a hint of a nod, but of course he wasn't cutting me any slack.

"Okay," he said. "It does sound as if you've thought about this a lot. But we also know that you don't always focus on the most obvious suspects. Anyone else on your mind?"

"Everyone who knew Raela may have disliked her," I blurted out. "She wasn't a very nice person."

Wayne snorted as Bridget shot me a grim smile. "Maybe, maybe not. That's not helpful in finding her killer, though. Everyone she knew didn't come to town and off her."

"True," Wayne said. "So, like Detective Bridget said, who else are you focusing on?"

"I'm still pondering," I said.

"How about the other boss in question, Dr. Arvus Kline?" Bridget asked. "Have you talked to him about her?"

Wow. Even after what they'd said before, they actually named someone they were considering—someone I hadn't mentioned. And someone I wouldn't have mentioned, since I knew he couldn't have done it.

"Only in generalities," I replied cautiously, then decided to state my opinion. "Arvie might not have been thrilled about the new competition, if you could call it that. But we have a wonderful clinic and all pet owners around here know it. He had no motive to kill her." I glared from one detective to the other as if trying to etch that fact into their minds, but I had no idea if I'd succeeded.

Arvie might even have been their second most favorite suspect, after Reed.

"Okay, got it," Bridget responded after a drawn-out silence.

I wanted in the worst way to ask them again who they were looking at—besides those I'd mentioned, of course. Or even, among those, whether they favored Oliver or Jon or Mickey Krohan, since Reed and Arvie were innocent.

One thing seemed apparent to me, though. Considering that Raela was killed by a drug used for euthanasia in veterinary clinics, it wasn't farfetched to focus on people who worked in veterinary clinics.

Being one of them myself—though they hadn't indicated so far that they actually considered me a suspect—I chose not even to mention that.

I realized that a thought I'd had earlier might be appropriate to air, so I said, "I imagine you know that the attorney Shea Alderson had Raela as a client when she was putting together her veterinary clinic. She might have said something to him about someone she didn't like, or who was giving her a hard time or was otherwise arguing with her. I assume you've interviewed him, too?"

Once again they didn't exactly answer, but they traded glances. Did that mean they had spoken with Shea—or they hadn't? And were they considering him as a suspect? I was, though Shea seemed more of a potential information source.

"Anyway, he might have some ideas," I continued. "I talked with him a little and I gather he may be bound by attorney-client privilege, but the fact that he didn't talk to me doesn't mean he'd act the same way with authorities like you." Although if they'd gone that route already, they probably didn't want to waste their time.

Well, I'd told them all I had in mind, except… "Look," I said. "I'm not about to tell you how to conduct your interviews, but if you—"

"Good," Wayne interrupted. "That's as it should be."

"But," I continued, looking him straight in the face, "I'd imagine Raela met a lot of people in town in her attempt to start up her vet clinic. I don't know who they are, specifically. I don't know if she intended to hire any vet techs, for example, or if she'd spoken to any other kinds of assistants. And since a number of people have already come here from San Diego, maybe she left a bunch of enemies there who'd be willing to follow her here to get rid of her permanently. And—"

"Thank you, Carrie." This time Bridget interrupted. "We appreciate your suggestions."

"And I'd appreciate it if you could act on them," I continued, despite realizing she was attempting to end this meeting. "Just don't assume that the people on your radar at first are the most likely to be guilty." I paused. "That's how I wound up helping you before, you know. Your primary suspects were just that—but they weren't killers."

That had to be true this time, too—right? I was all but certain that Reed was innocent.

I was still really bothered by that "*all but* certain." And I recognized that it applied to Arvie, too.

At least I was done here for now. Although I wasn't sure that was a good thing.

We started saying our goodbyes, but as I reached the door I turned back to the detectives. "I know you're not going to share with me the way I did with you. I understand why and all that. But if there's anything at all you can share with me, I'd really, really appreciate it. And if anything occurs to me that I think I should share with you, I'll do it."

"Good. Thank you. Goodbye, Carrie." And Wayne showed me out the door.

As I walked to my car, I rehashed the whole meeting in my mind—ending with my promise to share. I at least liked how I'd qualified it.

I would share with them only what I thought I should. And considering how they wouldn't share with me at all, well, my additional sharing could also be … nothing.

———

My Saturday evening with Reed was pleasant. I caught him up on all I'd been doing, questions I'd been asking, what had gone on with Oliver and the detectives and more. We'd even gotten into who else I should put on my suspect list to report to the cops—which really amounted to no one.

He once more expressed concern about my safety, but still, again, didn't really ask me to stop nosing around in my attempt to help him.

We didn't spend the night together. I'd left Biscuit at home with Neal, and Reed had to get back to Hugo.

And our respective states of mind were definitely relationship-directed, but not especially romantic. Not with an official murder accusation and more potentially hanging over Reed's head.

The next day at the shops went well, as usual—at first, at least. Our crowd was always enhanced on the weekend, and Dinah had the day off, so my other three assistants and I kept busy.

I kept thinking that one of the detectives would call and ask more questions. I kept hoping they'd call and instead give me some possible answers, but I knew better than that.

But today was Sunday, after all. I figured the police probably weren't investigating today unless there was some imminent danger to someone that suddenly became apparent.

So there'd be no further communication with either detective, at least not today. I did communicate with Reed, but neither of us was enthused about getting together that evening.

At some other time, my feelings might have been hurt, but at the moment I felt as if I needed some space.

And maybe some additional time, to think about other suspects or related information that I could provide to the cops … and therefore potentially, at least, get a sense of how hard they were investigating, and whether anything I'd said had helped them decide to focus on others besides Reed.

Or not.

I learned that the answer must be yes when Oliver stormed into the Barkery that afternoon.

"What did you say to those damned detectives?" he asked through gritted teeth, after I'd led him away from the line of customers toward the quieter area near Biscuit's enclosure. Fury blazed from his hazel eyes, and he looked as if his already receding hairline was disappearing even more—from stress?

"What do you mean?" I asked.

"I got a call from the guy cop. He wants to schedule another meeting with me—another interrogation. He didn't explain why, but when I demanded a reason, he kind of laughingly said something like I should feel glad it'll be with actual authorities so I can clear myself if I'm innocent. Does that mean an amateur like you turned him back against me? Does it?"

He'd drawn closer, leaning over me enough that I heard Biscuit growl from inside her enclosure.

"I don't want to talk about this." I glared at him with my hands on my hips. "No matter what I say, you're clearly ready to argue. I think I'll

219

call the detectives myself now." I yanked my phone from my pocket and held my index finger against it, then looked back at Oliver.

"You had better not be accusing me again," he hissed, "especially to the cops." And then he stalked out.

My assistants were grouping around, apparently ready to protect me, but I told them all was well. I hoped I was telling the truth.

I closed the shops on time that night and was glad that Neal was home from work that evening. After eating a quick casserole I'd prepared and walking Biscuit, we settled in to watch TV. Fortunately there were some silly sitcoms on, but we also saw a show about—what else? Cops investigating murders, this time in New York.

Hugging Biscuit on my lap, I made myself watch till the bitter end, partly since I knew there would be a satisfying conclusion. That was fiction, after all, on a TV show with good ratings.

"You okay, sis?" Neal asked more than once. He knew I'd gone to see the cops yesterday and that I was concerned about the apparent non-results of this trip. And I'd briefly mentioned Oliver's visit to my stores, without saying how much I'd felt threatened by him.

"Sure," I said each time he asked, soothed somewhat by Biscuit's close presence and trying to act as if it was true.

In some ways, it was, after all. I was maintaining a somewhat cordial relationship with the detectives. They had acted as if they somewhat gave a damn about my thoughts and suggestions, or at least hadn't told me they considered me not only an interloper but a stupid one to boot.

And they had left the door open for me to contact them again if anything else occurred to me.

They had also apparently started following up on what we'd talked about. They had contacted Oliver and started pushing him harder.

It turned out he wasn't the only one. At bedtime, I received a call from Reed. He, like Oliver, wanted to know what I'd said to the cops. Both he and Jon had been told to come back to the station for further interviews in the next day or so.

I didn't gather that the cops had even hinted about my conversation with them this time. I decided I would most likely contact the cops again tomorrow, to let them know what Oliver had done.

But when I did contact them on Monday, that wouldn't be the only reason. No, it was because I was scared—really scared—and needed their help.

TWENTY-FIVE

THE DAY STARTED LIKE all the rest—again. As always, early in the morning, Biscuit and I got out of my old Toyota at the small parking lot to the rear of my shops. It was still dark outside, but the narrow alley, lined with similar parking areas behind stores, was lit by small streetlights.

When my leashed dog and I walked toward the building, I saw an envelope taped to the back door that led into the kitchen. My name was on it, printed by a computer, I supposed: *Carrie Kennersly*.

Strange. If it had been hanging there the previous night before I left, I would have noticed it when I checked to make sure the door was locked. Someone had apparently stuck it there late at night—and undoubtedly unobserved.

I consequently felt worried even before I opened the envelope, which I didn't do immediately. I pulled it off without unlocking the door, since I had to enter through the front of the Barkery with my pup. I let her take her time sniffing on the way, and all the while my mind churned about what was in the envelope.

Well, heck. It could just have been an invitation to a party, or someone placing an order for Barkery or Icing treats without having the time to stop in to do it—although they could always order online or even by phone. Or it could be … my imagination was running wild, and I tried to calm it.

We reached the street out front and, under the somewhat brighter light there, I opened the door to the Barkery—after staring all around in case I might see someone with a bag of envelopes sticking them onto all the neighboring businesses. Which I didn't.

Out of self-protection, I also gazed into as many corners of the street and buildings as I could, looking for any movement except for the occasional car driving by. Was someone out there waiting for me?

Not that I could see. But the envelope made me nervous. For no reason?

Once the door was open and Biscuit and I were inside, I locked it again behind us after flicking on the lights. I let Biscuit off her leash, allowing her as usual to be loose in the Barkery before we were open for business.

Then it was time. I put my purse down on the counter and used my index finger to slit open the envelope.

A piece of paper was folded inside, which wasn't a surprise. I opened it—and gasped.

The printing on it said, *Stop contacting the cops about Raela Fellner or your dog will suffer the consequences.*

I dropped the page onto the counter and knelt on the floor. Biscuit immediately rushed into my arms and I held her tightly, murmuring loving things to her.

Nothing, nothing, could happen to my baby.

But should I listen to the command I'd been given? Would obeying it mean Biscuit—and I—would remain safe?

Not likely. In fact, if I just accepted what it said without attempting to find out who'd taped it to the door or without letting the authorities know I'd been threatened—well, Biscuit had been threatened, and that was the same thing—then that person would assume they had won and perhaps would make more demands.

Or, if that person was the killer, they might believe there would be no consequences to their actions, even if I was closer to figuring out who the murderer was than the cops were. And if that wasn't the case, why threaten me?

So, I concluded, the killer had to be Oliver. Maybe. But Oliver was too obvious, and the most obvious suspects hadn't been the killers in my earlier investigations.

That didn't mean it wasn't true this time, though. And—

Okay. This was getting me nowhere. Still holding Biscuit, I ducked behind the counter, since we were bathed in light here, inside the store, while outside it was dark.

Anyone going by—or hanging around—would be able to see us.

But I wasn't going to let that person win. My life was going to remain normal, and so was Biscuit's.

I had to keep her in the Barkery, so I fastened her leash so she had to stay behind the counter, then checked to ensure the door was locked. I turned out the lights.

And then, despite the warning on that horrible note as well as the early hour, I tried calling Bridget, then Wayne. But in both cases I only got the standard recording asking me to leave a message, which I didn't. And to be really brazen, I also tried Chief Loretta, but the result wasn't any different there.

So for now, I went into the kitchen, but I left the door just a bit ajar so I'd hear anything happening in the Barkery.

I washed my hands thoroughly, as I had to, wishing I could do the same to my mind, purging it of my thoughts and fears. And then after taking another peek inside the Barkery to ensure that Biscuit was there, lying comfortably behind the counter and secured so she couldn't run around—or, hopefully, be harmed—I got started baking Barkery dog treats.

But I stopped frequently to check on Biscuit. And when Frida came in to help with the early baking of the day, I felt highly relieved.

"Is something wrong, Carrie?" she asked almost immediately.

Despite Frida being a wonderful cook, I wasn't as close to her as, say, to Janelle or Dinah. I really liked Vicky and Frida, but I didn't feel as obligated to reveal everything to them, unless their safety became an issue, too.

Today, Frida wore a loose brown *Icing on the Cake* T-shirt over beige slacks, and her brown hair was pulled back into a pony tail as always. Her plumpness seemed to indicate that she appreciated the human bakery goods and other delicacies she created. She was kind, smart, and astute, and she'd know I was lying if I said all was well. So instead I just said, "I've got some things going on that are worrisome, but I'm fine. Thanks for asking, though."

I guessed Frida knew me well enough not to press for answers, but I did catch her looking at me more often than usual, as if attempting to read inside my head what my worrisome thoughts were.

Time passed more slowly than I would have liked, since I was waiting for it to be late enough in the day to actually reach one of the people I wanted to talk to—primarily, one of the detectives.

At seven o'clock, Janelle showed up and I opened the shops. She was stationed first in the Barkery, and without explaining why, I told her to keep a close watch on Biscuit and make sure no customers got too close to her. I popped in and out of the Barkery a lot, too, despite still finishing the early baking.

And then at eight, I again tried to contact the detectives, this time while in my office at the back of the kitchen, wishing I could bring Biscuit in with me. I'd have no privacy if I called from the shops, and I would worry about Biscuit's safety if I went outside with my dog.

I was really relieved when Wayne answered the call. I told him what I'd found on my shops' back door.

"Biscuit and I can come right away to the station to show it to you, and maybe you can have it tested for fingerprints. I'll tell you my suspicions about it, too." I would let him know about Oliver's rant yesterday, since, oh yes, Oliver was now not only at the head of my suspect list but was ripping the top off it. He clearly wanted me to stop looking into who killed Raela.

Assuming it was Oliver who'd left the note—and I was, indeed, assuming that.

"Umm—well, I understand your concern, but I have to leave in a minute."

"How about Detective Morana?" I asked.

"She's out on a case right now. But, look, why don't you plan on coming in this afternoon? I'll call you when I return, and then you can come in and we'll talk."

This afternoon. My heart was already beating fast out of fear for my dog. Would it last that long?

Of course it would. And at least I had a plan started—kind of.

"Okay," I said. "I'll wait for your call."

And figured unhappily that I'd be waiting for a while.

Not that I just sat around staring at my phone. But I did spend most of my time in the Barkery with Biscuit.

Would whoever left that note know somehow that I'd dared to defy it and called the police? I couldn't take that chance, even though attempting to get quick official help hadn't worked so far.

And I realized that even if the officials looked into it, and checked the note for fingerprints, that might not provide answers—and it wouldn't help that I'd touched that note myself while opening it. But at least I hadn't touched it a lot.

Fortunately, the stores were busy. Or unfortunately, in some ways, since I was even more concerned about security and ensuring that no one could get too near Biscuit, even people I knew. *Especially* people I knew. What if I was completely wrong about the suspects in Raela's killing and just the fact that I'd dared to make suggestions to the authorities had riled the actual murderer?

I kind of wished that Dinah was working that morning so I could talk part of the situation over with her as "research." I didn't really want to discuss it with my other assistants. Even so, Janelle knew the general situation, thanks to her relationship with Neal and some of our mutual conversations … and because I'd once helped her when she was a murder suspect. She was a wonderful asset, not only in the shops but to help bolster my mood.

In fact, she'd taken me aside as soon as I'd returned from my office after my brief phone discussion with Wayne. I must have looked as dejected and fearful as I felt despite my attempt to put on a happy face, even as we stood near Biscuit's enclosure.

"What's wrong?" Janelle had asked.

"Nothing," I'd responded.

"Well, whenever you want to talk about *nothing*, be sure to let me know. Meantime, just remember I'm here for you. If there's something you want me to do, or if you need to leave, just let me know and I'll help in any way I can. And if you'd like me to bring Go in to keep

Biscuit company, be sure to tell me." Go, or Goliath, was her beautiful purebred Labrador retriever, and he and Biscuit were good buddies. Janelle brought him in now and then when she was at work.

I thought about asking Janelle to take some particularly great photographs of Biscuit if she had some extra time—and then I quickly erased that from my mind. It felt too much like conceding it was possible that I'd lose my sweet girl to the horrible threat in the note.

That wasn't going to happen.

So I thanked her and hugged her and said all was fine. And then, for the rest of the morning, I made myself act as if that was the truth.

It worked just fine until Dr. Mickey Krohan came in. I was waiting on a customer in the Barkery, ringing up an order on our register, when I saw him enter and look around.

What was he doing here? Just shopping, probably. Even so, I almost shuddered when his eyes caught mine and he nodded in greeting. He walked all around the Barkery, past the partially occupied tables on the tile floor, past Biscuit's enclosure, which made me quiver all the more, and then to the counter where I stood. He went past me and stared into our refrigerated treat case, and that seemed to grab his attention for a while.

Fortunately, Janelle was in there with me. Once again, I sensed that she read my mood, but since she was busy with a family and their Yorkie, she only glanced at me now and then.

When I was done with my customer, I approached Krohan. Was this just a friendly visit or an opportunity to check out my shop, and me ... and Biscuit?

"Hi, Dr. Krohan," I said to him. "Welcome to Barkery and Biscuits." At the moment, I had no reason to be unfriendly to him except for my suspicions about everyone, particularly those who'd come from his San Diego clinic. Except Reed, of course ... maybe.

"Thanks." Krohan looked somewhat formal in his white shirt and dark pants. His light brown beard, the same shade as his short hair, appeared to have been shaved to appear barely there. "I've finally made my way here to check out your dog bakery. Can you tell me anything about your treats and how you developed them—and their ingredients?"

I laughed a little. "That could take a long time. But you can be sure that everything is derived from my job as a veterinary technician. I've learned what ingredients are healthy, and which are considered best for different kinds of canine medical issues, and so forth."

I did point out a few of the treats I'd developed that were not only my favorites but seemed to sell best, including some with carob, others with peanut butter, yams, pumpkin, and liver, in different combinations.

"Excellent," he finally said. "I have a couple of dogs at home, so when I'm ready to leave town, I'll come back here first and buy a selection of your goods. And I'm hoping to return to Knobcone Heights soon."

Really? That sounded odd. "That's nice," I said, not really meaning it. Despite his explanation about coming to town because he needed to find out what had happened to Raela, I still thought it just as likely that he'd come here because the local authorities had requested it.

"If my dogs and I like your products, I may be able to recommend that other people in the area buy some as well." The look in his brown eyes beneath his glasses appeared challenging, as if he wanted me to ask some questions.

Well, what the heck. I had some questions myself. "I take it you'll remain in touch with your former employees who'll now be working here, is that it?"

"Yes, and more. I'm thinking about taking over the clinic Raela tried to start here, as an adjunct to my existing vet practice. It's a good location, lots of potential patients whose owners are … well, let's just say they can afford our services. And the fact that there's already competition? I think there's room for both of us. Don't you?"

I tried to act friendly, in case I could learn something from him about Raela. "Well, as you can imagine, I'm ambivalent. I've been working as a vet tech at the Knobcone Veterinary Clinic for quite a while, although I'm part-time there now. I don't like the idea of competition for it. But if your practice would bring more customers here to buy from the Barkery for their dogs, or from Icing on the Cake for themselves, I'd certainly like that."

"Of course. Well, I haven't made a decision about it yet. For one thing, I most certainly don't like the idea that my former employee was murdered in this town. Or that the authorities questioned me as if I could have had something to do with it, though I can prove I was at home when she was killed."

If that was true, I could stop considering him a suspect—maybe.

I decided to remain cordial, just in case I did have to form some kind of business relationship with him.

Dr. Krohan left a short while later, and after a quick stop in Icing to make sure all was well there, I took Biscuit outside for a walk in the busy town square across the street—looking around very carefully, keeping her close beside me on her leash, and recognizing that the visit from Krohan, though interesting, hadn't done anything to make me worry less about my dog.

In fact, I worried even a little more, since it was possible his story had been just that—a story. Fiction to help throw me off my suspicions of him regarding who had killed his former employee and subsequently threatened my dog.

Biscuit and I returned quickly, and I sat and hugged her for a short while before getting back to waiting on customers in the Barkery.

And then I realized it was now somewhat late in the day—and I still hadn't heard back from Detective Wayne Crunoll.

So, around three o'clock, I called him again. He answered right away. "Okay, Carrie. You can come in now, but I'll only have a few minutes to spend with you."

That was better than nothing. And maybe someone around the station who worked in forensics would be able to grab fingerprints off the note or envelope.

"We'll be right there," I told him before he could change his mind.

TWENTY-SIX

"You're pretty brave," Wayne said as I sat in his office with Biscuit on my lap. White shirt, dark pants, and snide grimace—he wore what I sadly expected of him on a day he'd only reluctantly agreed to see me. "Or you love that little dog of yours less than I thought."

"No!" I shouted, then half expected a flood of uniformed cops to rush in to protect him. "No," I repeated more softly, glad we were still alone. "Just the opposite, on both counts. That's why I'm here. I need the police to help—to catch whoever left that note on my door. You surely understand. I know you care about your dogs." He brought "his wife's" dachshund mixes to my shops for treats often enough that I knew they were important to him.

"Yeah, they're okay. But you're not here to talk about them."

"You're right—and you know exactly why I'm here."

"Oh, yeah. To show off your plastic gloves."

Darn him. Why was he being so sarcastic?

Yes, I had worn plastic gloves to the station. I kept them around my shops to knead dough sometimes. And now I'd used them to handle the note and envelope, and even then I only touched the edges.

I didn't know whether the cops could get fingerprints off any of it, but if they could, most should belong to whoever had left the note.

I'd even handed Wayne a pair of those gloves to put on when I'd first handed him the message. At least, despite his attitude, he was careful in handling the note and envelope, gloves on, and he'd turned them over right away to a guy he'd called in from the KHPD forensics team.

Would they find prints? I didn't feel too confident about it. Whoever had done in Raela was probably fairly smart—or at least I couldn't assume otherwise. After all, whoever it was hadn't been caught yet... and might be a veterinarian. And most vets, of course, were intelligent.

"So who do you think left you the note?" At last, Wayne asked a logical, cop-like question.

"I don't know," I said. "Clearly someone who knew I'd been in touch with your department. Someone who figures I might have suggested them to you as a suspect in Raela Fellner's murder."

"There are several of those," he said dryly.

"Right." I hesitated. I'd brought up Oliver Browning before, so I added, "Look, Oliver confronted me the other day in my store because you'd been grilling him, so he's my first choice right now as a suspect. And he indicated he'd get back at me if I mentioned him to you, so please don't tell him. But I don't know for sure if he left the note, or if he's the killer, and neither do you. Is there anything you can do to hurry your investigation along and arrest the killer, whoever it is, before they find out I'm talking to you again?" Of course, I knew the answer to that. And since I was at the station, the killer might already know.

233

There was a knock on the door. When it opened, the forensics guy stood there. "Sorry, but the documents held no fingerprints except a few of Ms. Kennersly's." He looked at Wayne, then at me.

Surprise, surprise. I'd told them about the likelihood of some of my prints being there from when I'd opened the note.

The two men then talked briefly about the examination of those. The forensics guy had taken samples of my prints when he took the note. It all sounded okay to me, but I wished the results were different. They told me they would hold on to the note and envelope since these papers could wind up being evidence in the murder case. Or not.

When the forensics guy left, Wayne rose. "Sorry we don't have answers for you, Carrie—not regarding the murder and not regarding that threat to your dog." He actually sounded sorry this time, or at least his tone was gentler. "You know, we've told you before that we can't encourage an amateur like you to continue snooping into our cases, and now maybe you've been given a good reason to back away from this one."

For a fleeting moment, I wondered if Wayne could have left that note just to get me to stand down.

No, that had to be too cruel even for him. And this time, he and his fellow cops had acted less angry with me for looking into a murder. Maybe since I'd helped them find the culprits in the past.

"You're right," I said. "And I know you've been working hard on your investigation. But—well, what will you do to try to find the person who left the note?"

He just looked at me, wryness back on his face. "What do you think we'll do?"

"Very little," I responded, holding back the emotions that had suddenly leapt once more to the forefront of my mind: Frustration.

Irritation. Fear. And more than a bit of anger. This time it wasn't me who was in danger, but my dog—and the cops weren't jumping in any harder to help her. "I know you're busy and all. But you do realize, don't you, that looking into this might yield the actual killer?"

"Or it could result in whoever it is actually harming your dog," he reminded me—not that I'd forgotten that even for a moment.

"Which is why you should hurry, but—well, if you could also be discreet—"

"I've got a meeting coming up in about three minutes, Carrie," Wayne said. "And you're on your own with this, at least for now. Keep your dog safe. Although if you do happen to confirm who wrote it, let me know. If it's someone we're not already checking out thoroughly, we'll look into them more, and as a person of interest in the murder, too."

With that, he ushered Biscuit and me to the door of his office.

I stood in the reception area of the police station a minute later just trying to catch my breath—and looking around suspiciously at everyone who was there, to see who was looking at us.

I knew a few of them—cops and civilians—mostly from my shops. But none of my murder suspects were there.

Yet, would word get out to … whoever it was … and let them know I had disobeyed their instructions and showed up at the police station?

How could I protect Biscuit—and myself?

Dejected, I started to walk out. That was when Oliver entered the reception room from another hallway, followed by Bridget.

He'd been at the station, too? Maybe they were conducting the new interrogation Oliver had mentioned yesterday.

Had he become their main suspect?

And had he dared to threaten my sweet dog, who now was sitting at my feet?

Oliver stopped. Glared at me. Stomped across the room to stare down and point a long, accusatory finger at me. "Are you making false accusations again, Carrie? You'd better stop, or I'll make sure you do."

A threat—from the killer? From the person who had threatened Biscuit? Both?

"Just stay away from us, Oliver," I told him. "If you don't, I'll—"

"You'll be seeing me again," he spat back. "Count on it. Today. Or tomorrow. Or both … and often." And with that, he stomped out of the station as I stared at his back … and shuddered.

———

I tried ducking back into Wayne's office before leaving to tell him about this latest threat, but he wasn't there. Nor was Bridget, and she had apparently been the one questioning Oliver that afternoon.

I did manage, however, to get the receptionist to tell Chief Loretta that I needed to see her. To my surprise, she quickly appeared in the reception area and motioned for me to join her, which Biscuit and I did.

In a somewhat quiet corner away from the crowd, I told her what had happened. She was already aware of the threat against Biscuit, and she stooped to give my dog a quick pat.

"This is to go no farther than us. For your information, I granted a quick interview to Silas Perring of KnobTV this morning, which will undoubtedly appear on the news, but I didn't know of this latest threat against your dog. Right now, we're still checking into all leads but we aren't yet prepared to arrest anyone in Dr. Fellner's murder."

"I understand," I said, "but Oliver Browning just threatened me right to my face again, here in the police station. Surely you can do something about that. About him. That doesn't necessarily mean he's the killer, but—"

"Best I can say right now is that you should stay away from him. And don't make any accusations you can't prove. If you come up with any proof, of course—any evidence against Dr. Browning or anyone else—then come to us with it. Don't confront him."

"And don't tell him to stop making threats?"

"Do you have any proof he's the one who left that note against your dog?" The chief looked at me with her head cocked a little, which made me think she was just humoring me.

"No, but he personally threatened me right here, as I just told you."

"Did anyone hear it?"

"Probably. You can ask your officers who were around, and other people in the reception area."

But the chief slowly shook her head. "Sorry, Carrie. I have some business to attend to right now. If you want to ask around, go ahead." She headed back toward the hallway where her office was located.

I did ask a few people, including the officer behind the desk, if they'd heard Oliver's threats. No one admitted it, despite the expressions on their faces indicating they weren't telling the truth.

Because they simply didn't want to get involved? Maybe.

But I already was involved. I wanted to find the killer. And even more, I wanted to find out who'd threatened Biscuit.

What was I going to do?

Well, for one thing, Biscuit and I had hung around the police station long enough. I was glad I'd driven there, since it was easier to watch for anyone attempting to get close to us as we headed back

237

to my shops. Fortunately, I saw no danger—not even a hint that Oliver or anyone else I suspected was following us.

Nor did I see anything unusual as I parked behind the shops, then walked around to the front slowly enough for Biscuit to do what she needed to do before I put her in her enclosure in the Barkery.

I decided then that I'd be careful and concerned, sure. But I had to continue with my life—and ensure that Biscuit also continued with hers.

Even so, I needed some friendly faces and ears—so, standing on the sidewalk in front of my shops, I called Reed.

He didn't answer, though. He probably was busy with a patient at the clinic, and that was fine.

I went inside, and was waved at by Vicky. She was fortunately busy with customers. But seeing a hard-working assistant reminded me of the one who liked to write, Dinah, and I got an idea. Maybe there *was* something I could do to protect Biscuit and myself, particularly if I was correct in my suspicions about Oliver and perhaps Mickey.

After settling Biscuit in her enclosure, I approached Vicky and asked her to keep a close watch on Biscuit. She didn't ask why but immediately agreed and drew closer to my beloved pup. Then I hurried into the kitchen and back to my office, where I made a phone call and set up an appointment for tomorrow.

That was when Reed called back—a good thing. "Are you all right?" he demanded.

"Sure," I said, sort of meaning it. "How's the clinic today?" I wanted everything to be perfect there, particularly for the patients.

We talked for a couple of minutes about the animals he'd seen that day.

Then Reed asked, "Can we get together tonight?"

"Why do you think I called?" I replied.

We made arrangements that he'd pick up Hugo and bring him to my house. To keep things simple, he insisted that I just order pizza.

Good. I didn't have to go shopping, nor would I be out in public worrying about Biscuit. "Fine," I said. "See you later."

TWENTY-SEVEN

I soon became even more glad that we'd decided to stay at my house for dinner that night.

First, even though Neal realized I'd be there with Reed, he didn't ask if I wanted him to hang out with Janelle at her place. Instead, he announced that he and Janelle would join us for dinner.

He wanted some answers.

In fact, shortly after I arrived home but before Reed got there, Neal brought Janelle over and they both began bombarding me with questions. Janelle had recognized how upset I'd been at the shops even though I hadn't told her about the note, and she had alerted Neal. Now they both wanted to know what was going on.

I decided to tell them—for Biscuit's sake. And theirs. If whoever it was tried to do something horrible to my dog, I might not be the closest human around at the time. They needed to know—to protect themselves as well as Biscuit.

And so we all—including Biscuit and Janelle's dog Go—sat down in the living room. The humans all had glasses of beer. I'd avoided saying anything of import until then, but as I was about to start explaining, the doorbell rang. Biscuit and Go barked and ran toward the front door, and I dashed after them, picking Biscuit up and looking out the peephole before opening it.

Of course, I wasn't surprised to see Reed with Hugo there. I hadn't ordered the pizza yet—and I doubted whoever had threatened Biscuit, even if they knew where we lived, would be polite enough to ring the bell. I opened the door. "Come in."

As the dogs all traded sniffs, I glanced past Reed's back before he came in. Then we engaged in a brief kiss—after I'd closed and locked the door again.

I motioned for Reed to follow me into the kitchen, where I got him a beer and we waited for the dogs to take a few laps out of the water bowl. Then we joined the others in the living room.

That's when I asked what everyone wanted on their pizza. After we reached agreement—cheese, pepperoni, and green peppers—I phoned the order in to the town's closest shop.

Then I sat down again. I didn't really want to tell them anything, because I was afraid it would make the threat seem even more real. But I'd already looked the threat in the face, and then ridiculed and ignored it by telling the cops, which was exactly what I was warned not to do.

And so, sitting at the edge of the sofa and looking from one to the other of the people that I felt closest to, I told them about the note—and my fear for my beloved dog.

"What!" Janelle exclaimed. She plunked her beer glass down on the table beside the sofa and sank onto the floor, where all three dogs joined her. She hugged them, especially Biscuit, and that brought tears to my eyes.

The men reacted less emotionally, although I could see the anger and concern on their faces.

"No one can mess with my Bug," Neal growled. "What are we going to do about this?"

"I've already done something I probably shouldn't," I admitted, scrunching my shoulders. "I immediately went against what the note said and dropped in at the police station to let the detectives know, and to see if they could get any fingerprints off the paper—but they only got mine."

"You what?" Reed, who'd moved against me on the sofa as if in support during my revelation, now stood and glared at me.

I didn't need that, although I understood.

"I guess," I said somewhat humbly, "that I just refused to let whoever it was intimidate me. I'll do everything to ensure that Biscuit is okay, of course."

"What are the cops doing?" Reed pressed.

I gave a big sigh and drooped my head. "Not a damned thing."

Reed wasn't giving up, although he resumed his seat beside me. "Then we'd better—"

"Let me tell you everything," I interrupted, and described, blow by blow, my trip to the police station, including Oliver and his confrontation. And yes, I briefly mentioned Oliver's confrontation the day before, too.

"Okay." Reed placed his arm around me and drew me against him. "I was wrong. Very wrong. I encouraged you to investigate this time, since I'm a suspect. But I shouldn't have, even with your perfect track record in solving murders. Get out of it now, Carrie. And let all your friends know you've stopped. Somewhere along the line Raela's killer—and I'm still hopeful it's not Oliver—will learn about this, and hopefully he'll think he's won and leave both you and Biscuit alone."

"I'd like to believe that," I said. "And maybe I will let word get out that I've decided now to stay far, far away from the situation. Even if I don't."

"You've got to," Janelle said. "For Biscuit's sake." She was back on the sofa now, regarding me earnestly with her soft blue eyes. She probably was right.

But if I appeared to back out now, and let the world know, would that guarantee that whoever it was would stay far away from me—and Biscuit?

I knew better.

The pizza was delivered as we continued to talk. I put the boxes on the kitchen counter and we each served ourselves, placing plates with our pizza slices, and more beer, on the kitchen table.

I didn't eat much, and I ate quietly. I let the others discuss the situation and possible alternatives and suspects—and I noticed that neither Neal nor Janelle suggested Reed could even be a suspect, let alone guilty.

Eventually, we were done eating. After cleaning up, we adjourned again into the living room, where we turned on some news, but not for long. It was late enough that we soon talked about going to bed—here. All four of us.

First, though, the whole group went on an outing, We walked Biscuit, Go, and Hugo, everyone staying close together, including the dogs. Everyone was on heightened alert.

I saw nothing unusual on my street, and apparently neither did anyone else.

Reed stayed the night in my room, with Hugo and Biscuit on the floor. Neal and Janelle stayed together in his room, with Go joining them.

Reed and I engaged in nothing sexual, partly because we weren't alone in the house, I supposed. But it was also because, at least on my part, I wasn't feeling that way at all.

Being held close by Reed, sharing strokes and occasional kisses—well, that certainly helped me get through the night. And I hoped that someday soon, all of this would be behind us, Biscuit would be healthy, and a suspicion-free Reed and I would be able to resume our relationship as it had been heading before, including the physical part.

Boy, did I hope...

———

Reed woke up along with me early in the morning, and he and Hugo accompanied Biscuit and me outside. Again, carefully. Go stayed inside with Neal and Janelle.

A short while later, I was glad to see I was being followed as I drove to my shops. Reed was there to ensure that Biscuit and I got in okay.

I'd invited him to join me briefly at the shops before he took Hugo home and headed for the clinic, and I quickly made a pot of coffee. There were enough somewhat-fresh leftovers in the Icing display case that I was able to share scones with him, and we sat at one of the tables on the Barkery's tile floor, with the lights dimmed and the dogs confined in their usual spot on the far side.

"So what are you going to do today?" Reed asked almost immediately as we sat down with our light breakfasts. "And how are you going to start letting people know you're through with your latest murder investigation?"

He looked at me as if my doing this was a done deal, and I didn't glare back or argue. Instead, I sort of went along with what he said.

I hadn't told him yet about the appointment I'd made for this afternoon. But, heck, it was a self-protective measure. Plus, it was somewhat compatible with what he was demanding I do.

"I'm consulting a lawyer," I said. "Shea Alderson, in fact. I consider Oliver's verbal attacks on me here and at the police station to be threats, and I believe he could have been the one who threatened Biscuit, too. And maybe killed Raela, though I won't get into that with Shea. Since the police haven't given me any assurance that they'll try to protect me, let alone Biscuit, I want to find out what options I have to do it on my own."

"I'm really sorry Oliver is acting so miserably toward you." Reed's grip on his coffee mug tightened. "He might be at the clinic today to talk to Arvie. I'll talk to him."

I couldn't argue with that. Those two knew each other from before, and Oliver's initial presence in Knobcone Heights, at least, was thanks to Reed.

"Okay," I said. "Just—well, in case he *is* the killer, please be careful."

"I will. And you do the same. It'll be interesting to hear if there is some kind of legal action that can be taken to at least quiet him down, even if he's just reacting to the way the investigation's going and the suspicions against him—yours and any official ones."

"Let me know what he says," I responded. "That might make a difference in what I decide."

"I'd hate to see a lawsuit against Oliver on top of everything else," Reed said, "especially since I feel somewhat responsible for his being here. But if he's the one causing all this—well, he'll deserve that and more."

I couldn't argue with that, either.

And the fact that later today I'd be talking to someone else I somewhat considered a suspect?

Well, my list of potential suspects kept growing. But no matter what, Oliver remained at the very top. I needed advice on how to stop him. Fast.

———

Wouldn't you know it? Things were a bit slow at both shops that day, which gave me too much time to think.

And to worry about Biscuit—not that I'd stopped worrying about her for a second, but I was focusing even more on my fears for her than I had the day before, if that was possible.

Was Oliver the one who'd threatened her? Would I get any legal advice from Shea that would be helpful enough to keep Oliver—or whoever the note-writer really was—from harassing or harming me?

I had to. I couldn't keep going like this.

Janelle knew what was on my mind. She was helping out mostly in Icing that day, and she kept checking on me if I wasn't in the same shop as her, which I considered particularly sweet.

I was glad she and Neal were an item.

She had brought Go to work, too, so Biscuit wasn't alone.

Dinah kept pressing me to tell her what was on my mind—and she made it clear it wasn't because she was conducting any kind of research. She was worried about me, which I appreciated.

And her concern, plus Janelle's, caused Vicky, who was there that day working on our scheduling, to be concerned.

I reassured them all. Focused on baking and talking with the customers who did come in.

Took Biscuit for brief walks, and Janelle came along with Go.

Went to Cuppa's, both for a quick cup of coffee and to see my dear pseudo parents. I didn't tell the Joes what was going on, but since of course I'd brought Biscuit—watching all around us, both ways—she got an opportunity to see Sweetie.

And, after returning to the shops, was glad to see the time eventually roll around to the hour when I could finally head to Shea Alderson's office.

TWENTY-EIGHT

BISCUIT AND I DROVE there, even though it was within walking distance of my shops.

Shea's office was in one of the quaint, aging, and elongated Art Deco buildings that matched the Knobcone Heights Civic Center. I knew that some city council members, including Les Ethman, had individual offices in this building, and Billi had an office there that she shared with a few other representatives. It was a good meeting place for council members when they didn't want to be bothered with finding an open conference room, especially since it was only a block or so away from the Civic Center.

Interesting that as a newcomer to town, Shea had chosen this location. The other attorney I knew in the area, Ted Culbert, had an office on the other side of town, nearer to the lake and the Knobcone Heights Resort—another upscale location.

I realized that I'd actually left my shops earlier than I needed to, so after finding parking—at a meter along the street—I decided to peek into Les's office to say a brief hello and take up a little bit of time.

I wasn't certain whether dogs were permitted in the Civic Center or the buildings around it, but I also wasn't about to ask. I simply walked up the stone steps to the entrance with Biscuit leashed beside me, as if I knew exactly where I was going and had done it before.

Fortunately, no one questioned me. And once inside, since it was a general office building rather than an actual government locale, I didn't have to check in anywhere, even though I did see some men in suits patrolling, who might have been security.

I scanned the directory in the lobby and learned that Les's and Shea's offices were both on the third floor. I got onto the elevator with Biscuit and we were joined by several other people.

A few made a fuss over Biscuit, and no one gave us a hard time. Neither did anyone seem threatening, which remained my major concern. But since I didn't see people I recognized, anything going awry here didn't seem likely.

Most of us got off at the third floor. After glancing around, I recognized that both of the offices I was going to were to the right, so I headed that way. Les's number came up first, which was handy. Since it was during regular business hours, I opened the door and we walked in.

There was a desk in the room where I assumed a secretary might sit, although no one was in there. A door behind it probably led to Les's office. This one I felt more reluctant about just opening, so I went up to it and knocked.

"Come in," called the somewhat high, elderly voice I recognized as Les's.

I opened the door and Biscuit and I entered. The room was larger than the reception area, and Les sat behind a desk that looked just as I suspected one belonging to him would look: antique, polished, nearly empty of everything but a desktop computer and a few neat piles of paper. He sat behind it in a high-backed chair, but rose as we came in.

I really liked Les. He was always friendly, always on top of what was going on in Knobcone Heights. And he'd remained kind to me even when I'd been suspected of killing his brother's daughter-in-law—which I hadn't, of course.

He wore a light blue shirt and a huge smile. We approached each other and engaged in a warm hug. "Carrie! What are you doing here?" he exclaimed.

I didn't want to get into the particulars with Les, although I could have gained his sympathy if I'd mentioned my concerns about Biscuit. But I only had a couple of minutes before my appointment with Shea, and I didn't want to get into the scary situation just then.

"I've got an appointment with someone in the building," I told him. "I need to head there pretty quickly, but hoped I'd have a chance to say hi to you here." As Les bent to give Biscuit a pat on the head, I asked, "How's Sam?" That was his adorable bulldog.

"Fine, but I'll bet he'll really grumble when I tell him you brought Biscuit here. As you know, I generally leave him at home during working hours, although he gets plenty of attention from my housekeeper."

"I'll bet."

I was glad I'd come, even though we had to end our conversation a few minutes later.

"So when are we going to meet for dinner at the resort?" he asked when I started to say goodbye. Of course it would be at the resort, since his family owned the place.

"Soon," I assured him. "I'll give you a call, or you can call me anytime."

"Or text," he said. "That's what everyone does now, even more than emailing."

I laughed. "Okay, text me anytime."

Biscuit and I started to leave, and Les stood and followed. "I need to leave this door open," he said, pulling it open like an old-fashioned gentleman. "My assistant's running errands and I always like to make sure I know when someone comes into the office."

"Sorry," I said. "I hope I didn't startle you."

"No—and even if you had, there aren't many people I'd like to be startled by as much as you, Carrie. And Biscuit, too."

I laughed, and my dog and I exited the outer door.

Shea's office was near the end of the hall. Since he was relatively new to town, I wondered how he'd even gotten an office in this prestigious building, let alone one in such a good location. Probably just good luck in the timing, I figured—perhaps he was seeking an office when someone had just moved out.

When Biscuit and I reached the door with his number and name on the outside, I once more just walked in. As with Les's office, there was an outer room with a desk set up for a secretary or, in Shea's case, maybe a paralegal. But as before, the room was empty. Did Shea have any help? I wasn't sure, especially since the door at the rear, presumably to his actual office, was open.

Biscuit and I approached it, and I drew in my breath as Shea suddenly appeared in the door's center, startling me a little.

I had wondered, previously, what he would look like in a suit, and now I knew. He looked good in it, but then I already considered Shea a good-looking guy, and apparently Billi did, too.

"Carrie, come in," he said. "And you brought Biscuit."

"Yes. Mainly because she's part of what I need to talk to you about. I assume that Buffer and Earl aren't here, right?"

Shea laughed. "Right. It's professional and appropriate for you to have your dog at your work, but that's not such a good idea for a lawyer. Here, have a seat." He gestured toward a couple of chairs facing a desk in the middle of the room. His desk was newer yet more worn-looking than Les's, and there were plenty of piles of papers and file folders on it.

I sat where he'd pointed, and Biscuit took her place, as always, at my side on the floor.

"So what can I help you with? We can just talk in generalities now, but if you decide to hire me we'll need to go through some formalities."

"Right," I said. I assumed that would establish attorney-client privilege. Did I care about establishing that kind of lawyer-client relationship with Shea? Possibly, if the best way to get Oliver to back off would be to sue him, or at least threaten him with a civil suit since the cops weren't going to arrest him.

I'd decided that initially, I'd just ask Shea a few general questions—only enough to determine if I needed to go further and have him represent me. For now, I was just paying for his time and potential suggestions, not necessarily his loyalty.

"Someone has threatened Biscuit," I began. My little dog, hearing her name, stood and wagged her tail, and I bent a bit so I could pet her. "I think I know who it is, but I'm not sure."

Shea placed a tablet computer on his desk in front of him and apparently began making notes on it. "And you want to learn what can be done to get that person to back off before any harm is done, I assume." He glanced up at me.

"Absolutely."

We started talking in generalities, but I became frustrated that I wasn't finding much that was helpful in what Shea said. Apparently he recognized this.

"Look," he finally said, "why don't we just come to an agreement that I'll represent you for this on a limited basis. Then we can get into more detail."

"Good idea." I leaned forward over the edge of his desk. Biscuit was settled back down on the floor beside me. "The only thing is that … well, I think you can guess what I believe was the origin of the problem. The threats I received, including that note, resulted, at least indirectly, from Raela Fellner's murder and the aftermath. You already confirmed that you were her lawyer."

Shea nodded. "That's right, on a limited basis regarding opening her veterinary clinic here. But of course I still can't get into any detail about that."

"Can you still represent me, if my situation is somewhat derived from your client's death?"

"I don't see any problem with it. What you and I will be talking about shouldn't touch on anything I'd have to keep quiet about under attorney-client privilege with Raela, even if she were alive. You're not opening another vet clinic, I assume."

"Very true," I told him.

"Then let's do it," he said. "Though in the unlikely event that we get into any iffy areas, I'll have to back off." He brought out an agreement for me to sign. We went over it briefly, and its contents and price sounded okay—or at least I hoped so.

After a short while, Shea was my attorney on this matter: the threats against Biscuit, assuming we could determine who was at fault, and any potential related threats against me, including those from Oliver.

"Okay," he said. "Tell me who you think left that threatening note and why."

He of course knew about Raela's new clinic and was familiar with my clinic. I went into a brief explanation about Raela, Jon, and Oliver's connection to the Knobcone Clinic due to Reed's former employment with them in San Diego and Arvie's search for a new vet.

"As her lawyer, I'd imagine you were one of the first people to hear about Raela's death," I said to Shea. He nodded slightly.

"Well," I continued, "I need to let you know I have a kind of odd nonrelationship with the local cops, especially a couple of the detectives, related to the other murders that have happened in town over the past year. And—well, I guess I can be forthright with you since you're now my lawyer. I've been discreet in how I talk about this in general, but I have to say, I did a better job than the authorities in finding out who those murderers were."

"So they think you're going to do their jobs and solve all murders around here?" Shea's tone sounded amused, though he maintained a blank expression on his face.

"Not really. They're not particularly happy about me, a total amateur, outclassing them in solving these cases."

"Interesting," Shea said. I couldn't interpret the look he shot at me with his pale blue eyes. Maybe he was trying to see inside me to figure out how I could do better than the trained cops. Well, if he could learn that, I wished he'd reveal it to me, too.

"Anyway," I said, "you may be aware that after Raela was found, the detectives spent nearly an entire day questioning those of us who work, in whatever capacity, at the Knobcone Clinic. I gathered this was because Raela was new enough in town that she hardly knew anyone, but she'd met all of us—and rubbed most of us the wrong way. She'd complained very loudly one day, at our premises, about Reed and Arvie not even considering her for an interview. And she made a scene in our lobby, handing out flyers for her new clinic. I guess the cops wanted us to point fingers at one another—and maybe have someone stand out as the probable killer."

"Yes, I heard about that." Shea typed something on his tablet. Then he looked up again. "But I still don't see where this is going."

"Well, the thing is," I said, "I've been getting pretty frustrated recently."

"Because the cops, unlike you, are zeroing in on your boyfriend Reed Storme as the likely killer." This time, Shea's expression looked strangely challenging. "But you're willing to do anything to make them look in a different direction."

"Because he's innocent," I retorted. I certainly hoped so, and it seemed that enough time had passed by now that if there had been any genuine evidence against Reed, the cops would have found it.

Or so I told myself.

"Maybe." Shea sounded as convinced as the cops.

"Anyway, Reed didn't threaten Biscuit. No way. But I decided to visit my contacts at the police department—those detectives—and they wanted to know where I stood with my suspicions. So I named everyone I considered to be suspects, and why, and I gather that even though they'd already talked to all of them, they jumped on them again with more questions. Got pushier, maybe."

"Yeah, really?" This sounded like sarcasm from Shea, but I kept going.

"In fact, they may have treated each one of them as if they were the prime suspect. That's what I think, anyway. I also think that Oliver took it personally. He was very angry when he was told to come in for another interview, and the next day I got the note that told me to stop speaking to the cops and threatened Biscuit."

Again, my dog heard her name, and this time edged closer to me, lying with her head on my sneaker-clad foot.

"I see." Shea paused, not looking up at me. "Did it ever occur to you to listen to the police? I assume they told you to back off, even if you had an opinion about who the murderer was."

That seemed a strange thing for my new attorney to say. "My reason for talking to you isn't so you can tell me to stop what I'm doing," I stated. "My closest friends and family do enough of that. I'm involved now, like it or not. Maybe it was a mistake, but I did go back to the station again and tell the cops about the threatening note. They weren't helpful at all."

"You did what?" Shea demanded. "Don't you think going back to the police was a little foolish?"

Maybe so, but I also thought the lawyer I'd hired ought to be more sympathetic. Instead of insulting me, he should try to come up with other ways I could protect my dog and myself.

"What I need," I continued, "is to hear what kind of legal action I might be able to take against the person threatening Biscuit, and any suggestions you might have as to how to figure out who it is—in case it isn't Oliver after all. I saw him again, by the way, at the police station after my most recent visit and he was even nastier."

Shea's look hardened, and he shook his head before returning his attention to his tablet.

Something inside me was starting to do somersaults, though. As I continued to watch Shea, waiting for his suggestions and legal advice, I went over, in my mind, the few comments he'd made since I'd started recounting what I'd done.

He had already heard about the detectives' first visit to the clinic after Raela was killed. He was pointing to Reed as the probable killer. He was apparently aware that the cops had gotten pushier with the suspects I'd suggested they ought to talk to again.

And he also gave me a hard time about talking to the cops about the note.

I then recalled that in my first visit to the station, I'd told Wayne Crunoll that although I couldn't get a lawyer to violate attorney-client privilege, I didn't know whether lawyers were bound by it when questioned by authorities like the police. I'd suggested that the cops talk to Shea about anything Raela might have told him that could have spurred someone to murder her.

What if they had? What if Wayne and Bridget had pushed Shea the way that Oliver felt they were pushing him?

Oliver hadn't liked it, and he'd claimed not to be the killer—of course. But what if Oliver was telling the truth?

And what if Shea had a reason to be mad that I'd suggested the cops talk to him, and possibly push him? And to be mad that I'd disobeyed the instructions in the note and talked to the cops again?

Oh, no. Surely this was just my wild imagination.

But that same imagination had helped me solve three murders already. Was it happening again—with my mind going in a different direction than I'd previously imagined?

I needed a break to think about it.

I needed to get out of there.

"You know what?" I said. "I think I acted too hastily in coming here. I want to ponder the situation a little more before I start any kind of confrontation with Oliver or anyone else, legal or otherwise.

Just go ahead and bill me for a full hour of your time. If I decide to go forward with this, I'll contact you to make another appointment."

I made myself smile at him as I gathered my purse and Biscuit's leash—but it was already too late. Shea had somehow gotten around his desk, and he swooped up Biscuit into his arms.

My perfect, friendly little dog knew something was wrong and wriggled, even growled—highly unusual for her.

"What are you—" I started to demand, but Shea interrupted.

It was then that I saw he had a small gun in his hand—and it was pressed right up against Biscuit's chest.

"Guess who threatened your damned dog to shut you up," he said with a sneer. "And now we're going to get out of here. I thought about meeting with you someplace else, but since you wanted to hire me, I figured it wouldn't look official enough. And I thought it would be okay, since you didn't know anything, but ... well, I gather you've guessed."

"That you killed Raela?" I saw his gaze harden even more. "It was a guess, yes—before. And I can't say it's more than a guess now, so if you'll just let us go ... "

Shea seemed to ignore what I said and began to talk again. "It would be awfully hard to come up with a good excuse as to why I had to shoot you and your dog here at the office. But if you're a good girl and leave quietly with me, we can make it look like we're just happily leaving the building together. I'll let you go when we're out of here and I can just slip away."

Yeah, and I was a monkey's uncle—or aunt. Or pet dog.

Never mind that. Shea was right about one thing. Staying here to get shot wasn't a good idea.

"Okay," I said quietly. "Let's get out of here, and I'll expect you to live up to that promise."

And if I bet my life and Biscuit's on it, I was sure we wouldn't be around much longer.

TWENTY-NINE

As we stepped through the door into the hall, Shea stopped and looked the opposite way from how I'd come. "The damned emergency stairway has an alarm," he growled, "or we'd just be able to slip out that way."

And he'd be able to kill Biscuit and me in there with no one any the wiser about who'd done it. I was grateful for the alarm.

Was there a way I could stop him from doing anything rash if I tried to get help while walking in a fairly public direction—without anyone getting hurt, including us?

Where were all the people who'd been roaming the hallway when Biscuit and I had arrived? Wasn't another elevator supposed to be emptying somewhere around here?

Surely there would be someone who'd walk by or pop out of an office and see what was going on—then safely duck back in and call 911.

But I saw no one. And I didn't dare do anything that could lead to this SOB of a lawyer harming my dog.

My phone was in my pocket, but Shea would see if I tried to grope for it and push any buttons.

What was I going to do?

A stupid idea came to mind—but it was better than no idea at all. Did I dare to do it? If I was the only one who'd possibly be hurt, there was no question at all. But Biscuit?

And Les?

No time to ponder. We were halfway to the elevator, near the door I sought. I was walking right beside Shea so I could keep an eye on what he was doing with Biscuit—and he unfortunately could keep an eye on me.

Suddenly, I grabbed the arm that held the gun targeting Biscuit, since it was closest to me. I yanked quickly downward, so the weapon was aimed away from my dog and me as I grabbed onto it.

"Hey!" Shea shouted, not letting go.

At the same time I reached out to my other side and slammed open the door to Les's outer office. "Help!" I screamed. "Les, call 911!"

Now Shea was wrenching my hand that had hold of his gun. He'd dropped Biscuit, and my poor little dog had landed sideways on the hallway floor. She stood up right away and started barking.

That, plus my screams, apparently raised a lot of attention. Some of the other office doors started to open.

The gun. Shea was stronger than I was, and as hard as I tried to keep hold of it—without doing anything to the trigger—he now had control over it.

And aimed it at Biscuit.

"No!" This time I leaped onto him with all my weight, my arms around his throat, somehow slamming him to the floor. The gun went off.

I half expected, half hoped, to feel the bullet hit me, since that would mean Biscuit was okay.

It didn't.

But someone in the doorway to a nearby office, a man, also began shouting. Had he been hit?

As I'd feared, I didn't want to be the cause of anyone else being hurt.

"Carrie!" That was Les's loud, authoritative voice. I managed a glance toward his doorway and saw him standing there, phone in one hand and folding chair in the other. Really? But he used the metal chair as a weapon, zooming forward and striking Shea's back with it.

Shea, on the floor, turned to aim the gun at Les. No. I couldn't let him shoot Les. But I didn't have a weapon I could use against him now.

Wait. I did have a weapon, one I had never have thought of before, and her name was Biscuit. I didn't even have to do anything to get her to attack. My perfectly sweet, kind, loving little dog had continued growling, and now she leaped up to where Shea sat on the floor and chomped down onto his gun hand.

"Ow!" he shouted, trying to shake my dog off him, but it was enough disruption for me to jump onto him, too, and smash his hand down to the floor, holding it in place under my foot.

"KHPD!" shouted another voice from somewhere beyond us. This fast? Yes! Three uniformed police officers, guns drawn, waved all the people in the hallway out of their way, and in seconds they took control of Shea.

And me, and Biscuit, too, but that was okay.

"So glad you're here, officers," Shea panted as they cuffed his hands behind him after taking his weapon. "I'm a lawyer. That woman made an appointment to see me and drew a gun on me. I know her, and I think she's involved with that murder that occurred here."

"Oh, can it, mister." Les was now in the hallway with us, shaking his head. "I'm City Councilman Les Ethman, and I can vouch for Ms. Kennersly. She's all right."

"That's Carrie Kennersly?" asked one of the cops, looking at me. He grinned. "Hey, can I be brash enough to assume we've now got a genuine murder suspect in custody?"

"We'll see," Les said as he winked at me and helped me to my feet.

———

Fortunately, when the shot had gone off, it had hit the wall and not any person—or dog. The cops confirmed it and called in a crime scene investigation team.

And then, even knowing who I was, and apparently aware of my reputation for solving murders, the cops "invited" me to the police station. In other words, one of them was assigned to accompany me there right away.

"I'll be bringing my dog Biscuit, too," I told Officer Maki, an attractive female uniformed cop of Asian heritage. "She's very much involved in this situation, including my outing of Mr. Alderson as the top suspect in the murder of Dr. Raela Fellner."

I now knew that Shea had done it, and I'd let the cops know in the statement I'd provide. But Shea hadn't actually admitted it to me, and I didn't know his motive. Most important, I wouldn't be able to hand over any evidence to prove it.

Most lawyers don't murder their clients even if they stop getting along. But Shea had, at least once. And he'd seemed willing to go for twice.

Since we were near the Civic Center, the walk to the police station didn't take very long—and that was undoubtedly why the cops had gotten there that quickly. I asked for a special concession not to be given a parking ticket when the time on my meter ran out—I hadn't anticipated staying in the building longer than it took to talk to and possibly hire Shea.

Once in the station, I was shown immediately into a conference room where both of my favorite detectives joined me, and so did Chief Loretta.

"So what happened?" The chief was the first to speak.

I told her why I'd gone to the lawyer in the first place, and how my suggestion that her detectives talk to Shea—and apparently push him to divulge all he could about Raela and her relationships with others—seemed to be what made Shea snap and try to shut me up.

"He would have been better off if he'd threatened me and not Biscuit," I concluded.

All of the cops were pet parents. All of them laughed.

Bridget Morana was assigned to get my statement, including my description of how Shea had turned on Biscuit and me, and how he'd made it clear that he was the one who'd left the threatening note against my dog.

But would this prove he was Raela's killer? Not necessarily. And despite his threatening me with a gun, even shooting it within a public building, I worried that this lawyer, who apparently knew the legal system, would be able to post bail or otherwise get back on the street quickly.

———

It was almost six o'clock by the time Biscuit and I returned to my shops, and my assistants had started closing up. I'd called to let them know I'd be late, and included a hint about why.

I'd found, after leaving the police station, that I was both jazzed and somewhat depressed. No, I wasn't at all unhappy that this latest murder investigation, or at least my involvement in it, seemed to be drawing to a close. But I wasn't thrilled that the things the cops were mainly looking for—evidence and, most especially, motive in relation to who killed Raela—still hadn't been found.

I knew I didn't want to be alone that night, so when Janelle had answered her phone, I'd told her to get my assistants together to meet at the resort for dinner, and, of course, to invite Neal, too.

Then I'd called Reed. "I have some potentially really good news to report," I told him, and invited him to join us.

Finally, I'd called Dinah, the best research expert I knew. She'd been able to break away from some customers to talk to me, and I not only invited her to dinner directly but also gave her a brief rundown of all that had happened that afternoon—knowing that when I told the same story to everyone at dinner later, no one would be surprised. Dinah would reveal all—or at least all she knew.

I finally shot her the real zinger, the reason I'd called. "Please don't tell anyone else about this," I said, "but I've got some potentially fascinating research for you to conduct. It might even lead to the final resolution of the murder case."

And then I told her what I needed her to do.

When Biscuit and I arrived at the shops, Dinah was sitting at one of the tables in the Barkery at her laptop. The last customers were leaving, so that was fine.

"Find anything?" I asked.

"Working on it," she said with a grin.

As I put Biscuit into her enclosure, a thought struck me. I quickly called Bridget and told her the quandary: Buffer and Earl, Shea's dogs, did not have their caretaker. "I can call Billi Matlock of

Mountaintop Rescue to take them in for now at least, if that's okay," I said.

"I'll get back to you soon," Bridget said. Which she did. She had asked Shea what he wanted to do, and though he wasn't talking about anything yet, he gave permission to have his dogs placed at Mountaintop Rescue . . . for now. Till he was out, he'd told the detective.

Right. Well, we'd see about that. But for now the most important thing was making sure his definitely innocent dogs were cared for.

———

Dinner at the resort had become a large party—nearly all my wonderful assistants, friends, and family in Knobcone Heights were there, including Reed, Arvie, Billi, and the Joes. Neal had booked us an area on the patio so I could bring Biscuit. Of course. No way was I leaving my pup at home, even though the person who'd threatened her was in custody.

Nearly the whole gang had heard some of what had happened, but, wine glass in hand, I stood and gave them a detailed rundown.

"But," I said as I finished, "I have to caution you not to go around accusing Shea of anything other than threatening Biscuit and me, and of course what he did to us this afternoon. Any connection between him and Raela's murder is still just speculation."

"Maybe," called Dinah.

I felt my eyes open wider. "Have you found something?"

"Nothing definitive . . . yet. Wait till tomorrow."

They all toasted me, sweet people. And we all indulged in a wonderful dinner.

Previously, I'd asked Dinah who her research resource was at our veterinary clinic and not gotten an answer. Nor did Dinah seem inclined to share her information now, even as we were all expressing an interest in her research abilities. I figured I might not be the one to prove who the killer was—but it wouldn't matter, if Dinah could help to stitch up the many loose ends in this murder case.

Afterward, Reed drove his car behind mine to my house, where I left my car and then went home with him. When we were alone inside, after walking the two dogs near his house, he kissed me and scolded me and thanked me for perhaps solving the case and getting the cops off his back—at least for now, and hopefully forever.

"You know I love you, Carrie, don't you?" he asked as we got ready for bed.

"I certainly hope so, since I love you," I responded.

There was no mention of any commitment like marriage or moving in together, and that was fine with me. But love? Well, that could be a commitment unto itself.

Despite knowing that my schedule for the next morning required rising early, as usual, I didn't fall asleep for a while, even when I heard Reed's breathing elongate, indicating he was sleeping.

Would the cops discover any evidence to link Shea to Raela's murder?

Was Dinah actually finding any potentially helpful information in her research?

Where was my relationship with Reed headed?

And this was the final murder in Knobcone Heights I would get involved with—right?

THIRTY

I DID MANAGE TO get to the shops on time the next morning—very early, as always. I believed Vicky was supposed to join me first, and though she had been at the dinner the previous night, I felt sure that my top scheduler would be on time.

Which she was.

Dinah was to arrive next, but Janelle beat her. Interesting.

Both shops had a lot of customers by the time Dinah arrived looking exhausted but full of smiles. "I think we need to go talk to your cop friends," she said. "They might have found some of this online, too, or they could, but this could save them some time—and help keep your buddy the lawyer in jail."

She gave me a quick rundown of what she'd found as I made sure Vicky and Janelle were prepared to take full control of the shops. I decided to let Biscuit stay in their care, too. I was positive—almost—that the person who'd threatened her wouldn't be around my shops ever again.

What Dinah had found, to my surprise, didn't prove that Shea was a killer at all, let alone Raela's murderer. But it was enough to get things started with the police that resulted in an outcome I hadn't foreseen.

First, we went to Chief Loretta's office. Bridget was away from the station working on the investigation against Shea, but Wayne joined us.

"I looked Shea up on the California State Bar website," Dinah said. "His credentials there indicate he's been practicing law in Knobcone Heights for around eight months, and before that he came from Corverville in Northern California, a town near Eureka. The media reports there suggested some somewhat shady things about him, though without any specifics, and so I made a few quick calls this morning."

Even if I'd thought to Google the guy before hiring him as my lawyer, this probably wouldn't have made any difference. Nor would it have pointed to Shea as a killer.

Dinah went into more detail—and the upshot was that the District Attorney of Corverville had agreed to show up in Knobcone Heights the next day to speak with the police.

And the consequence of that? Well, about a week later, Dinah and I were invited back to the police station, on the condition of our complete silence about what we were about to watch through one-way glass. The window was like the kind they show on television, where people can look into an interrogation room but those inside can't see out.

Inside the room, in addition to attorneys from the local District Attorney's office, were Shea and the lawyer he'd hired to represent him: my attorney friend Ted Culbert. Interesting that Ted would take on Shea, but maybe lawyers felt obligated to help other lawyers.

The discussion inside the room took a while, with lots of questions and objections and all. But between what Dinah had discovered and what I heard during the interrogation, I gleaned quite a lot:

Apparently, the Corverville DA had told the local authorities, including the Knobcone Heights District Attorney, that yes, Shea Alderson had practiced law in their town. Over a year ago, he'd taken on a client who'd been bribing local officials and needed representation when caught. *Allegedly* bribing, although some officials had been convicted. The guy had also been wily enough to plant evidence that indicated Shea was the one doing the bribing—or so Shea had claimed. There was enough doubt about it that Shea managed to save himself and stay out of jail, but he wound up leaving the area because of how badly his reputation had been damaged by the media only hinting of nonspecific allegations. None of his local clients had stayed with him.

The only good information about Shea online and in media reports was that he took on representation of animal shelters for low or no cost.

And that wily client of his? Well, he'd been killed in what appeared to be a hit-and-run accident with his own car. The perpetrator hadn't been caught even when the car in question was located, despite all the suspicions against Shea.

It was around that time that Shea had left, claiming he couldn't stay any longer because of the way townsfolk now thought of him. He found a new home in Knobcone Heights.

It turned out Dinah wasn't the only person who'd researched Shea's background and found the problems. Raela had done so, too.

And in exchange for her silence, she'd gotten Shea to represent her in the opening of her new veterinary clinic—in leasing the property it was on—in getting things started to make sure her veterinary license was adequate to run a vet hospital. And more. And more. For compensation that kept getting reduced.

Apparently, Shea had eventually had enough. He'd visited Raela at her new clinic early one morning. Unfortunately for her, Raela had allowed Shea to watch her deal with some of her initial patients, including one very ill dog that had to be euthanized.

And so Shea knew where the pentobarbital, and the hypodermics to administer it, were kept and how to use them.

At the beginning of the interview, Ted Culbert told his client to be quiet, especially since there was apparently no physical evidence linking Shea to the crime. But when the Corverville DA came into the room, Shea told his counsel where to go and decided to make a full confession to get a plea deal. He even admitted to threatening Biscuit with that note and making sure to leave no fingerprints.

Shea had known what he was doing. He was, after all, a lawyer who, he claimed, respected the legal system.

Not people, perhaps, but the legal system.

So, yes. I had helped to catch another murderer.

———

I'd also visited Mountaintop Rescue several times over the past week, to check on Earl and Buffer as well as to bring some leftover treats.

And to see Billi. The day after watching the interrogation, sitting in her office sipping coffee, I shared some of the things I'd learned about Shea Alderson. I labeled everything as "suspicions," though, and I didn't mention that Shea had confessed to murdering Raela in order to avoid the most onerous sentence, which I assumed could be the death penalty even though that sentence would probably not be carried out in our state. This information hadn't gotten into the media yet, so to let Billi absorb the news slowly, I pretended not to be aware.

Billi did seem concerned, but apparently she hadn't really been interested in Shea except as a friend and fellow animal lover —fortunately.

"If he's convicted, do you think he'll get to see any dogs in prison?" I asked Billi. I figured a city council member was more likely to know this than a veterinary assistant. "Some institutions bring in canines that inmates help train as service dogs." Maybe Shea would be allowed to do that if he had good behavior.

"I suppose it'll depend on which prison he's incarcerated in," Billi said.

I wondered how a lawyer who was a murderer would do in prison. I supposed it wouldn't be as bad as it would be for an imprisoned cop. Maybe.

"How did you learn all this about Shea?" Billi finally asked.

I just grinned at her. "I'll tell you when I can." Then I changed the subject, discussing the adoption event we were holding that coming Saturday.

It was as great as the last one. Maybe greater. Quite a few cats were brought to my shops in carriers, and dogs were leashed on the Barkery floor. We had volunteers helping again, as well as my assistants, and the Barkery was full of people and leashed pups there to hopefully find new homes. Of course, Shea wasn't one of the helpful volunteers this time, but his two dogs Earl and Buffer were there to be adopted.

No matter what else Shea might be, he was someone who loved dogs, especially his own. He'd signed the paperwork to relinquish them for adoption.

I gave him a lot of credit for that. It had to have been hard. Apparently harder for him than murdering a human.

I wasn't surprised, but I was pleased when Mayor Sybill Gabbon came in right as our event opened. She wore a suit with her moderate-height black heels and, as usual, looked very mayor-ish. But instead of coming over to say hi to me, she knelt on the tile floor and began playing with the dogs who'd been brought from Mountaintop Rescue.

"Hi, Mayor," I said, hurrying over to her. Billi joined me. The mayor apparently really did love animals—which was something that always raised people in my estimation.

Unless they also happened to be murderers of humans.

"Hello, Billi. Hello, Carrie. As I mentioned last time I saw you, I'm interested in adopting a dog—and I'd even consider more than one, especially since Corwin just loves dogs. He told me I could choose on his behalf before he gets here." She hugged the canine who was closest to her, who happened to be Shea's pit bull, Earl. Interesting. I wondered…

"Mayor, one of the reasons we're holding this event is that two of the shelter's latest rescue dogs belonged to Shea Alderson, the person who allegedly—"

"Committed the most recent murder in town. Yes, I'm aware of that, and these killings have to stop." She rose and stared at me as if I'd had something to do with causing the murders, not solving them. But then she relaxed. "I understand that you once again had something to do with finding the alleged perpetrator. Congratulations, Carrie. And now please introduce me to that man's dogs. I'm sure that becoming orphaned that way has to be hard on them."

"You just hugged one of them," I informed her. "That's Earl. And the other is Buffer, that yellow Lab mix." I pointed just beyond where Earl sat. Both leashes were being held by Janelle.

"Let me play with them both a little," Mayor Gabbon said. She knelt once more, and I wondered how she did it in her skirt and heels. But Janelle released the dogs' leashes, and the mayor was soon almost rolling on the floor with them, laughing and hugging them.

So our usually remote, aloof, and inaccessible mayor wasn't so bad after all.

And I liked her a whole lot more a little later, when she told Billi that she wanted to adopt both dogs.

"Great!" Billi said. "Let me get the paperwork together."

I joined her at the counter where she was filling out the adoption forms. "So, are you going to do a major interrogation about how these dogs will be treated, and a home check to make sure all's prepped for them?" I asked.

Billi knew I was kidding—sort of. "I'll ask a few standard questions and maybe leave things open for a home check, but someone in the public eye like our mayor had better be a good dog mama or the world will know. And I'll want to know more about why her son is moving home—and what kind of a person he is."

"That's what I figured. So this should have a good result." It appeared that the murder, as bad as it was, hadn't ruined all the lives involved.

Which made me smile—even as another visitor skipped up to the counter and asked to adopt a little doxie mix who was a newbie to the shelter.

———

Reed popped in toward the end of the adoption event, when almost all of the cats who'd come and most of the dogs had found new homes.

I couldn't help asking, "What's going on with Oliver? Is he going to keep that new veterinary clinic going?" If so, I wondered if Ted Culbert would be able to help him now with any legal and licensing issues.

"No," Reed said. "Arvie just hired him to join us at our clinic." Which made me smile.

No one seemed to know what was going to happen with the new clinic. Apparently Dr. Mickey Krohan had been asked if the files at the San Diego veterinary hospital contained anything about Raela that could be used to locate any heirs—but even if any were found, I figured it was unlikely her relatives would keep the new place going.

And Dr. Mickey himself? Well, though he'd said he might take the new clinic over, he'd now told Reed he had no intention of doing so.

Reed and I had a date scheduled for that night. We'd been spending a lot of time together that week, even at the clinic when he had to handle emergencies in the middle of the night and needed the help of a vet tech.

I was always exhausted the next day, of course, when I went to my shops—but it was worth it. Being with Reed. Assisting this wonderful vet in saving animals' lives.

Sharing a lot with him—including a relationship that appeared to be going somewhere.

I still wondered where, but I was happy about taking my time to find out.

I recalled only too well his telling me not long ago that he wanted us to spend some quality time together—maybe away from

Knobcone Heights—and to talk about our future. But things had been chaotic and uncertain then.

Well, those things had been resolved.

And I believed it was finally time for a little travel ... and talk.

THE END

BARKERY AND BISCUITS DOG TREAT RECIPE

Peanut Butter Dog Treats
½ cup whole wheat flour
Dash ground ginger
¼ cup creamy peanut butter
2 tbsp unsweetened applesauce
2 tbsp water

Preheat oven to 350°F.

Combine flour and ground ginger.

Combine peanut butter, applesauce, and water. Add to flour mixture. Mix with spatula until well combined.

Use your hands to knead dough and press into a ball.

Place dough on a flat surface and press until about ¼ inch thick (or use rolling pin).

Use favorite cookie cutters (bone-shape, heart) to cut dough into desired shape. Can also cut dough into thin strips and twist to shape into spirals.

Bake for 15–20 minutes until golden brown.

Store in airtight container or in refrigerator.

Tip: Can also make with ripe banana instead of applesauce.

Makes about 60 small dog treats.

ICING ON THE CAKE PEOPLE TREAT RECIPE

I've included this because I'm a chocoholic and really love these brownies. The fact that they're relatively simple to make also earns them lots of points in my opinion.

However, *they are definitely not dog treats!* Chocolate is poisonous to canines. But enjoy these as great people treats!

Make-in-My-Sleep Brownies
4 squares (1 oz each) unsweetened chocolate
1 cup margarine (2 sticks)
2 cups sugar
4 eggs
1 cup all-purpose flour
2 tsp vanilla
1 tsp salt

Melt chocolate and margarine in microwave. Cool.

Add remaining ingredients. Mix well.

Pour into greased jelly roll pan (15" x 10"); or line pan with non-stick foil for easy removal.

Bake 325°F for 25 minutes.

Sprinkle with powdered sugar while still warm.

When cool, cut into squares.

ACKNOWLEDGMENTS

As always, I want to thank my wonderful agent Paige Wheeler, as well as the delightful people at Midnight Ink who work with me: editor Terri Bischoff and production editor Sandy Sullivan, and the publicists, including Jake Kent.

And since I admire people who cook and develop recipes, particularly since I'm not among them, I definitely want to thank my friend Paula Riggin, who provided both recipes this time: Peanut Butter Dog Treats, which my dogs Mystie and Cari loved when they tried them, and Make-In-My-Sleep Brownies, which my husband Fred and I loved and shared with others.